TRUE LETTERS FROM A FICTIONAL LIFE

Kenneth Logan

HARPER TEEN
An Imprint of HarperCollins Publishers

HarperTeen is an imprint of HarperCollins Publishers.

Library of Congress Control Number: 2015955157
ISBN 978-0-06-238025-8

Typography by Erin Shell
16 17 18 19 20 PC/RRDH 10 9 8 7 6 5 4 3 2 1
❖
First Edition

For my mom and dad

CHAPTER 1

Tim Hawken's arm draped around my shoulders meant nothing to anyone but me. I could see our reflection in the window as we leaned against the kitchen counter. Our pal Kevin's parents had split town again, so ten scruffy kids from Vermont and New Hampshire were sliding around the O'Dea house in woolen socks and stuffing too much wood in the stove. An army of empty beer bottles gathered in ranks next to the sink. Four or five of them were mine.

My sort-of girlfriend, Theresa, and her parents were driving through a blizzard to visit tiny colleges in western New York. She'd been gone almost the entire spring break. She kept sending me text message updates like *We just fishtailed!!*

I abbreviated *wow drive safely* to *wds*. We spend enough time together that a lot of people assume we're dating. Sometimes Theresa thinks we're still a couple, too. She's made a big effort to make things work out between us. One afternoon last June, she showed up at my house on her bike with a bouquet of flowers and a canvas bag full of Matchbox cars for my little brother. "My mom made me clean out my closet," she explained. "I don't want them, and you know how much I love my little Rexy."

"And you know how much he loves being called Little Rexy," I said, eyeing the flowers. I was a little embarrassed to receive them, but sort of pleased, too. "You know he doesn't even play with the cars. He just hoards them."

"Whatever makes him happy. I also brought your mom flowers from our field. She loves irises."

Hands in my pockets, I peered into the bag. "You got anything to eat in there?" She kissed me on the cheek, and my mom sang Theresa's name from the open front door. She loves Theresa. I think she loves me more when I'm with her.

I ducked out from under Hawken's arm and got another beer from the porch. The snow swirled in whistling gusts outside. "It made sense for the school to cut cross-country and track," Mark was explaining as I came back in. "There's no money for it, and running's not even a sport." Mark has many opinions, and he shares them generously. No one outside our circle of friends challenges anything he says, though, because he looks and acts like a boxer about to enter the ring. He's shorter than me, but he's ripped, and he won't let anyone forget it. There's a photo of a bunch of us at a party last winter, standing on a snowy porch. We're all wearing down jackets and woolen hats—except for Mark, who's shirtless. He lives and drinks with his father up the road from the Hawkens, and he stays with them whenever his father kicks him out. "For real," his rant continued, "I'm glad our school's done with running. And with runners. Bunch of faggot homos."

Hawken winced and said, "I know you're trying to be thorough, Markus, but that's redundant. And don't say that kind of crap. It makes you sound stupid."

"Fine," Mark said. He defers to Hawken as though Hawken is his older brother. "But it's true. Those guys are ridiculous. All they can do is run? How is that a sport? They don't have to do anything other than move their legs and breathe. No catching. No throwing. There's no contact, no danger, no—"

"Dude," Derek interrupted. "You play a sport where most of the team just stands around in a field." I was impressed that Derek was staying so calm. He's super fast and was one of our star track runners, although everyone was always telling him that he should play basketball instead. That drives him crazy. "I'm not that tall, and no one's seen me dribble or shoot," he'd gripe to me. "They're like, 'We have one black guy around here, and he's not even any *good* at being a black guy.'"

I joined Derek's assault on baseball. "Seriously, you don't

have to be an athlete to be a good baseball player. Some of those guys can barely jog around the bases."

"But they can crush the ball out of the park," Mark snapped. "You ever hit a 95-mile-per-hour fastball out of the park in front of 600 gazillion people?"

"600 gazillion people?" I asked quietly. "No, never in front of that many people. Half that many, maybe."

Next to me, Derek snickered.

"That takes some serious strength and coordination," Mark went on, looking furious. "Serious strength and, you know, like, calmness."

"Composure." Hawken helped him out.

"Yeah," Mark said angrily. "Composure."

"But is composure a sign of athleticism?" asked Derek. "If I'm a world-class chess player, am I considered an athlete of great skill, too? Or if I'm a superb actor, must my athleticism be thought outstanding as well?"

"Or if I'm a brain surgeon?" I began, but I stopped there because I was going to crack up.

Mark stood and went to the porch for another beer. "Why are you ganging up on me?"

"Pediatric rheumatologist?" Derek continued, deadpan.

I suddenly felt sorry for Mark. It was too easy to get him going. "We're not ganging up on you, dude. We're just defending the cross-country team. Have you ever run a 5K over a bunch of crazy hills before? It's really hard."

"I could totally do it," Mark said.

"I'm sure you could finish." I shrugged. "Eventually."

"Ooooh," Hawken lowed. "Do I hear a challenge? Is there going to be a little race between you two?"

"What?" I yelped, alarmed. "I didn't say anything about racing anyone!" This was Hawken's way of evening the score for Mark. He always came to Mark's defense in sneaky ways.

"I don't know if I'd outrun those super-skinny cross-country freaks, but I could beat Liddell."

"Oh, *there* it is. There's the challenge that James Liddell cannot refuse!" yelled Derek. "There's going to be a race! Tonight! Tonight!"

"Right, through the snow." And then, in the accent I've honed while spending entire sleety Saturdays watching the English Premier League, I said, "Fetch me my cleats and chill some champagne!"

"No, for real," said Mark, trying to sound casual. "When the snow melts, I'll race you. If you think baseball players aren't athletes, let's race."

"I didn't say *you're* not an athlete, Mark. I just meant that you don't *have* to be an athlete to play baseball."

"Whatever. I'm down to compete, but if you're going to be a wuss about it . . . I guess I shouldn't be surprised, you being a soccer player and all."

"Ooooh," Hawken sang again, rubbing his hands together. "I'm pretending that remark did not apply to me. You guys have to race now for sure-ity!"

"There's the Mud 10K!" shouted Derek. "We were

talking about running it anyway."

"That's 10K. We're talking about 5K," said Mark.

"10K, 5K—what's the difference?" yelled Hawken. "It's not until June. There's plenty of time to train."

"Oh, I'm not training," Mark said. "I'll just run it." He gulped from his beer, banged it on the counter, and fixed his stare on me. "You in?"

"June?" I asked with a smirk. "Sure, I'll race you in June."

"Done!" hollered Derek in delight. "Shake on it! Shake on it! Hawken and I are witnessing this! It's epic!"

"Sign this contract!" shouted Hawken. He was scribbling something on a napkin.

I read over his shoulder, shaking my head in disbelief:

We, _____

and _____

do here by commit myself to racing each other in the mud 10k in June 2016. Failure to do so will result in sever bodily harm.

He handed me the pen, and I reread the agreement.

"Are you editing my napkin contract?" Hawken asked.

"Only a little," I muttered, changing the *myself* to *ourselves* and adding an *e* to the end of *sever*. I couldn't help it. I left *here* and *by* as two words—making that change would've crossed the line into obnoxiousness. I signed my name in the first blank.

"That's illegible," commented Derek.

"But we all witnessed it," said Hawken.

I slid the contract to Mark.

"What the hell?" he said a few seconds later. "This reads like a marriage certificate or something."

"Which would be perfectly legal here in the Great State of Vermont," Hawken pointed out. "But it's not a marriage certificate. It's a napkin. So just sign here, please. Careful not to tear it."

Mark's tongue stuck out between his teeth as he signed, as if he were eight years old.

Before anyone could reconsider, Hawken snatched the contract away, scurried to the center of the kitchen, thrust the napkin over his head, and shouted in a high, hurried voice, "This is a legal document!"

A couple of Kevin O'Dea's pals from his new school walked in and stopped in their tracks, looking confused.

"We need outside-nonpartisan-unaffiliated-and-wholly-neutral witnesses to sign this," Hawken declared. He beckoned the two boys we hardly knew over to the counter and explained the situation. They grinned and signed their names beneath the oath. "Date those signatures, please," Hawken directed solemnly.

When it was done, Mark and Derek drifted away to talk to a couple of girls in another room, and Hawken and I leaned back against the kitchen counter, his arm around me once again. We watched the snow pile up in the dark, and he pretended to groan, but he was grinning.

"Why can't we have snow without cold?" he said in the scratchy voice that girls say is adorable. "I like snow. I hate being cold."

In the window's reflection, we were a translucent couple among black trees, copper cabinets, and gray snowflakes. He's just a little shorter than me, maybe five foot nine. Neither of us combs our hair, but his is darker brown, and his eyes are blue while mine are green. He smiles more easily than I do. It always looks like he's on the verge of breaking into a grin.

I took a swig from my beer and asked, "You feel like going for a walk? This might be the last snowfall of the year."

"Yeah, a walk would be good. But it's only April, dude. It's barely mud season. The snow ain't done."

We were on the porch tying our boots when Derek stuck his head out the door.

"Where are you two headed? You're not driving home tonight, are you?"

"Nooo way!" Hawken laughed.

"No, we're going for a walk, dude. Just sobering up, sobering up."

It was only ten o'clock, so Derek squinted, shook his head, and pretended to spit at us, then shut the door. As I pulled on my gloves, Hawken asked, "Where's your pirate key?"

He used the big, old-fashioned key to my desk drawer to crack us open a couple more beers.

A snowplow scraped past on the road below as we left the house. We slid down Kevin's driveway, leaving long swoops in the three inches of wet snow covering the ice and frozen mud. When we reached the easy walking of paved road, I slung my arm around him.

We had the road to ourselves. As we rounded the first bend, I had just finished saying that I wasn't sure if I should date Theresa, when I heard myself ask, almost whisper, "You're still not dating anyone, huh, Hawken?" I don't know if my stomach's jumping made my voice shake. "You could date anyone you want, you know."

"Ha! I don't know about that, man."

"Sure, you could. You're smart. You're athletic. You're wicked funny." The beers helped me get the next words out. "You're cute." I gulped from my bottle, and Hawken cracked up.

"Thanks, thanks." He clinked my bottle.

"No, I'm serious," I continued, encouraged. "Everyone has a crush on you."

"Oh, yeah?"

"Everyone." I tried to sound casual. "Even me."

I didn't hide behind the beer bottle or laugh nervously or try to change the subject, and Hawken fell into his raspy little laugh.

"Even you, huh? James Liddell has a crush on me? The girls will be crazy jealous, man."

"Well, I'd be jealous of any girl who's with you." I tried

9

laughing, and he stopped walking. We'd reached a dark stretch between streetlamps.

Hawken stepped away and turned toward me so that I had to drop my arm. I took a sip of my beer and studied the snow caught in the laces of my boots, but he nudged me with his elbow to make me look up, to make me look him in the eyes, and he said, "For real, huh?" He didn't sound scared or angry. For a moment, I thought I'd been right.

"Yeah, man," I said quietly, and shrugged and shivered all at once. "What can I do? Who can blame me?" The soft tone of our voices and the scrape of our feet, the hushed seriousness of it all—suddenly I felt like we were ten years older. I wanted to hold his hand.

He looked off into the forest and scuffed the pavement. I was sure he was about to say, *Yeah, me, too. I've had a crush on you, too.*

"Dude," he said instead, "I'm flattered as hell." And then he kicked my foot, lightly, twice. He was smiling.

He couldn't see the chasm that had opened behind my ribs. He didn't get it. I managed to find my voice. "You're all right with all this, man?"

"James, I'm fine with it." We started walking again, an arm's length now between us. "You know my brother's gay?"

My legs went even weaker. It seemed like a big leap to bring up his gay brother. A crush didn't make me gay.

"No, I didn't know about your brother," I muttered.

"Patrick lives in Brooklyn with his boyfriend, Liam. I'll

introduce you to those guys next time they visit."

I stopped, gazed up the road, and said, "We should head back, huh?"

Hawken was quiet for a moment. "Sure."

He wouldn't say a word to anyone. I trusted Hawken. But I wished I'd been smart and kept my own mouth shut anyway. Everything would have been easier if I'd just stayed quiet.

Our boot prints grew less distinct as we retraced our steps in silence, and by the time we reached the bottom of Kevin's driveway, the snow had erased our tracks completely.

It was just as I would pretend. The walk out had never happened.

CHAPTER 2

Derek dropped me back home early the next morning, Sunday, and I had to shovel our driveway. I'd guzzled a ton of water before I crashed at Kevin's, but I was still hungover. I'd lost count of my late-night beers. I leaned against the shovel, eyes closed, and tried to trick my brain into thinking it was getting sleep. Rex, who's ten, was supposed to be shoveling, too, but instead he was digging holes all over the yard, allegedly looking for his left glove. "I know where it is!" he kept yelling. "It's right over here. Near this tree. That's where I left it yesterday."

"Rex," I hollered for the tenth time. "Get over here and help!"

He looked up, like a startled squirrel, and shouted, "Wait! Wait!" He flung his shovel in one direction and ran, stumbling, fifteen yards in the other. "It's definitely right over here." And he dug maniacally, throwing snow back between his legs.

I chucked my shovel in a drift and plodded toward him. He didn't look up until I was reaching for him. And then he only stopped shrieking when I had his face pushed into the snow and his arm wrenched behind his back. I yanked him onto his feet, and his wet wool hat fell by his boots. Gasping, red and teary, Rex looked as though he had coughed the hat up.

"Go get your shovel." I pushed him forward, then glanced up at the kitchen windows, where my mom stood watching us, arms crossed. Rex must have seen her, too, because he collapsed back to the ground in tears.

"C'mon, dude. You're ten years old."

But I knew what I'd hear as soon as I walked into the house: *I don't care what Rex did or didn't do. You're seven years older than him. Act like it.*

This past Christmas I gave Rex a shock collar, the kind that gives dogs an electric jolt when they bark. Figuring I'd return it afterward, I kept the receipt. I got him a couple of Beatles albums, too, but as soon as I saw how excited he was tearing off the penguin wrapping paper, I knew the joke was going to go over badly. He looked all confused when he had the collar unwrapped, and then he yelled, "We got a dog?"

My older brother, Luke, just stared at me and said, "Thank you for ruining Christmas."

Rex and I don't always fight. A couple of summers ago, my parents' friends invited us to stay at their lakeside cabin way up in Vermont's Northeast Kingdom. We were there for a week. Every morning I'd wake up to Rex hanging upside down from the top bunk, his hair as crazy as his laugh. Luke would sleep late, but we'd scramble out of bed just as it was getting light and run down to the dock in our hoodies and bare feet, even though it was freezing. We'd reel in sunfish all morning until our dad got up and wandered down to us, nursing a cup of coffee, not saying a word, just sitting and smiling like I'd never seen him smile before. Rex kept singing "Come on, little fishies, come on, little fishies," each verse higher than the one before, and I remember my dad breathing this great big sigh and grinning a little bigger. That was good. That was fun.

While shoveling the driveway, I tried concentrating on the still water of that lake instead of cursing at myself for all the dumb things I had said at the party. I could still hear Hawken: *You know my brother's gay?*

Later that night, before I went up to scribble in my notebook, I slugged orange juice straight from the carton and paused, yet again, to study the photo my mom had stuck beneath an I Heart Vermont magnet on the fridge door. It's Theresa and me standing in front of a bush of pink flowers, my arm around her. It wasn't even the prom or anything. It was a dance in the school gym, which smells like basketballs and the guys who bounce them. Theresa wore a blue summer dress, and my tie, by chance, matched it perfectly. Theresa's beaming. So was my mom when she took the photo. At seven fifteen every morning, I go to get milk for my Cheerios, and there's the boy I'm supposed to be, my arm around the girl I'm supposed to be with.

Theresa and I became friends in third grade, and our first kiss was on Halloween in seventh. She was the Jolly Green Giant. I was an outlaw. She left green makeup on my charcoal five o'clock shadow, and our friends gave us a hard time about it all night. We'd learned to be much more discreet by the time we started sleeping together the summer between our sophomore and junior years.

As happy as I was to be with Theresa at that point, I wasn't sure *why* I was so happy about it. I wasn't sure if it was because she was Theresa or just because she was a girl— sleeping with any girl was good news about who I was, who I might become. But it never felt right. It left me feeling guilty. Back in December, when I realized that I wasn't *in love* with Theresa, I started to find excuses to avoid ending up in bed with her. I can't explain any of this to her, though, so things between us have been tense.

"She's using you, too," my brother Luke pointed out. I'd given him part of the story, phrasing it carefully: *I don't want to make her think we're forever. She's not the only one on my mind.*

"Don't give yourself all the credit," he continued. "She's getting what she wants, too. She might change her mind tomorrow and dump you for a guy on the baseball team."

"Not the baseball team. Stop."

"It could happen. And you'll be left wondering how you could've been used so shamefully."

Luke was speaking from experience. His junior year, he dated this girl from another school. They met at some youth environmental conference. He let her write her name on his notebooks. He allowed her to adorn him with yarn bracelets. The entire time, he played it as if he were in control. Then one day, she sent a text message. They were done. She had met someone else, someone at her own school. It would be easier for everyone that way. Good-bye. Luke's one-line response—*You have my bird field guide*—was met with silence. He invited me to witness the burning of her school photo in the backyard.

But there were enough good moments with Theresa to make me wonder why I'd want to be with anyone else. Back in the fall, Theresa invited her friend Kim and Derek and me over for a dinner party when her parents were out of town. They trusted her not to throw a big party, and they weren't being naïve—she really was responsible. "Wear something nice," she told us.

"What do you mean?" I said. "Like matching track suits?"

"Derek, make sure he looks presentable." He nodded. No

wise-guy comment or anything. He liked Kim a lot, and so did I. She's hilarious, and she's pretty without trying hard. No makeup, no flashy clothes. She wears T-shirts and jeans and her hair in a ponytail. She doesn't like nasty gossip, she doesn't complain, and she doesn't like drama. But I think Derek's scared to date a girl who might be smarter than he is.

There was jazz playing when we arrived. I could hear it through the closed front door. "Music's too loud," Derek muttered, picking a piece of lint off my jacket. He'd basically dressed me. Wear that pair of jeans. That white button-down. Black blazer. No tie. He was wearing a red tie beneath a navy V-neck sweater. Khakis. Normally, he looks like he's in an Adidas ad. "Since when do you wear a watch?" I asked. The door opened, but he would've ignored my question anyway.

"Oh, well, well, well. Don't we look nice, gentlemen!" I'd seen Theresa in a skirt only a handful of times before, never when she was just going to be hanging out with me. The aroma of roasted chicken filled the warm house. She was also cooking a soufflé, red potatoes, and something with shallots. I'd never heard of shallots.

"I love shallots," I said, staring at the glass of white wine Theresa held. "I believe they're pronounced sha-LOW. And we're drinking wine? Out of grown-up glasses? This is all very fah-ncy."

"My brother bought the wine for us," announced Kim, coming out of the kitchen holding a tulip glass of red. "And we have both kinds."

It looked like Derek was about to say something, but he didn't.

"We're hanging out in the kitchen," Kim continued. Derek watched her disappear back down the hall. Black skirt, red stockings. He detoured through the living room to the stereo, and the music dropped to a comfortable level as I entered the kitchen.

"Red or white?" asked Kim.

"I don't know." I shrugged. "I'm not a wine drinker. Maybe half and half? That has to be called something, right?"

"They mix Coke and red wine in Spain," said Kim.

"He's not doing that," Theresa said quickly. "He'll have red. Don't break that glass, James."

"I'm more worried about spilling on my shirt."

"Try sipping instead of guzzling," Theresa instructed. "This could be a big night for you—learning how normal people consume alcohol."

"Big night, huh? I'm all for that."

"Dinner will be ready in half an hour or so," Theresa said, tying an apron around her waist. "You guys hang out. I'm going to tackle a few of these dishes." We all protested, insisted on a turn at the sink, but she held up a hand to silence us. "Please just relax. I got them." She handed me a bowl of Doritos and my wine and shooed us into the living room. "Derek," she said, "I was telling Kim that you're going to be an astronomer." And then she went back into the kitchen.

This was the first Derek or I had heard of his plan to

become an astronomer—a professional, full-time, for-real astronomer—and for a moment, as he settled into the couch, he looked at a loss for words. "Oh. Sure. I have a telescope."

"He and his dad *made* a telescope," I interjected.

"And I like looking at the stars with my telescope."

Kim and I waited for more. Derek was looking at me as he sipped from his glass. Was his hand shaking?

"The telescope is pretty cool." I helped him out. "You can see planets with it. What other kinds of stuff can you see with it, dude?"

Kim was watching us with a pained smile.

"You can see planets with it, yeah," said Derek. "The moon is cool." And then he downed his entire glass of wine in a single swallow.

"We looked at Saturn the other night," I explained. "It was kind of blurry, but it had rings, just like, you know, they tell you it does."

"The aperture is only four inches," he explained. "A bigger telescope would give you a clearer view."

"It's nice to talk about something other than sports for once," Kim observed mercifully. "Most of the guys from my school—all they want to do is talk about their teams."

Derek beamed at me. I got up to refill his glass.

"I thought we were sipping," hissed Theresa as I put the bottle back on the kitchen counter next to her.

"Some of us aren't ready to sip yet," I whispered back. "He's like a different guy around her. All of a sudden so nervous."

"Your job is to put him at ease!"

I swirled his glass in front of her.

He downed two more glasses of wine before we sat down to eat. Red tablecloth. Dim light. Nothing burned. I was helping Theresa bring the food from the kitchen to the dining-room table and found myself grinning. I felt good about everything. *This is how it could be all the time,* I remember thinking. *This is nice. I have everything under control. I do like Theresa. I like her long hair, and I like when she wears a skirt, and I like listening to jazz in a warm kitchen while she cooks. We could do this all the time.*

Halfway through the meal, I picked up Derek's glass and my own and started to get up from the table. "We are out of wine, my friends," Theresa announced.

"What?" Derek and I yelled simultaneously.

"How can this be?"

"Theresa"—Derek pointed at her—"why are you so greedy?"

"Really? Are you positive we're out of wine?"

She was positive. And no, there was not a wine deliv-ery service we could call. I knew better than to suggest we borrow from her parents' cabinet, but I eyed it until Theresa frowned at me.

We spent much of the rest of dinner comparing the gym programs at our respective schools. At Kim's school, you didn't have to take gym if you played a sport, whereas we had to take it no matter what. I'd received a C one term for consistently failing to wear the proper uniform. This happened while I was the leading scorer on the soccer team. There was no greater injustice imaginable. Kim suggested I transfer to her school, and then Theresa pointed out that I'd have to wear a yellow-and-black soccer uniform and be called a Yellowjacket.

"Crap, that's right." I sighed. "Sorry, deal's off, Kim. I'm not going to be a Yellowjacket. Your players look terr-ee-blay."

"That's all that really matters to James," Derek said. "How he looks on the field."

To prove his point, he produced a photo on his phone of me fixing my hair while about to take a penalty shot.

Kim's brother texted to say he was on his way to pick her up, and Theresa suggested that I give her a hand with a few things in the kitchen. I gave Derek an all-teeth smile and got up, leaving him alone with Kim and his chance to ask if she wanted to hang out again sometime. As I stacked dishes by the sink, Theresa slid up next to me and whispered, "You look very handsome."

"So do you," I whispered back. "I mean, you know," I mumbled. "Beautiful."

She put her hand on my waist as she reached around me for a dish towel, and her perfume made me slightly light-headed. *Stay right there,* I wanted to say. *Just like that forever.*

"Is he going to ask her out?" Theresa mouthed. I clasped my hands together as though in prayer, then I wrapped them around her waist and spun her to the counter. We kissed while they talked and giggled in the dining room.

This was a perfect evening. I told Theresa it was perfect. She rubbed her cheek against mine and kissed my ear. "Thanks," she whispered. "You were perfect, too. Except that you drank most of the wine, you jackass."

"No!" I protested. "That was Derek!"

They entered the kitchen while we were cracking up and I was gripping Theresa's wrists to prevent her from bopping me on the head.

"Okay," said Kim, ignoring the fight. "I'm out of here. Thank you again for a wonderful evening." We each got a peck on the cheek. "C'mon, Derek," she said, taking him by the hand. "You can wait with me on the porch."

After they left the kitchen, we stared at each other wide-eyed and grinning. "Stay here tonight," Theresa whispered.

"We *have* to stay over. Derek's not driving anywhere. He's going to be asleep on the couch in twenty minutes."

Sure enough, he came back in and stretched out on the couch to chat, but soon he was asleep and smiling. Kim ended up canceling their first date—some family thing—and Derek took it as a flat-out rejection, never called her back. Thinking he'd lost interest, she started going out with a kid at her own school, and Derek pretended not to care. But lying there on the couch, he was goofy with happiness. We covered him with a blanket and went upstairs to curl up in Theresa's bed.

You could see the stars from her window. "Maybe he'll

show her Saturn through his telescope," I said. "Then she'll be his forever."

"Oh, yeah? Is that how he made *you* fall in love with him? Astronomy?"

I thought of Hawken's stunned expression when he looked up from the telescope after first seeing Saturn. The way he put his hand on my shoulder in excitement. "Something like that," I muttered. It was the first time all night I'd let myself slip into thoughts of him.

April 10th

Dear Mom,

Oh, hi. It's your son. James. The middle one. You might remember me as the one who trekked muddy boots across your freshly washed kitchen floor last night. Or as the kid who complained while you dragged me through the mall last weekend after buying me new soccer cleats. Sorry for being a jerk.

At one point during the Shopping Death March, I made fun of some people walking into the bridal shop. That set you babbling about how time flies, and how soon we'll be buying a suit for my own wedding. You might've noticed that I didn't have much to say about any of that. Maybe you're right—I hope you're right—maybe I'll be buying myself a tuxedo ten years from now.

I do like the way people behave toward me and Theresa when we're together—everyone's voice changes to music, and we get all sorts of smiles. And we're not even really dating.

You know, I try hard at everything and, believe me, I'm trying hard here, too. What I wish would happen is that tomorrow morning I'll wake up and everything will be totally effortless. Thanks again for the cleats.

James

Back in freshman year, I fell into the habit of writing letters to people and then stuffing them in my desk drawer. I started doing it after I read a book about Abraham Lincoln. He used to scribble angry letters to cabinet members, pouring his guts onto the page, saying everything that had been rattling around his head, and never send them. Then he'd go talk to the guy calmly.

The key to that desk drawer is one of those old antique jobs with a long hollow shaft and a clover head. It once belonged to a pirate, I'm pretty sure. Just in case anyone gets nosy, I keep it with my house key in my pocket.

From where I sit and scribble every night, I can see out my window, up the hill into the woods. It's not just a backyard with some trees. It's a forest that sweeps north, practically unbroken, to the tundra. A few miles from my house, Vermont's two biggest highways and two big rivers converge. Snow to our west melts into the White River and splashes into the Connecticut, the river that drains the northern hills. My dad calls our valley the Shire, because he says we live such cozy little lives, like a bunch of hobbits sipping tea by potbellied stoves in our burrows. He's right, in some ways. But everyone else calls the place the Upper Valley.

When I was about ten, I was looking out my bedroom window when the whole snowy world glowed blue beneath a full moon. A moose cow and her calf emerged from the trees and loped along our yard's edge, then slipped back into the forest. I watched them trudge up the wooded hillside until I couldn't tell their legs from saplings, their bodies from the shadows. Now, whenever I pass that window, I peek out to see if they're there, standing on the shore of that sea of trees that laps at our lawn. One day, my dad says, that forest will swallow up all our little roads and houses. It took me a long time to realize that he meant lifetimes from now, not so much "maybe by next September." Still, I think about it every time I mow the grass and every time I help my dad repair our old stone wall. It falls apart ten yards into the woods, where it once separated sheep pastures that hemlock, maple, and ash have already reclaimed.

CHAPTER 3

Hawken caught up to me in the hallway on the way to English on Monday afternoon.

"Did you read that play?" he demanded.

"Yeah."

"All of it?"

"Yeah, I liked it."

"Quick summary, please?"

"Oh, boy . . ."

Just then, Aaron Foster came out of a classroom and swished down the hall in front of us. He was wearing skinny black jeans, a lavender V-neck sweater, a gray scarf, and white tennis shoes, no socks. The snow hadn't even melted yet.

Hawken grabbed my arm and opened his eyes and mouth wide, as if the stars and planets had aligned before him. I honestly didn't know what was wrong with him until he leaned into the stare and then slowly turned his head from Aaron to me.

Feeling sort of sick, I looked at the ground and whispered, "Stop."

I should've handled it differently. I should've smacked him in the head or tripped him or something to at least acknowledge he was being funny. I knew he wasn't actually suggesting that I date Aaron Foster, but it was like a bad dream coming true. We walked a few yards in silence.

"Hey," Hawken whispered. "I was only kidding."

In ninth grade when Aaron arrived in our school, fresh from California, he was always scribbling in his own notebook, usually with a purple gel pen, making a show of being a writer. He hung out with this girl Lisa Schultz, who's friends with Theresa. She's pretty cool most of the time, but she wears combat boots and somehow she got a tattoo on her bicep when she was fifteen. She dates boys, which confuses them. Anyway, Aaron and Lisa would sit around writing together. He would stare at my friends and me for a bit, eyes narrowed, then go back to scribbling. There was another Aaron in our class back then, Aaron Gillespie, so to distinguish between the two, Aaron Foster was quickly dubbed "Gay Aaron."

That nickname died out eventually, but I still never went out of my way to talk to him. The few times I *had* to speak to him, I looked over my shoulder, wondering who was watching.

He still hadn't looked back at us when he reached our classroom, opened the door, and disappeared inside. I glanced back down the hall, but the only other people were way at the other end, so they couldn't have witnessed the exchange between Hawken and me. But who knew? Maybe some kid had been stuffed in a locker during lunch and had observed it all through the vents.

There were two empty seats left when we got into class: one on either side of Aaron Foster. Hawken and I settled in to his left and right. We still had a couple of minutes before class began, and Mr. Breyer wasn't even in the room yet, so Hawken scooted his chair next to Aaron, leaned across his desk, and demanded, "Hey, you two. What happens in the play? For real. He might give us a reading quiz. I don't want to fail again."

Aaron laughed politely and drew little circles on the cover of his notebook. He wasn't used to being included in our conversations, though it wasn't all our fault. Soon after he'd arrived, he'd called Hawken a retard. I remember Hawken looking as though Aaron had spat in his face, but before he could say anything in response, Derek pinned Aaron to a locker and whispered a threat that began *Listen, you little fairy* and then dropped so low I couldn't hear the rest. Meanwhile, I had turned to Hawken and offered this heartfelt comfort: "You are not what he just said." I'm sure that reassurance made him feel all better.

That was at the end of ninth grade, when we were all smaller and stupider. If we held grudges for all the idiotic things we said and did as freshmen and sophomores, the hallways would be silent. No one would be talking to anyone else. Hawken certainly wouldn't be talking to Derek or me. A few months before we stuck up for him against Aaron, the two of us had been demolishing a bag of tortilla chips in my kitchen. My mom came in and asked how Hawken was doing.

"Good," I said with a mouthful of chips. "Hawken's just Hawken."

"He doesn't seem upset in class?" she asked. "He's not getting teased?"

"Tim Hawken?" Derek asked. "No. Of course not."

"His mom says he's having a hard time. Some kids have been giving him trouble because he goes for help with reading."

Derek and I glanced at each other. He grimaced. We often joked with Hawken that his reading problems made him special. "You're just a special kid," we'd said a few days earlier, cracking up. "Your specialness makes us love you even more. Dr. Seuss says you're one of the most specialist specials there is!" I remember Hawken laughing along with us.

"Naw, he's fine," I said.

"Well, he might be playing it tough at school, but he's having a rough transition. So look out for him."

Derek and I quit that kind of joking around from then on. I've never apologized to Hawken for the crap we said to him. I don't know how.

But either Hawken had forgotten, or he never mentioned it. He felt comfortable enough to demand emergency reading assistance, anyway. "Come on," he pled. "Seriously. This is why they put us you-try-so-hard readers in class with you you're-so-good readers. You're supposed to be helping me. A quick summary. Go!" I shook my head helplessly, and Hawken reached across, grabbed Aaron's arm, and shook him. "Aaron! C'mon, man. Rescue me!"

Aaron looked over at me. "I don't even know where to begin. I mean, it's Shakespeare. It's kind of complicated. . . ."

Mr. Breyer walked in.

Aaron whispered in a hurry, "Everyone falls in love but they fall in love with the wrong people."

"No kidding, Foster," whispered Hawken. "But what about the play? The play!"

Aaron laughed out loud.

"You both suck at this," muttered Hawken just as Breyer called out, "Split a piece of paper with a friend and number it one through five! A quick reading quiz. Hawken! Let's go, kid. Head off the desk!"

As we were leaving class, Breyer called Hawken aside. I stopped, too, ready to chat. "Hey, he'll catch up with you, James," Breyer said gently.

So, I waited out in the hall. And five minutes later, when

Hawken came out, he had black shadows under his eyes that I'm not sure had been there before. He turned down the hall without noticing me, and I had to walk fast to catch up with him. "Hey, man," I said. "You okay?"

He didn't answer right away. "He doesn't get it. He just thinks I'm lazy. Like I don't even try to do the reading."

I walked in silence with him for a bit. *You don't try to do the reading*, I wanted to say. *You get everyone to do it for you.* Instead, I said, "He knows that you have, like, a reading disability, right?"

"Yeah, but I don't think he knows what that means. Anything he assigns us to read takes me, like, three times as long to read as everyone else. So I try to skim it. Or I find summaries online. Or I ask for help from you guys. Otherwise, all I would do all day is sound out words, sound out words, sound out words. It's exhausting."

"I could read out loud to you," I offered.

"I have audiobooks a lot of the time. I have one for this play. That's what he was just on my case about. But it rots. It takes forever to listen to those things. And the Bruins were on last night . . ."

"Oh, dude." I pushed him. "My sympathy for you is gone!"

After school that day, Derek, Theresa, Hawken, and I went sledding down the abandoned logging road behind my house. The previous two springs, we had all run on the track team, but to Mark's delight, track and cross-country had been cut due to budget constraints. The letters to the editor and school board had been fierce but ineffective.

Derek and I stopped at Ike's Gas on the way to go sledding. Plastic orange toboggans are among Ike's meager merchandise. I was standing next to Derek as he paid for the sled when the cashier said cheerfully, "Sledding, huh? I didn't know you people liked the snow."

I was confused, but Derek didn't even hesitate. "No, ma'am. We don't like no snow." I'd seen variations of this routine many times, and it makes everyone super uncomfortable. Derek's parents forbid him from doing it. I wanted to pick him up and carry him out of the store. "Dat white stuff is mi-tee colb. MI-TEE colb!"

"Dude, let's go," I interjected. I knew exactly where he was going next.

"But you know what I do loves?" He spread his arms wide. "I loves white folk. *All* you white folk. I loves you."

The lady behind the counter had gone deep red, and she wouldn't look at us as she handed Derek his change. I grabbed Derek's shoulder and hustled him out of the store.

"Why do you do that?" I asked as we strode to his car.

Derek sneered. "'I didn't know *you people* like the snow?' You've got to be kidding me."

"I mean, it was a dumb thing for her to say, but—"

"You have no idea," Derek interrupted. He wasn't angry with me. It was a statement of fact. I *don't* have any idea.

I've seen his back stiffen when someone sounds surprised that he does well in school, and sometimes I've wondered what's caused him to fall stonily silent in stores and restaurants.

I'm not sure which is harder for him, though: being black in a state where almost everyone's white or being Christian in a state where so few people go to church. Both of Derek's parents are doctors at Dartmouth-Hitchcock, the big hospital. They're super nice and also super religious. On the way to my house, we drove past Derek's "Sabbath House of Fun," as he calls it. His mom and dad used to take me there on Sunday mornings if I had stayed over on a Saturday night. And then they would ask me what I learned. Derek stopped talking to me about God years ago. There's still a palm leaf cross on his bedroom wall, but the picture of a blond-haired, blue-eyed Jesus that used to hang above his pillow disappeared soon after we entered high school.

Theresa and Hawken were kicking a ball around on the driveway when Derek and I arrived at my house. Hip-hop thumped from Hawken's car stereo. He tried juggling the ball with his boots on—it didn't work—and the ball rolled beneath his car. Theresa got down on her stomach on the gritty wet driveway and fished the ball out. She used the outside of her foot to send the ball skidding back to Hawken. He kicked it back under the car.

Derek led the way up the trail behind my house to the sled run. The old logging road tumbles out of an overgrown meadow. In the summer and fall we sometimes make a little fire there and watch the stars. When you sit on top of the big granite boulder in the middle of the field, you can watch cloud shadows shift across the foothills of the White Mountains. My family doesn't own the property, but I consider the place mine.

Derek and Hawken rode in one sled; Theresa and I rode in the other. These are the usual teams, and they're pretty evenly matched. Derek and Hawken are aggressive sledders, but Theresa's light. We catch enough air on a few jumps to knock the wind out of ourselves upon landing. Normally, we end up lying tangled together in the snow, laughing hysterically.

When we hiked back up to the starting line after our fifth or sixth run, I stretched my arms out and fell backward into a drift.

Hawken jumped onto the empty sled and pointed at Derek, alone in the other. "Just you and me. The Final Race."

Theresa leaped on the sled behind Derek. "No, Derek and me against you guys!" She was pointing at Hawken and me. Hawken's smile didn't change. It was as though it had frozen to his face. He stared off down the hill. I was supposed to climb on his sled, wrap my arms around him, and careen down the road in a tight embrace. We'd done it plenty of times before.

"I'm sitting this one out," I said.

"James!" Theresa roared.

"It's all you guys," I said, and, as she screamed in protest, I pushed her and Derek down the first twenty yards of the run. Hawken leaped up, ran with his sled to catch up, and dived onto it when he was level with them. He'd opened up a lead by the time they screamed around the first corner. I fell backward in the snow and made myself think about Theresa's smile instead of Hawken's.

When they arrived back at the rock, we all agreed it was time to call it quits. We slid down the trail to my house. I could smell wood smoke, and the clouds were still pink, the sky a weak blue. The worst of the winter was over. The darkest part, anyway. Spring would arrive in a few weeks. Life would get easier.

CHAPTER 4

Derek and I were tiptoeing through the school parking lot's slush the next afternoon when a truck roared toward us. We trotted out of the way, but the driver still slammed on his brakes and slid. Ready to yell, we both looked over at him, but he was staring at Aaron Foster, who had slipped in the slush just ahead of the truck.

He was sporting a typical Aaron Foster ensemble beneath his unbuttoned blue peacoat: tight white jeans and a purple T-shirt. He gave the driver a weary glare as he got up, and then he continued walking to his car. His trousers were soaked.

"Faggot!" the driver shouted as he accelerated out of the parking lot.

I started to walk over to Aaron's car, but he had hopped in quickly and his reverse lights flashed white. As he backed past me, he kept his head turned, but when he looked forward to drive away, I could tell he was holding back tears.

"Good grief, dude," I muttered.

"But why does he wear that stuff to school?" said Derek. "All those girls he hangs out with—not one of them has the sense to give him good advice about how to avoid attracting attention."

"Maybe we should say something to him."

Derek shrugged. "Man, my father would have something to say to me if I went to school dressed like that."

I nodded. But watching that scene in the parking lot made me feel sick. That night I ended up scribbling Aaron a letter.

Tuesday, April 12th

Hey, Aaron,

We don't know each other all that well, so it probably seems weird that I'm writing you a letter. I hope you won't take it the wrong way. I'm probably going to end up saying something stupid and insensitive, but I swear I'm writing with good intentions.

I'm sorry that you're always getting picked on, and I'm sorry you had to deal with that kid in the parking lot today. And I'm sorry that I was one of the guys who used to give you a hard time. But honestly, why do you wear such flaming queer outfits to school? You're inviting trouble. In a perfect world, you could wear whatever you want, I guess, but look around you, man. This isn't San Francisco. It pays to try to fit in a little.

Here's another thing I don't understand. If you're gay, and I've heard that you've admitted it, then why do you have to act like a girl? If a boy likes other boys, why would he be attracted to a guy who walks and talks like a girl? There are probably a few other gay kids in the school, but I'm sure they're scared to come out because they don't want to be associated with you.

Here's what I wish you'd do: go buy yourself a pair of loose-fit Levi's and a plain blue T-shirt. Buy a pair of Chuck Taylors and scuff them up in the street. Wash all that gel out of your hair, dry it with a towel, and use your hands to comb it. Do some sit-ups and push-ups. Listen to Led Zeppelin. Watch a hockey game. Then you can come sit with us at lunch.

James

Of course I didn't send the letter—I never sent any of them, but Aaron reached the same conclusions all by himself. When he walked into English class the next morning, I actually didn't recognize him for a minute. He wore loose jeans, a white T-shirt, and a blue hoodie. His blond hair, usually standing in spikes, fell deflated across his forehead. He looked pale and sad, but I couldn't help thinking that his life was about to improve dramatically.

Mr. Breyer assigned Aaron to my small group to do peer review work on essays we'd just written. Our third partner was a girl named Tara, whose contributions to peer review consist mostly of loud gum chewing and eye rolling. She once yelled at me for using the word *constitutes*. She said I was being stuck-up.

"Hey, man," I whispered to Aaron once we'd pulled our desks together and before Tara had made it across the room. "I'm sorry about what happened yesterday. You know, in the parking lot."

"Yeah, some people are jerks," Aaron said without looking up.

"I would've said something to the guy, but—"

"I don't want to talk about it," Aaron interrupted as he dug through his backpack. He pulled out a math notebook and a pack of colored markers and put them on his desk, as though he'd need them in English.

"Okay," I said quietly. "I like the new look."

Tara arrived just then, and they started chatting it up about her new shoes. I'm not sure if Aaron even heard my last comment.

The next period I had health class in the same room. One moment I was listening to Tara mispronounce *paragraph*, and the next I was listening to the baseball coach wing a lecture about sexually transmitted diseases. To his credit, Coach Williams had gone online to find photos of genital chancres. Those woke me up, as did the back row's fake puking sounds. For a minute, it seemed like Williams had some valuable information to pass along, but then, as he was talking about the importance of condoms, he dropped a bomb that made me gnaw the end of my pen flat. "Condoms are especially important for gay men because of the AIDS." And then with his hand raised, like a Boy Scout taking an oath to tolerance, Williams swore, "I don't have any problems with guys who like other guys. If that's your choice, that's your choice."

I sat there thinking about all the nights I'd spent trying to fall asleep, trying to reprogram my dreams, willing myself to feel the way about girls I knew I was supposed to. The word *choice* had never occurred to me in relation to the way I felt about boys and girls. It was involuntary. Like a reflex. I wanted to turn in my seat and gauge Aaron's reaction, but I just stared at my desk, punishing myself with the flavor of Bic plastic and ink.

CHAPTER 5

That evening I had to go interview my neighbor, Mr. Kelly. I was writing my history term paper on the Vietnam War protests. My dad had suggested I interview Mr. Kelly, who lives up our road and always stops to talk to my parents when he's walking his dog past our yard. My dad said the old guy would give me a version of history "I hadn't listened to carefully."

I tried to warm Mr. Kelly up by saying that it must have been fun to be young in the late sixties, when the hippie scene was at its height. Looking at me in disbelief, he barked: "Were you there, Manfretti?" He says I look like a guy he knew in college, so he calls me that: Manfretti. "I don't remember seeing you back there in all that late-sixties' fun. Let me tell you what your peace and love dipshits were all about.

"My father and his brother and his buddies fought in the Pacific Islands against the Japanese. My uncle never came home from that war. He died out there battling the Jap Empire. And if you think they were nice guys, the Japanese, fellas we should've sat down with and offered a joint and bootlegs of the Grateful Dead to, ask the grandparents of your Korean and Chinese friends. But don't mix them up. They do not like that. Believe me.

"At the end of the war, the entire country's celebrating that it's all over, and the economy's going gangbusters, everyone's got a new refrigerator and television, and my uncle—still dead.

"Twenty years later, the children of my father and uncle's generation—*my* generation—go off to college. These kids have been afforded more leisure time than anyone anywhere has ever had—their parents are working their tails off to send them to school to read poetry and study art. And what are the kids' responses to all that comfort and privilege? 'Screw your System. It's broken. Nothing's right. You're all Oppressors.'"

"But what about the Civil Rights Movement?" I asked. "Those guys—"

"I'm not talking about the Civil Rights Movement! Don't mix up the kids sitting scared as hell at lunch counters and the faggots sprawled stoned on college greens. Reading and thinking and talking bullshit about human rights is not the same thing as fighting for it. The hippies didn't get it. They joined a circus that pretended to be part of a fight. If a fight looks like a lot of fun, you should be suspicious. 'If you ain't scared standing up for what's right, you ain't standing up for much.' Mark Twain wrote that."

Mark Twain did not write that. I googled it as soon as I got home.

I recapped that conversation at dinner, and my dad smirked, but my mom's fork clattered to the table and she pretended to scream. "Ask Mr. Kelly if dropping napalm on civilians and sending American boys to die in the dark of Viet Cong tunnels keeps America strong and free! James, he's equating World War II and the Vietnam War. They're not the same thing."

"I don't know. I wasn't there." I shrugged. My dad started cracking up.

"Oh, go read about it." My mom sighed.

Sometimes it's hard to tell if she's actually annoyed. She gets fired up about politics. "Mr. Kelly told you part of the story. Not everyone he calls a hippie was lying around stoned. A lot of them saw the Vietnam War as a betrayal of the values Mr. Kelly's *blessed* uncle"—she was becoming sarcastic—"fought to defend."

Rex was banging his spoon against his water glass. My mom put her hand on his to still him. When I looked up, she was staring at me hard. "They were questioning whether it made sense to promote freedom and peace by dropping bombs from the sky. And whether an economy still fueled by manufacturing missiles was an economy they wanted to be part of."

This kind of reaction was why my brother Luke and I often called my mom "Mother Comma Esquire." She drops into aggressive lawyer mode without warning. I'd been separating my mixed vegetables into small piles during her rant: a little pile of corn, a little pile of lima beans, a little pile of red pepper pieces. "You're going to eat all those," my mom said, returning to her own dinner.

I ate them in four fast forkfuls and asked to be excused.

"Forget about your history paper." My dad chuckled as I got up. "Please your mother: just lie around upstairs and smoke some pot. Be a revolutionary."

"Go write up your interview!" my mother yelled, putting her hands over Rex's ears. Now I knew she wasn't really angry.

"I heard *pot*!" Rex hollered. "I want some pot!"

I went up to my room, leaving them to deal with their youngest son. Before I tried to decipher my scribbled interview notes and type up a coherent transcript, I found an index card and on it, in big capital letters, I preserved Mr. Kelly's advice and tacked it to the wall above my desk:

> *IF YOU AIN'T SCARED STANDING UP*
> *FOR WHAT'S RIGHT,*
> *THEN YOU AIN'T STANDING UP FOR MUCH.*
> *—NOT MARK TWAIN*

★ ★ ★

In the yellow light from the porch, I could see sleet falling, and I could hear it rattling on the deck. I don't know if it was sleet or freezing rain or what, actually, but it made me ache for summer, when my mom would be tying back tomato plants at this time in the evening, and Rex would be up in his tree in the corner of the yard. I know it's an ash tree only because he told me. We were on the driveway just after it rained last fall, and I picked up one of those winged seeds, tossed it in the air. "I love these helicopter things."

"Samaras," Rex corrected me.

"What?"

"They're called samaras. That one's from a maple. They fly like that so the seeds grow far from the tree. Luke told me."

"Oh." I picked up a smaller one. "What about this guy?"

"Ash." He pointed to his favorite climbing tree. "Probably from Patrice Bergeron."

"You're naming trees in the yard after Bruins players?"

"Not all of them." He pointed to a sickly pine at the back of the yard. "I named that one after the goalie for the Flyers because Dad says he's going to chainsaw it soon."

That kid knows more about animals and plants than anyone I know. A couple of summers ago, I was mowing the lawn, and Rex came out of the woods, barefoot and grinning, his hands cupped in front of him. I turned off the mower and bent down to see. He'd caught this tiny, shiny gray snake with a bright yellow ring around its neck and an orange belly.

45

"Whoa! Look at him! Where did you find that little guy?"

"Back at the old fire ring in the clearing. They like hanging out in the charcoal. Isn't that weird?"

"That is weird. Does he bite?"

"No, he's just a little ring-necked. He's wicked gentle. I want to see him eat. I'm going to catch him something."

I stood up from my crouch. "And you're going to go put him back, right?" Rex didn't answer. He peeked between his fingers. "Remember what Luke said after the Red Eft Fiasco." Rex had caught and imprisoned three bright orange newts without telling anyone. Luke found him crying inconsolably over their little shriveled corpses.

"Snakes like being outside, dude. You wouldn't want to be put in a glass jar, right?"

"But it'll be safe and decorated."

"Come on. Let's go put him back. You can show me where you caught him."

He cupped the snake against his shirt with his right hand and took my hand with his left. He doesn't do that anymore.

Sleet strafed my bedroom window. If that snake still had any slither, it would be curled way down in an old chipmunk hole somewhere. Luke says the deer and moose curl up in low spruce stands or willows when the weather's really ugly. All those creatures out there just know what to do—they don't have to figure it out. As Rex said, it's so weird.

CHAPTER 6

The next day after school, Derek and I headed to the weight room, only to find it crowded with baseball players, including Mark.

"Ohhhh!" Mark bellowed as I entered. "James! What are you doing in here? You in training for our 10K now?"

"Sure," Derek replied for me. "We got to turn young Liddell here into one of you *real* athlete-types."

While I spotted Derek on the bench, Mark tore into Aaron Foster for his abrupt shift in style. "What's up with that fag? Overnight he becomes a real boy? Who is he? Pinocchio?"

The younger kids on his baseball team were in hysterics.

The older guys just smirked. A year or two ago I might've joined in. What bothered me most was that Coach Williams, the baseball coach who teaches my health class, was right there, trying to fix one of the stationary bikes, and he said nothing. Maybe he wasn't listening, but the word *fag* usually gets a response from even the most dazed and weary teacher. In the locker room and gym, for some reason, the word attracts as much attention as the clang of weights.

"Mark, give him a break," I said eventually. "That kid takes a ton of abuse. Who can blame him for wanting to fly under the radar for a while?"

"Fly under your *gay-dar*, you mean?" Mark laughed.

The sophomores and freshmen howled.

I shook my head, tried to smile, and looked over at the coach.

Nothing.

It bothered me all afternoon and evening, so after I'd finished my homework, before I went to sleep, I ended up scribbling another letter, this time to my soccer coach.

> *Thursday, April 14th*
> *Dear Coach Greschner,*
> *Thanks for agreeing to coach our indoor team. Even though we're playing only once a week, it feels good to kick the ball around, keep my touch.*
> *One of the things that's bothering me lately is that I feel like I'm hiding on our team. I never really totally relax around*

those guys. I guess I'm scared someone's going to see through
me. I've thought about telling you and the rest of the team
what's going on, but I'm not sure I can get the right words to
come out of my mouth. The idea of talking in public about
everything rattling around in my head sort of makes me want
to throw up, and I'm still not totally sure I know what's true
about me.

  Anyway, that's it. I wish I could talk to you directly, but
I don't know how you would react. Kids yell stuff in the locker
room, on the bus, on the field all the time, and no one says a
word to stop them. Not even you. I don't know. Maybe I'm
not the only one who's thinking about all this stuff, but it sure
seems that way. Thanks.

  James

On Friday, I was staring blankly across the lunchroom when
I spotted Aaron walking away from the serving line with a
plate of pasta on his tray. He wore a light blue button-down
and khakis, still playing it safe. While he was looking around,
trying to find his giggly girlfriends, another boy walked past
and, without even turning his head, hit the tray so that the
spaghetti tipped all over Aaron. The plate clattered to the
floor and every head in the lunchroom turned.

  The long, low chorus of *homo* began at the baseball players' table, but then boys on the other side of the lunchroom
picked it up, so it quickly sounded as though it was coming
from everywhere. Aaron looked so pale that I thought he

might pass out, but instead he walked quickly out the door.

It was a shame that Aaron didn't witness what happened next. It might've made him feel a little better. A couple of teachers were all over the baseball team. They escorted four of them down to the principal's office, and kids booed at the culprits and clapped as they filed out. The booing was loud. When I got up to go find Aaron, a few senior girls were screaming at a group of freshmen sitting by the soda machines.

There's a boys' bathroom right around the corner from the cafeteria, and that's where I found Aaron. I opened the door ready to make a joke about doing laundry with paper towels and purple hand soap, but Aaron wasn't trying to clean his shirt. He had both hands braced on one of the sinks, and he gasped as though he'd been held underwater. When he turned to duck into the only toilet stall, his shirt looked as though someone had machine-gunned him across the chest.

"Aaron," I said softly. "Aaron, hey."

He couldn't draw a steady breath, but he managed to beg from inside the stall, "Leave me alone, please."

"Dude, it's James Liddell." As if that would be any comfort to him. "I'm sorry—I'm sorry that just happened."

"Please just leave me alone," he said again, and then added in a tight high voice, "James."

I stood there for a little while longer, listening to him fight himself back to normal. Then I took off my sweater and slung it over the stall's metal wall.

"Hey. Here. Take this. You're never going to get that shirt cleaned."

No response.

I took a deep breath. "Hey, man, I know you don't want to talk right now. I don't blame you. But maybe another time, yeah?"

Still nothing, but he drew a longer, steadier breath.

"There's a party at Kevin O'Dea's tonight." I didn't know what else to say. "Maybe I'll see you there?"

No answer.

I left.

English came two periods later. I sat in the back row that day. In the few minutes before the bell rang, most of the class huddled at the front of the room, looking at photos of Mr. Breyer's baby.

Aaron walked in, eyes still puffy and red-rimmed, but calm. He wore my green sweater. When he spotted me, he made himself smile for a second and walked over. Without saying a word, he placed a pink alligator PEZ dispenser on my desk.

"What's this?"

"Fair trade until Monday," he explained, tugging the collar of my sweater.

"Fair trade?" I laughed. "Is this a fifty-dollar PEZ dispenser?"

"It's very dear to me. And your sacred sweater's way too big on me. And on you, actually. I'm sorry that I've waited so long to tell you. We'll switch back on Monday."

I nodded. Kids were finding their seats. Aaron took the desk one up and across from me.

"Hey," I whispered. "Come to that party tonight." I wanted to be nice, but maybe I got carried away. I never saw Aaron at parties.

Breyer told us to turn to the previous night's reading.

Aaron swiveled quickly and hissed, "Where is it?"

I scribbled directions on a scrap of paper, poked Aaron with a pen, and handed the note across the aisle to him.

Then Breyer called me to the front of the room to read aloud.

As I walked into the gym after school, Mark was coming out the same door. He was shirtless, as usual, and he grabbed my arm. "Liddell! Why is Aaron Foster wearing your stuff?"

It's a plain green woolen sweater—I hadn't realized that it had become my signature look. "I gave it to him. Someone spilled spaghetti all over him." I pretended that I hadn't seen Mark at lunch, jeering with the baseball team.

"Yeah, but"—and here Mark grimaced—"Aaron Foster? You lent your sweater to that kid? Who knows what kind of dirty it'll be when you get it back."

"I think it'll be okay," I muttered and tried to walk away, but Mark still gripped my arm.

"You should be careful, James." He was talking quickly, but he sounded sincerely concerned. "You don't know what people might say."

"Yeah, I know, dude." I could hear Hawken's voice in my head: *He's just trying to help.* "Thanks, man."

He slapped my butt as I passed him. "I don't work tonight," he said, "so I'll see you guys later."

The impressive thing about Mark is that he's had a job, at least one job, since he was eight years old. He's weeded gardens, stacked firewood, shoveled snow, cut lawns, cleaned gutters, and painted fences for years. Now he's a dishwasher and prep cook in a restaurant, and he's been trying to start a dog-walking business. Hawken took a photograph of him untangling the leashes of two Pekingese while a golden retriever mounts his leg. We're not supposed to mention that photo anymore, but it's the screensaver on Derek's laptop.

The confusing thing about Mark is that as much as he can be a moron, he can also be really funny and nice to people you'd never expect him to be friendly around. He always works the elevator for this disabled boy who's in a wheelchair. He's the only person I have ever seen helping that kid and his aide with the elevator. And in class, he makes friends with the girls sitting next to him, even if they're not popular. There's this one girl, Sam, who's pretty overweight and wears sweatshirts with puppies and horses on them, and I've seen Mark leaning in to listen to her, asking questions quietly. She seems really happy to talk to him, and he's not up to anything, as far as I can tell. He really does know how to talk to people, how to listen to them, when he's not threatening to cripple them. I don't know why he can't be the same way around us guys more often. It's as if he thinks we're all competing to be alpha dog in a furry pack that only he believes exists.

CHAPTER 7

When I emptied my pockets after school that afternoon, the coffee can I chuck my change into was three-quarters full. One of the things that ended up in the change can was Aaron's alligator PEZ dispenser. My keys live in that can, too, so I figured I'd see the gator when I grabbed my keys on the way out the door on Monday morning. I'd stuff him back in my pocket to trade with Aaron. I hate PEZ, and I love that sweater.

Kevin O'Dea used to go to our school, but this year he transferred to a rich private school in New Hampshire. We don't see much of him anymore, except when he throws parties.

His parents had gone out of town again, so he invited half the kids in the Upper Valley to his place. That half invited the other half.

Derek and I discovered an old telescope in the garage and, to take a break from the crowd, we retreated to the tree house in an old hemlock. The moon was bright that night. I had just managed to bring the mountains around the Sea of Serenity into focus when we heard shouting coming from the other side of the house.

"Someone's probably having trouble getting his car past all the other ones and wants, like, thirty people to back out," Derek guessed. We had parked on a back road over the hill from Kevin's place, knowing we'd be stuck if we parked on the long, narrow driveway.

"Whoever's yelling is pissed."

"That's Mark," Derek replied.

And then the real screaming began between four or five boys. A bottle broke. Derek and I both stood up and let go of the telescope. It tipped out of the tree house, spun twice in the air, and clattered onto the ground. Through the kitchen window, we could see a crowd rushing into the living room, where windows looked out onto the driveway. A girl shouted "Stop! Just stop it!" and another yelled "Oh my God!" over and over and over again. The music fell silent.

"What just happened?" Derek asked flatly.

But he didn't move and neither did I. We could hear a kid yelling, "He didn't mean it! He didn't mean it!" Another kid shouted, "Shut up! Shut up and get the cars out of the road so an ambulance can get through!"

It's tough to say how much time passed before we started down the ladder. Inside the house, we could see girls in tears being comforted by stiff-shouldered boys. Kevin O'Dea was running around with a black garbage bag, and another boy was chucking beer bottles in it. He used his whole arm to sweep a dozen cans off the kitchen counter.

As Derek and I rounded the house, engines started up along the length of the driveway. Descending cars sent light beams careening across the treetops. We saw Mark sitting in his car, cradling his hand, flexing his fingers. Hawken stood by the door, whispering to him. He held a handful of snow to his own jaw and as we approached, he waved us away.

Boys from Kevin's school stood on the edge of the light, about ten yards away from where a boy in a green sweater lay in the snow. A kid wearing a volunteer fire department jacket knelt next to him, holding a fleece to the back of the boy's head and talking into his phone. I squinted at the kid lying on the ground.

"That's . . . that's Aaron Foster," I whispered. Aaron looked like he was gazing up at the moon and stars. His eyes were half open.

"I don't know his name," the boy said. "But he might've cracked his skull."

I pointed to Mark in the car. "Did that kid punch him?"

"Yeah, but he's so hammered he doesn't even know where

he is, never mind who he hit."

"I got hit, too," a second boy said. "My lip's bleeding. Look."

"I got elbowed in the jaw wicked hard," said another. "By you, I think."

"Did Mark punch Hawken?" I asked. "The kid holding snow to his jaw?"

"I only saw Hawken tackling Mark in the snow," said the kid tending to Aaron.

"As if he would've been able to steer down the driveway even if all the cars *had* moved. He's so wasted he threw a whiskey bottle against the side of the house."

They all started talking over one another.

"Where'd all the blood come from?"

"Didn't you hear Aaron's head hit the ground? He cracked the ice."

"Is Aaron breathing?"

"He's dead."

"Is he dead? He's not dead!"

"Hey," the kid holding the fleece to Aaron's head interrupted, looking up. "Would you all shut up? This is really, really bad." His yellow winter gloves dripped blood in the snow.

Everyone went quiet.

Theresa found Derek and me shivering in the dark among drunk kids we hardly knew. She leaned against me. "He was asking Hawken and Mark where you were," she whispered, nodding at Aaron. "He'd been here only, like, five minutes." She squeezed my hand.

Sirens yelped at the bottom of the driveway. The ambulance had to wait for the last of the cars to clear out.

"We can't help. We should split," Theresa whispered to Derek and me as the sirens grew louder on their way up the hill. The three of us slipped behind the house and climbed over the ridge back to the car. I felt bad leaving Aaron there, but it wouldn't help anyone if we got busted.

We jumped into the bushes along the road when a couple of cop cars flew past. Theresa, who is usually our self-appointed designated driver, took us home. We learned later that the police weren't letting cars leave even after they turned off Kevin's driveway onto the main road. They blocked the street. Two kids got DUIs that night. Ten got charged with underage drinking.

My parents were reading when I arrived home. They sat with me in the kitchen until one, talking through everything.

Conflicting stories would emerge from that night, but the story I knew then was that Mark had been yelling for kids to move their cars so he could back out. No one cooperated. Drunk out of his mind, he pushed the kids nearest him, and when one of them pushed back, he went nuts. He hit Hawken. He shattered a whiskey bottle against the house. He clocked Aaron in the jaw, and Aaron's skull cracked the ice.

My parents looked more worried than I had expected

them to be when I told them about Aaron. "Was he breathing?" my dad asked. "Was he conscious? Did he respond to what was said to him?"

I shrugged halfheartedly. I wanted to reassure them, but I couldn't.

"He cracked his head on an icy driveway and was unconscious, James. People die from hitting their heads like that. A hockey player died a couple of years ago after hitting his head on the ice during a fight." My dad didn't seem to notice that I had put my head in my hands. He just kept talking. "Swelling beneath the skull puts so much pressure on the brain that sometimes doctors have to drill a hole—"

"What if Aaron's dead?" I interrupted.

My parents didn't respond.

"What if he's dead, and Mark gets charged with murder?" I hadn't cried in front of my parents in years, but my voice was tight. I got up for some water.

"Mark's not going to get charged with murder," my mom said softly. She's a lawyer. "But he might spend a lot of time in court. He might get sentenced to a few months in corrections. How did he get that drunk anyway? How is he getting his hands on bottles of whiskey?"

"I have no idea. Probably through someone at work." Like everyone else I know, Mark has connections. My brother Luke's pal buys beer for us sometimes and charges us only a cheap six-pack. "I didn't have anything to drink, anyway," I lied. "Neither did Derek or Hawken. And I'm sure Aaron didn't either. He'd been at the party for, like, five minutes."

"Aaron's the boy you all think is gay, isn't he?" my mom asked carefully.

I nodded.

"Do you think Mark punched him on purpose? Do you think he hit him because Aaron is—"

"No," I interrupted again. I told them that Mark's a good guy, that Hawken's good friends with him, that he's really funny, that he dressed up as a skunk for Halloween one year. During a field trip to the science museum in fourth grade, Mark and I spent the entire time together, watching the leaf-cutter ant colony.

They didn't say anything.

Derek came to my place Saturday afternoon. His parents said that Aaron was still in the hospital under observation. They work in a different department there, so that's all they knew about him.

Mark, we heard from Hawken, had been arrested and then released into his father's custody. Hawken had only had one beer that night and was chewing gum when the cops arrived. No underage drinking ticket for him.

Derek and I tried doing research for our history papers, but I'd get to the bottom of a page and realize I hadn't taken in any of the words at all. My mind was full of ambulances and beeping hospital machines. I caught Derek staring at the ceiling.

We ended up sitting at the kitchen table talking with my

mom for a while. It made me a little nervous to hang out with her and my friends. She can say embarrassingly insensitive things. Most famously, at my sixth-grade birthday party, she commented to Derek's mom in front of the other boys: "Well, I'm just glad James is good with his feet because he certainly can't catch or throw." I'd heard that one repeated a lot over the years.

"Aaron's not going to die," Derek said.

"How do you know?" I asked.

"It just doesn't seem like that's meant to happen."

"What? What is that supposed to mean?"

My mom looked tense, but she was staying out of it.

"I just don't think he's going to die," Derek said.

I let it go and just stared out the kitchen window into the woods. I thought for a second that moose was back again—I stood up, peering into the fading light.

"What?" said Derek, following my gaze.

Just a tree. "Nothing," I said, sitting back down. "I wonder what Mark's doing." We'd heard he'd gotten a two-day in-school suspension.

"Mark?" Derek said. "He's probably watching ESPN right now, cursing at competitive poker."

"At least he didn't try to get away last night," I offered. It's what Hawken would have said if he had been there.

"Mark couldn't reverse down the driveway because of all the other cars. That's why he was throwing punches in the first place."

"But he didn't run off into the woods. Hawken kept him calm until the cops arrived."

"Right. Hawken, who he had just decked, had to calm him down," Derek said. "Mark's like a bad pit bull. A bad *drunk* pit bull. There's always the chance he could suddenly go berserk."

"He's had a rough time." I don't know if I was defending Mark or defending Hawken for being good friends with him. "Mark's dad kicks him out all the time. He showed up barefoot at Hawken's door at two in the morning last November."

"Was he like, 'Hey, Hawken, how much can you bench-press?'"

"No, he was like, 'Dude, I want your mom.'"

My own mother lost her patience and slapped my arm. "I don't know how you two can be laughing," she interrupted. "Have either of you tried calling Aaron?"

"He's in the hospital. He can't answer his phone."

"Well, his mother?"

"What are we supposed to say?" I asked.

"I'm sure she'd like to know that his friends are concerned about him."

"Mom, we're not really his friends." I pictured him wearing my sweater as I said it, but I went on. "We've never hung out with him. Not once. I don't even know his number."

"He only hangs out with girls. Maybe because he acts like one," Derek explained.

My mom shook her head. "It must be really hard for his parents."

"What do you mean?" I asked.

"Well, him being gay." She sighed. "And now this."

That was her attitude. That's why she never talked about gay people—they have a sad affliction.

"I'm just grateful you boys are all normal," she went on. "I don't know how I would deal with that sort of . . ."—she searched for the right word—"complication."

I started breathing again when Derek spoke.

"Aaron doesn't like boys," he said. "But he really, *really* likes boys." And then he started laughing, and I pretended to laugh, too.

My mom didn't. "You two are terrible."

"What do you want us to do?" I asked. "Sob into each other's arms?"

"You should call his mother." It wasn't a suggestion.

"Do you think they'll let Mark keep his job?" I asked.

When Mark first announced that he had landed a job at a restaurant, we all assumed it was a fast food joint over in West Lebanon, but it turned out to be a really nice place up in an old mill town on the Connecticut River. The town used to be one of those places with a supermarket that smells like cigarettes and sells produce wrapped in cellophane, even in the summer. Just off Main Street, right next to what must be the last video rental store in the state, there's a methadone clinic. But a couple of years ago, the town underwent a sort of revival. Sumac, the little restaurant where Mark works, opened up. One of the local bars started brewing its own beer and bringing in live music. Someone renovated the old theater. A decent pizza place appeared. The *Boston Globe* mentioned Sumac in an article about the best farm-to-table restaurants in New England, and Mark carried the piece folded up in his pocket for a few days to show anyone he could trap.

Hawken, as always, came to his defense. "Let him be happy about it. He's proud of something other than baseball for once, and he's not getting any support from his dad." Evidently, his father was happy that Mark was earning money, but he had nothing nice to say about the restaurant. Once he told Mark not to bring any arugula-eating boyfriends home from work. "I was impressed that he knew what arugula was," Mark said with a shrug.

"That job's the one good thing he has going at the moment," Derek said. "I hope they don't fire him. Otherwise, he'll be out getting laminated all the time and throwing punches at anyone within swinging distance."

My mom shook her head. "Sometimes I wish you boys would make some new friends."

"Look at where we live," I said, my arms spread. "Where are we going to find new friends?"

She stood up, cleared away our glasses.

That evening, I found Aaron's home number in our school directory. I had my end of the conversation planned and went over it in my head as the phone rang and rang.

"You have reached the Fothterth." It must have been his little brother's voice. "Pleathe leave uth a methage."

"Hey, thisisJamesLiddelljustcallingtoseehowAaron'sdoing-thanksbye."

My dad always yells at me for speaking too fast on the phone. I thought about calling again, trying to leave a slow, clear message. I hadn't even mentioned my number. *I'll call him another day*, I thought, walking into my room. Suddenly, I felt like I was being watched—I froze and looked up. Aaron's alligator PEZ dispenser was looking right at me. It blinked.

I shook my head. I needed to get out of the house. Derek said he was going out with his folks. I called Hawken. No answer.

What I felt like doing was hanging out at Derek's and playing around with his telescope again. The first time he brought Saturn into focus for us, the view gave me a jolt. "That's really Saturn?" I asked. "We're really looking at Saturn?"

Hawken elbowed me away and peered into the telescope. He stood up, looking alarmed. "That's crazy. How can that be?" Hawken gazed at the fuzzy point of light Derek had pointed out. I gazed at Hawken, just his nose and his wide blue eyes peeking above the collar of his zipped up fleece. He pointed from the telescope to the planet. "It's crazy that we're looking at *that*."

"It's kind of hard putting the two together," I agreed.

One moment, rings and sphere. The next, tiny speck of light. You view something twice and even though it's the same thing, the two views have nothing to do with each other. That happens with people, too, I guess. You think you're seeing someone accurately and then—suddenly—it turns out you had only a fuzzy, tiny idea of the real thing. Mark arrives at your front door barefoot one night in November. Hawken comes home crying because you made fun of his reading problem. You find Aaron hysterical in the bathroom. You walk with your pal in the snow one night and he tells you—all sorts of stuff. Total clarity for a moment. And then, in a blink, the distance opens up again.

As I was trying to sleep that night, I wondered how Aaron was doing. Why had I invited him to that party, anyway? He wouldn't have gotten hit if I'd just kept my mouth shut. I had wanted to do something nice, but it was stupid of me. I knew who'd be there. Why did I think he would've had a good time? And now he might die. Would someone call here if he did? I wondered what Mark was up to—whether he was lying awake in the dark, too. What would he do if they put him in a cell? Push-ups and sit-ups? I wondered what Kevin's parents had said when the police phoned. When I closed my eyes I'd see Aaron, the yellow gloves behind his head dripping blood onto the snow.

Hawken and I had an indoor soccer game that Sunday. Our school soccer coach agreed to be our indoor coach, too, but other than that, the team has nothing to do with school. Most of the teams are sponsored by local businesses. They pay for the uniforms and registration fees, and we walk around wearing their ads. Our team's sponsored by Henry's Towing, so every Sunday I don my blue T-shirt with a big truck on the front and Number 10 on the back. We play in a sprawling metal-sided, hangar-like building just off the highway, about thirty minutes from where we live. You're not allowed to spit because it's artificial turf, this green plastic grass with what looks like potting soil beneath it. The ball moves fast on the stuff, but if you fall or slide, you get a wicked burn that lasts a week. It's one of my favorite places on the planet. I always go into the game saying that I don't care if we win or lose, but the reality is I hate losing. My casual attitude gets left on the bench with my sweatshirt. Hawken's always reminding me to calm down, to not curse at myself or others.

That Sunday we played Done Right Plumbing. Their goalie wore bright green goggles and threw himself at people's knees. I swear he wanted someone to leave in an ambulance. Toward the end of the first half, Hawken tried to feed me a ball, but it was a few feet too far ahead of me. The goalie dived and curled over it, but I was running full speed toward the ball too, so I ended up falling, landing on top of him. For a few slapstick seconds, he was trying to stand up while I was trying to climb off him, and when we finally disentangled ourselves, he snarled, "You run like a girl." Before I'd even thought about it, I stepped forward and pushed the kid so hard he stumbled backward and fell, his goggles flying off. He lay there on the plastic grass, looking at me with his mouth half open, stunned.

The next thing I knew I was at the center of a cursing and jostling crowd of red and blue shirts. Someone slugged me in the back and a cleat dug into my foot. The ref grabbed my arm, yanked me out of the maelstrom, and made a big show of drawing a red card from his wallet, as though he were a magician pulling a rabbit from a hat. Some parents behind the glass applauded. When I reached the bench, Coach Greschner glared at me and growled, "What's wrong with you?" I didn't answer. My team played a man down the rest of the game, and the other team scored five goals in the second half. We lost 7–2. Their goalie gave me the finger as he left the field at the end of the game. Since we play every team two or three times a season, I knew I'd face him again.

CHAPTER 8

Mondays at my school always begin with an assembly in the gym. Derek and I crept in late and slumped against the wall in the back, just as Ms. Reed, the principal, updated the school on Aaron's condition. "Aaron is still in the hospital. His doctors say that he was very lucky only to have fractured his skull. It's still unclear whether his concussion will have lasting effects on his health. Some of those effects could be very serious."

Nearly five hundred kids lined the bleachers, but at that moment, the gym might as well have been empty. The principal let the silence linger for a bit, and then went on to say that we would have shortened classes on Wednesday. Whispers grew to shouts in seconds. We would have shortened classes on Wednesday, she repeated loudly, so that we could meet in small groups to talk about social choices. The school had invited counselors from a local agency to lead the discussions, and we'd learn more about it later.

I had English first period that morning. Mr. Breyer was sitting on his desk, nursing his coffee and staring out the window as we filed in. "No one sit at this desk, please," he said, pointing to the center desk of the front row. When everyone was seated, he stood, nodded to the one empty spot, and said, "Let's keep that one open until Aaron's back. We'll start today with a ten-minute quick-write. You may choose your own topic, but I'll suggest a few." DRINKING, he wrote on the board. FIGHTING. HOSPITALS. CRYING FATHERS.

He's never been one to let us off the hook.

When the time was up, he asked for volunteers to read. Three kids read about fighting *and* drinking. One kid talked about a kung fu flick he'd seen on Saturday. We all laughed a little in relief, even Breyer. I didn't read mine. It was about what a jerk I'd been to Aaron over the years.

That night after dinner, my mom insisted I try calling Aaron's mother again. "I'm sure she'd appreciate that his friends, his classmates," she corrected herself, "are concerned about him."

I dialed his number, hoping for his little brother's methage again. But his mom answered.

"Hey, uh, Mrs. Foster, this is James Liddell. I go to school with Aaron, and I was just calling to see how he's doing and all."

I didn't get the warm response my mother had led me to expect.

"Well, he's not doing great, James." She put an edge on each word. "He's still in the hospital with a fractured skull. And they're not sure what kind of long-term damage he's going to suffer. He's really, really not good."

"Um, I'm really sorry to hear it," I stammered.

"James, why did you boys invite him to that party? Is that what you and your group consider fun? Making kids think they have new friends and then beating them up?"

I didn't answer for a moment. I felt sick. "No," I managed. "No, none of this is fun. That's not how it was at all." And then I looked at my phone and hung up. No good-bye or anything. How could she think we'd do that? That I'd do that? Is that who people thought I was? I couldn't concentrate on my homework, so I tried writing a letter to Aaron, but it didn't really make me feel any better.

I decided to go for a late run to clear my head.

"Did you to talk to Mrs. Foster?" my mother asked as I headed out the door.

"Yeah," I replied without looking at her. "No change. She said thanks for calling."

I caught Lisa Schultz on the way out of English the next morning. "Hey, Lisa," I called. "You got a second?"

She stopped and looked me up and down, as if I were a total stranger on the street.

"Hey, listen," I said, leaning against a locker. "Are you in touch with Aaron's mom at all?"

She nodded.

"Would you let her know that I gave Aaron my sweater that day because—"

"I remember," she said. "It was nice of you."

"Yeah, thanks. And I guess it was a bad idea inviting him to that party—I feel terrible about it now, but—"

"I get it," Lisa said. She punched my arm. "If I see his mom, I'll tell her, Liddell."

"Thanks," I called as she disappeared down the hall. I'm not sure she did get it, but it was the friendliest interaction we'd ever had.

Classes went on more or less as usual until Wednesday afternoon, when we were assigned to small, mixed-grade discussion groups. Teachers led some of them, but mine was led by an outside counselor. She didn't seem much older than us, and her voice shook as she explained that we didn't have to say anything, that we could just listen to everyone else, which is what I planned to do.

It was in that group that I first heard someone other than my mom suggest that Mark had meant to hit Aaron, that he'd punched him because he was gay. There was only one kid making the claim, a kid named Noah, but he was vehement. He had a nose ring, like the kind they put on pigs to keep them from rooting in the dirt. I'd seen him around—he's a freshman or sophomore—but I'd never spoken to him. His hair was dyed grape-green last fall. This semester, it was Bomb-Pop blue.

Hawken was in my group, too. He shook his head when Noah accused Mark of targeting Aaron, and pointed out calmly and quietly that Mark had punched him, too.

Noah was on the edge of his seat. "He didn't hit you hard enough to put you in the hospital, though," he insisted. "He went after Aaron."

"No, he didn't," Hawken said evenly. "I'm not saying they're friends, but Mark doesn't hate him. And he took a swing at everyone within reach."

"That's just your opinion," snapped Noah.

"How is that an opinion?" I jumped in, my voice raised. "He hit Hawken, too. He wasn't throwing punches at gay kids. He was throwing punches at everyone there."

"You're a freaking homophobe," Noah shot back.

"You've gotta be kidding me." I turned to the counselor, but she looked terrified.

"Boys, I need to ask you to lower your voices," she managed, pushing her hair back behind her ears.

"This school's full of homophobic idiots," snarled Noah, ignoring the counselor. "It's amazing that it took this long for the redneck jocks to start attacking people."

"Redneck jocks?" I laughed, and Hawken stood up. The blue-haired boy's eyes grew wide. Hawken didn't even look at him. Instead, he said quietly to the counselor, "This group's not helpful. You're letting that kid spread rumors." And then he picked up his backpack and walked out.

I followed him. As the door closed, I heard the counselor pleading, "Okay, okay, I need to ask everyone to just take a deep breath and refocus."

We walked down the hallway in silence for a few yards. "I knew this was going to happen," Hawken said eventually. "I knew kids were going to start saying Mark had it out for Aaron."

"Yeah, I sort of figured people would draw that conclusion, too."

"The thing is, it matters. If the story becomes that Mark punched Aaron on purpose, he could be in even more trouble. I'm not defending what he did, but he didn't even know who he was hitting."

"It'll be okay, dude." I didn't know what else to say.

"He doesn't hate gay people."

I didn't say anything.

"He talks to my brother when he's home."

I talk to his brother when he's home. I had no idea that he was gay until Hawken told me.

"Mark's dad made him call Aaron's mom, you know. Apologize and all."

"Whoa. How did *that* go?"

"He said it was terrible. She let him have it. He won't tell anyone this—he's never going to let down his tough-guy image—but he *does* feel bad about what happened. He didn't mean to get that drunk. He cried when he apologized to me. He couldn't stop. He was curled on my bed with his face in his hands. It was awful."

"Mark?"

"Yeah, Mark. Everyone thinks they have him pegged. That guy back there in the conference room? The kid with blue hair? Mark and I changed his tire in the parking lot last year because he didn't know how to do it. It's screwed up."

Later on, Mark was walking down the hall a few yards ahead of me. Kids looked up, saw him coming, and got out of his way in a hurry. I don't think he even noticed.

Theresa and I hung out after school that day. She lives down the road from a general store that sells milk, bread, and beer to locals, and it sells postcards, maple syrup, and moose miscellanea to tourists. We walk down there when we have nothing else to do. I picked a big chunk of ice and snow from the snowbank on the roadside and threw it way up in the air. It thudded on the pavement but didn't break, so we kicked it down the road for a few yards. Theresa picked up another chunk of snow and tossed it way into the air, and this one exploded—*poof!* We stood over the aftermath. "Look at those lines shooting away from the center," she said, and she took a photo. "Like a white-hot starburst."

"In cold black space," I said. "It's freezing out here."

Theresa bought a hot chocolate. I got a small black coffee.

I'd just started drinking coffee, to my parents' chagrin. When I put the cup on the counter, Theresa grabbed a pack of gum from the candy rack. "You have to start chewing gum if you're going to start drinking coffee," she explained. "Otherwise, your breath's going to smell like Mr. Nash's, that substitute teacher." I nodded. You don't argue with girls about that kind of thing. I dug in my pocket for a few crumpled dollars, but Theresa beat me to it.

"No, let me get it!" I said, pushing money toward the cashier.

"Nope, I got it," she said, patting my arm. "You deserve it for being nice and cute."

The dude behind the counter shook his head and said, "Take it while you can, Liddell." I didn't know his name. He'd graduated from our school a couple of years before. He probably knew my older brother.

"Soon it will be ice-cream season," Theresa mused. "Until then, all my money goes toward hot chocolate."

I watched the cashier look her up and down. He seemed to be looking forward to ice-cream season, too, when Theresa would stand outside the store licking vanilla cones in a tank top and shorts. He glanced at me, eyes narrowed, and I smiled. It was one of the reasons I liked hanging out with Theresa. I enjoyed other guys' jealousy.

On the way home, knives of light sliced the sky from a gold-rimmed cloud. "I've been trying to paint a sky like that," Theresa said. "Every time I try, the painting comes out looking like one of those posters with some kind of inspirational quote beneath it. Or a Bible verse."

"Well, you could give it to Derek."

"Oh, that's perfect. His parents will love it. I can paint him a whole series of clouds and sunbeams and title each one. *Inspiration . . .*"

"*Righteousness,*" I hollered in my deepest tone.

"*Striving,*" she boomed, shaking her fist.

"*Straightness,*" I yelled.

"Straightness?" She laughed.

"I mean, like, straitlaced. Straight-ahead?" She laughed harder. "Straitjacket."

She took my hand in hers. I didn't mind it when we were alone in the house or at the movies or something like that, but cars kept whizzing past. I let her hold my hand for fifty yards or so, and then dropped hers to reach for gum. "Wintergreen?" I offered. She shook her head.

A car pulled over. My mom. "Hey, you two!" she called. Rex was already climbing into the backseat. My mom drove us back to Theresa's, where I grabbed my stuff, and Theresa kissed me on the cheek as I left. "See you," I said, and squeezed her arm. She looked hurt as I closed the door, but it would've been dishonest to kiss her back.

That night, I had trouble sleeping. I was thinking about how things between Theresa and me were disintegrating—*poof!*—like that chunk of snow on the asphalt, but it was happening in slow motion, and there wasn't anything beautiful about it. It was more like Aaron's skull cracking the ice, a noise that I could hear in my head, and that made me cringe, even though I hadn't even been anywhere near it when it happened.

I started to drift off to sleep, and I could see Aaron lying there. He got up from the ground, took off my old green sweater and held it to his face, as if smelling it. Blood from the sweater's wool stained his pale cheeks.

CHAPTER 9

Theresa called for a repeat dinner party at her place that Saturday night. Her parents were out of town, and once again it would be just Derek, Kim, Theresa, and me. I agreed to go only because it was a second chance for Derek with Kim, but I knew Theresa saw the night as a chance to fix things with me. My plan was to play it cool, go home at the end of the night, avoid giving her the wrong idea.

Theresa told us not to bring anything to drink because she had it covered, but given that she'd run out last time, Derek and I decided to bring a few bottles of wine just in case.

When we got out of the car at Theresa's and were fixing

our ties in the driveway, Derek stopped me from bringing the wine in with us. "Just in case she really does have it covered."

Once inside, we followed Theresa into her kitchen. "Mind if I pour us some wine?" I asked.

"Oh, dear," said Theresa, a finger to her lips, pretending she hadn't even thought about it. "It appears that I am fresh out. But there's some beer in the fridge."

I looked over Derek's shoulder as he pushed aside cartons of orange juice and milk. He found four beers. "Is this the fridge you were talking about?" he asked.

"Dude, you left your car unlocked, right?" I whispered.

Three minutes later everyone was holding a glass of four-dollar red, but only Derek and I looked really happy about it. Kim's smile was nervous. "C'mon, Theresa, cheer up! It's a glass of wine!"

"It's three *bottles* of wine."

Derek offered a toast, "To the Boy Scouts, who exhort us to always be prepared." I laughed loud enough that Theresa winced, and I apologized, but she told us to get out of her way, to go hang out in the living room. When I came back into the kitchen twenty minutes later to uncork another bottle, she looked tense. "Can we save that one for dinner?" she asked.

I pointed to the third bottle on the counter. "We got plenty. You seen the corkscrew?"

She stepped in front of me, fixed my collar and tie, and kissed me. "Hi," I responded. She was waiting for me to kiss her back. So I did. "The corkscrew? Where does it live? This drawer?"

She turned back to fixing a salad. "You know," she said, "it'd be nice if you were somewhat sober at the end of the night."

"Hey! This bottle's a twist-off anyway—I don't even need the corkscrew!" I started to leave and then stopped. "Do you want me to help?"

She shook her head. Silently.

Looking back on the night, I don't think I even drank that much, but I hadn't eaten anything all day. I remember coming back into the kitchen, taking over the job of sautéing Brussels sprouts, and feeling like I was doing an awesome job. While I cooked, I told Kim a long story about how Derek once rescued dozens of puppies from a burning skyscraper—"he's that good of a guy." Derek kept telling me to shut up, but he was laughing, and at one point Kim giggled with her forehead on his shoulder, and he put his arm around her. I remember shouting that I'd discovered my passion, that I was going to apply to culinary school, which made even Theresa crack up.

I don't remember everything I said at dinner but I do remember talking about the semiformal dance Theresa and I were going to the next weekend at Kim's school. The dance was to raise money for a kid who got hurt in a snowmobile accident. I really didn't want to go. "Are you *sure* kids from other schools are allowed in?" I asked.

"They just want your money, James. Wear that tie, and you're good."

"Hey," I yelled, pointing at Kim and Derek. Theresa hushed me. "You guys should go! Do you have a date, Kim?"

She drank from her glass and shook her head at the same time.

"That would've been good, but I can't go," Derek said quietly. "I'm going to see my aunt in Boston with my parents. She's not doing well."

"Ah, crap," I cried. "Well, next time then. Maybe Hawken should go."

Derek dropped his fork, and Theresa glared at me.

"Not with Kim." I laughed. "I just mean it'd be fun if he came along, too. You know. For the hell of it." No one seemed to think it was a good idea. "I'm sure that messed up snowmobiler kid would appreciate Hawken coming along," I muttered.

Later, after telling a story about one of Hawken's amazing goals in soccer, I remember closing my eyes and telling myself, *Don't bring him up anymore.* And I remember Derek saying, "Liddell, put down your glass, take out your phone, and call home to say you're staying at my place. Right now." I remember Rex answering, shouting the news to my parents, and then shouting into the phone, "They said okay."

Not long after, Theresa whispered, "James, you're slurring." I vaguely remember hugging Kim good night when her brother picked her up, and I remember lying on the couch, leaving Derek the job of talking to Theresa in the kitchen. The room started to spin, and I tried to stop it by pressing my foot into the floor.

Then I woke up at 5:40 a.m., my mouth dry and a wrecking ball swaying inside my head. I was in Theresa's bed, wearing only boxers. What had I done?

She was there, too, her back to me. Was that taste just wine? It wasn't vomit. At least I hadn't been sick. I stood up, felt dizzy, and grabbed the bedpost to steady myself, then shuffled to the bathroom. When I came back, Theresa was awake and facing me.

"Morning," I croaked. "Sorry to wake you."

"You okay?" she asked.

"I'm good. I mean, I want to die, but I'm good." I tried to laugh, dropping onto the bed. "I got really drunk, huh?"

"You got *really* drunk."

"Did I have a good time?"

No response.

"I mean, did *you* have a good time?"

She didn't answer right away. "It's not all that nice climbing into bed with a corpse, you know?"

I was probably supposed to apologize by taking her hand in mine or something. I didn't. "I didn't even drink that much," I groaned. "I don't know what happened." How much had I talked about Hawken? What had I said about him?

"You were a drunken idiot. That's what happened."

I rolled away from her. Part of me was relieved—I hadn't done anything to make her think we were any more serious than before. But I didn't like her calling me a drunken idiot. I once saw a guy at a Bruins game, years earlier, who was so drunk that he fell over the seats in front of him and spilled beer all over these little kids. My dad turned to my brothers and me and said over the shouting and crying, "And *that*, my friends, is why you don't want to become a drinker."

Birds were beginning to chirp in the gray light. I rolled over onto my back. "You have any Advil or anything like that?" She didn't offer to get it for me. She just told me where to find it, and I nodded, flung my arm over my face, and tried pushing against that wrecking ball to make room for sleep.

That afternoon I drank gallons of water, fell into a coma for two hours, and then forced myself to go for a long run. I'd read that it's a good way to feel better after a night like that one. I don't know if it's because you sweat the poison out of your system or because it just feels like the right punishment, but either way it works for me. I threw up on a back road at the top of the biggest hill. It was self-inflicted misery that I was somehow proud to suffer. The rest of the way home was torture, too, which made me feel even better. When I got out of the shower, I actually felt pretty good, if not exactly relaxed.

I couldn't stop thinking about how I just had to get over

Hawken and either make things work with Theresa or tell her we were done. Those thoughts were on a loop in my head. They kept me awake that night. Eventually, I turned my light on and tried anesthetizing myself with the collection of Nathaniel Hawthorne stories that I keep by my bed for just such emergencies. But even that didn't work. I got up and started writing a letter at 2:00 a.m., and, looking back, I think I was trying too hard to sound cheerful.

> *Sunday, April 24th*
> *Dear God,*
>
> *Since you're all-knowing and all-powerful, omniscient even, it may be unnecessary to put what's going through my head on paper. I suspect you already know what I'm thinking and feeling. That is, of course, if you actually exist. To be honest, I have my doubts. You have to admit, given this world of suffering, it can be tough to believe there's any sort of Loving Grand Design. But let's assume for at least the length of this letter that you do exist and you're not the sicko that all the violence in this world suggests you must be. Heck, from now on, for decorum's sake, I'll even give you the respect of capitalizing the pronouns that refer to You.*
>
> *So—You already know what I'm going to write, but I'll go through the motions of doing it anyway. I guess that's what praying is all about, huh? You're probably not impressed that I have to ask about the point of prayer, but You can take that up with my parents. They fell away from*

religion before I had any say in the matter.

Anyway, I'm writing to ask for a cure. "For Aaron?" You ask. Well, yes and no. Please let him get better soon, yeah, but the work's not done after that.

I want a cure for boys who like other boys. I've read that three percent of the population's afflicted, so it's not totally selfish. Gagging syrups, nauseating serums, caustic powders, horse-sized pills: I'll take 'em. I'll wash 'em down with orange juice. Just make my life a little easier, would You? I mean, how the hell am I supposed to handle all this? I don't know if it's Your fault that I like guys, but I don't think it's mine.

Here's what I'd like to happen: Tomorrow morning when I wake up I want to be with Theresa. I want to call her. She's on my mind all day. I sit next to Hawken in math, and he interests me as much as the dull numbers on the blackboard. He smiles at me, and I do not want to put my arm around him. Theresa sits down next to me at lunch, and I get all nervous and happy, the way I usually do when I sit next to Hawken. When I kiss Theresa at her locker after school, I'm all grinny the way Derek used to get when he'd kiss what's her name. Oh, that's a good one: I can suddenly remember Derek's girlfriends' names without any trouble because I think they're cute, too. Maybe Derek and I swap girls at some point. You might not be as into that part of the plan, but You get the idea.

I'm glad We have an agreement. (Do I capitalize We because You're involved, or does my own inclusion in the term sink it to the lowercase?) I'm looking forward to waking up straight tomorrow morning. I'll strut downstairs into the kitchen, pour myself some cereal, and when my mom asks, "What's happening at school today?" I'll say, "Mom, I don't know, but I want to go screw me some girls."

You're the one who said go forth and multiply. Just trying to be obedient.

Your faithful servant,

James

CHAPTER 10

I barely saw Theresa the rest of the week, and Derek mentioned the dinner party only once, during an afternoon run. "You were funny for about forty-five minutes, and then I wanted to murder you. I didn't because I figured Theresa would want to do it herself." I tried to change the subject. Had he talked to Kim since then? "We've texted, yeah. But you should be more worried about whether Theresa's finally going to lose her patience with you," he warned. "If I were you, I'd be on my best behavior at that dance on Friday. It might be your last chance with her."

Hawken and I had a rare midweek indoor soccer match, so I drove us down to the field with my dad. We were listening to the oldies station. It's a habit we've developed because there are so few options on the radio dial up here and Rex jammed a bunch of nickels into the CD drive a few years ago. While we were pulling onto the highway, the song "Just My Imagination" by the Temptations came on, the one with the chorus: "It was just my imagination / Running away with me." It was weird, because I'd had that song stuck in my head all week. There had been moments in the days after Aaron got punched when I'd been convinced that I was going to wake up in my bed to find that nothing had happened.

"I was reading the town's online forum this morning," my dad said suddenly. "There was a thread about bullying at your school." And then he asked point-blank, "Is Aaron really gay?"

I glanced at Hawken in the rearview mirror. He made his eyes wide. They were exactly the same color as his bright blue fleece. I took a few seconds to think about my answer.

Aaron acts gay. He dresses gay. He walks and talks gay. I'd heard that he has declared more than once, publicly, "I am gay."

"I don't know," I mumbled.

"Why do so many people *think* he's gay? Does he have a boyfriend?"

"I don't know," I said again. Not a word from Hawken.

"I mean, is he really effeminate? Your mom said he dresses sort of differently from other boys in your class, but he might just have a different sort of style, right? It doesn't necessarily mean he's a homosexual."

Neither Hawken nor I responded, but my dad went on doggedly. "The reason I wonder about it is because some people are saying that Mark punched Aaron because he's gay, right? But how would Mark know? How would Aaron even know? He's, what, sixteen? Seventeen? I mean, it's clear that he goes out of his way to be different, and if kids are bullying him, it might be because they feel threatened somehow by Aaron's decision to flout social norms. But if Aaron blended in a bit more, the other boys might not feel so aggressive toward him, right?"

"I don't know," I muttered.

"I'm not at all defending Mark for being a belligerent drunk. I'm not saying that he deserves our sympathy for throwing punches, although I have to say I do feel sorry for anyone who's messed up his own life for a while, not to mention someone else's. But I wonder whether Aaron's sexual orientation makes any difference here. If Aaron were straight and dressed and acted the way he does, wouldn't he be just as likely to earn your classmates' contempt?"

"I don't know."

"And if kids like you two, who dress normally, walk and talk normally, do well in school and in sports, try to makes friends with everyone, if either of you were gay, you probably wouldn't be a target of violence, would you? I bet, in fact, that no one would care very much that you were gay. They wouldn't feel like you were challenging them, the way that Aaron seems to."

"It's true," Hawken finally chimed in. "I don't think anyone would care that much if one of us were gay." He uttered those last words uncomfortably slowly. We made eye contact in the rearview mirror again, and I felt like I could read his mind: *Tell him.* I scowled just enough for him to see, and he put his forehead on the cold window. I wanted to do the same thing.

"Slow down, James."

Glancing at the dashboard, I saw that I was doing seventy-five. I slowed down.

If I'd been alone with my dad in the car, I wondered, would I have taken the chance to open up? Would I have found the guts just to start talking and say, *Well, as a matter of fact . . .* I wondered if Aaron had told his mom. I mean, unless his mom's brain-damaged, the news wouldn't be a big surprise to her. He could probably just say, "Mom, I'm gay, and also I need more glitter nail polish." He wouldn't be turning her world upside down.

"It must be hard for Aaron's parents," my dad mused.

I looked back at Hawken. He frowned and sat up straight. "His father's not in the picture," he said. "I think his parents are divorced."

"Rocket Man" by Elton John came on the radio just then, and my hand collided with my dad's as we both lunged for the dial. He cracked up. My brother Luke used to play that tune on the piano so often that my dad finally banned it. I was relieved when he did. Elton John made me uncomfortable.

When we got back from the game, my brother Luke called from college. He's two years older than me, and he goes to college in Maine. I'd spoken to him briefly last week and told him about Aaron and Mark. I'm sure my parents had talked to him about it, too, but they must not have described Aaron in much detail. Luke got under my skin that night, so I ended up climbing out of bed at 12:34 a.m. and scribbling him a letter.

I didn't really start writing right away. I did what I often do—I just sat there with my notebook open and my pen in my hand and stared out the window, off into the forest, waiting for that moose to come back out of the trees. I know it gets cold out there, but wandering over the hills, not worrying about who you're going to be in ten or twenty years, whether you'll keep your friends and family—I've spent a lot of time imagining myself setting off into those woods with just a backpack.

In some ways, Luke's changed a lot since he went away, but in others he's exactly the same. We've never been the kind of brothers who have to be kept in separate cages so we won't claw or bite each other, but for a while, when I was in middle school, we weren't all that close. It wasn't until the fall of my freshman year, when Luke was a junior, that we became pretty tight. Our relationship changed in a single afternoon, a perfect Saturday in October, when the hills were red and yellow against a bright blue sky, and Luke nearly burned the house down.

My parents had gone to a wedding and left him in charge. About an hour after, Rex began demanding lunch, and Luke announced that he would make his specialty, grilled cheese. "You have a specialty?" I asked.

"I'm developing it today," he explained.

Sometimes to keep Rex in one place, especially at meal times, we tied him to a kitchen chair and told him we were playing "Kidnapped on Planet Xiphoid." And sometimes, when Rex wasn't in a high-pitched screaming mood, we blindfolded him, too. Luke had just shoved bread topped with cheddar into the toaster oven and was pulling anything red or peppery from the spice rack, and I was just tying the last knots over the blindfolded prisoner's wrists when I smelled smoke. I turned around and screamed. Flames shot from the toaster oven and licked at the curtains and kitchen cabinets. Luke looked up from the spices, leaped to the sink, and filled a pitcher with water.

"Unplug it! Unplug it!" I yelled, and lunged across the kitchen to pull the plug from its socket just before Luke threw water at the inferno and mostly missed, soaking a row of cookbooks. Rex stood with his chair and ran for the door, but hit the wall next to it instead. I knocked the flaming oven off the counter so it banged to the floor, and then I grabbed my favorite hoodie, my all-time favorite gray hoodie, and with half a dozen whumping blows, beat the flames to death.

Luke kicked the smoking oven and cursed at it.

Breathing hard, we surveyed the damage. Blackened cabinets. Charcoal-stained rug. Sopping-wet cookbooks. Blindfolded seven-year-old brother tied to kitchen chair.

Luke started to giggle.

"You nearly burned the freaking house down," I panted, still shaking with adrenaline. "The curtains almost caught fire! The whole place could've gone up! What's funny about that?"

"Imagine mom walking into the kitchen right now," he said, wiping sweat from his forehead with his sleeve.

I started to laugh, too. "They're going to kill us."

Luke pointed at Rex, face to the wall, the chair still tied to him.

"I don't want to play this anymore," Rex called over our laughter.

It didn't take long to mop up the water, air out the house, and dispose of the toaster and rug, and Rex agreed it would be wise to skip his role in the drama when we explained the burned cabinets to our parents.

My mom had to sit down when she saw the damage. "The one time we leave you in charge you nearly burn down the house?" she shouted at Luke. "How is it that the toaster oven has worked perfectly well for fifteen years and suddenly, today, when you happen to be on your own, it goes up in flames?"

"Maybe because it was fifteen years old?" I suggested.

"Maybe because it hated you and saw its chance to kill your children?" proposed Luke.

"It's caught fire before," my dad muttered. My mom swung to face him. "Crumbs catch fire," he said with a shrug.

Maybe it was my willingness to share the blame. Maybe it was our telling and retelling of the story to everyone at school. In any case, Luke and I spent more time together and laughed at each other's jokes more easily after that day.

I started writing to Luke at a little past one in the morning, while Aaron's pink PEZ alligator peeked at me over the rim of the coffee can.

> *Wednesday, April 27th*
> *Hey, Luke,*
>
> *I just spoke to you a little while ago, but here I am writing a letter anyway because you started doing this thing tonight that I haven't heard you do in a long time and, to be honest, I was glad when you stopped doing it. You started lisping like some sort of drag queen and calling me darling and stuff like that, and I could hear your buddies cracking up in the background. It's not that big of a deal or anything, but I kept wishing you'd stop. That's why I was saying, "Luke. Hey, Luke, listen," really patiently, but sometimes it's pretty tough to shut you up, you know? I sort of wanted to hang up.*
>
> *The thing is, I might as well tell you since you're not getting this letter, I'm pretty sure I do like boys, and listening to*

you lisp makes me think we're probably not going to be friends some day. I know you're just joking around, but it makes me worry that when you find out, we're never going to speak again. And, frankly, if you continue lisping, that'll be fine. Most of the time I do like hanging out with you, Luke. I like being your brother, but I don't know how our lives are all going to work out. Maybe you'll realize that just because I like boys, it doesn't mean I'm going to become a flaming fashion designer. Or maybe we'll talk only once every couple of years when we happen to cross paths in the driveway at Christmas. If I'm still allowed home.

I get pretty scared about all of this. Remember that time you announced you were going to become a Yankees fan, just to annoy Dad? His response: "I'd have an easier time if you came home and told me you were gay." It was probably a forgettable comment for you. I remember exactly where I was standing in the living room. I'm still hoping I wake up totally straight tomorrow and none of this will be an issue. That'd be great. Until that happens, though, do me a favor and quit the lisping.

Okay, Luke. We're all set, then. I've had my moment of super-mature honesty, so now I can go back to being your annoying little brother. Always loyal to that role, I have stolen a jacket and a lamp from your room, and I think Derek might have pocketed some of your stuff as well. We were digging through your sock drawer a couple of weeks ago, hoping to find a lighter, but all we found was a copy of Playboy. Derek pointed out that you're the only person on the planet who

actually buys dirty magazines anymore. Anyway, it answered
any doubts I had about your sexuality. I had to feign interest
while Derek examined every page. Very awkward. He wanted
to borrow it, but I made him return it to your hiding spot.

Those are the moments when I really worry about myself.
I wasn't all that interested. I just wanted a beer. We ended up
drinking warm Michelob Lights that we'd stolen from Derek's
garage. Of course, his dad noticed them missing and went
ballistic. But it was light beer—fewer calories. Parents never see
the bright side of delinquency.

Talk to you soon, dude.
James

Breyer started English class on Friday with good news. He'd
just hung up the phone with Aaron's mom, and the doctors
said Aaron could probably go home that weekend. "What a
f-f-freaking relief." Breyer laughed. We'd never heard him
come even close to cursing, so we all cracked up. Everyone
was suddenly in a good mood as we pushed desks aside for
little performances of scenes from *A Midsummer Night's Dream*.
Breyer assigned us our roles, and Hawken and I ended up in
the same group. We had to act out the play within the play—
Hawken was Pyramus, and I was Thisby. Hawken stabbed
himself and sprawled on the floor and I had to kneel right
next to him and say:

Asleep my love?
What, dead, my dove?

O Pyramus, arise!
Speak, speak. Quite dumb?
Dead, dead? A tomb
Must cover thy sweet eyes.
These lily lips,
This cherry nose,
These yellow cowslip cheeks,
Are gone, are gone.
Lover, make moan.
His eyes were green as leeks.

Breyer took me aside beforehand and instructed me to perform that passage in two different ways: once to get a laugh, and once to "hush the room with sadness," as he put it. He said it would be really hard to manage the second, serious reading, but I nailed it by getting all quiet and whispering some of the words. I didn't touch Hawken while he was lying there, but I had to remind myself not to stroke his hair or anything. When we finished, everyone applauded, genuinely—it wasn't the usual polite golf-clap. Hawken was smirking as he stood up, and he pretended to punch me in the gut.

I'm sure Breyer was exaggerating, but he said that it was the best reading he'd ever heard, that I'd managed to rescue even the "green as leeks" line from sounding totally ridiculous. He caught me on my way out of class and asked me why I'd never done any acting. "You were really good just now," he said. "Why not give the stage a shot? You wouldn't have to quit the soccer team to do it."

"I don't really like acting," I mumbled at the floor. "Besides, that wasn't really acting." Breyer thought I was just being modest.

"I think you have a talent for it."

"I get lots of practice," I muttered.

"Really?" Breyer raised an eyebrow. "How so?"

My heart was beating fast as I looked at the clock. "I'm going to be late for chemistry."

"Another time?"

"Yeah." I nodded. "Another time."

Sitting in chemistry, I thought about what I would say to Breyer. How would I tell him without clumsily dropping the weight of my secret in his lap? *I liked reading* A Midsummer Night's Dream, I scribbled next to unbalanced equations. *I've always wanted to wake up one day in a world where I liked the right people, and they liked me in return. I worry it'll never happen.*

CHAPTER 11

That evening was the semiformal dance at Kim's school. I stole a skinny gray tie from Luke's closet and looked through his stuff to see if he had a flask. No luck.

We'd been at the dance for about an hour or so, jumping around to hip-hop tunes and Top 40 stuff that I never listen to willingly, when a guy stepped hard on my foot, and I turned and glared at him. He was still dancing, doing exaggerated disco moves, not just hopping in one spot, but he put his hands up apologetically, grinned, and patted my shoulder as he turned away. I nodded at the back of his head, and the kid across from him, who was wearing a yellow tie, smiled at me and saluted. He was the kind of cute kid I always had to remind myself not to stare at. I nodded at him, too, more slowly, and turned back to my own little bouncing group. When I looked back over my shoulder at him, he was still dancing and staring right at me. He smiled widely and shrugged.

I nodded at him again, uncertainly.

Kim mouthed "water" and pointed to the refreshments table. Squeezing through the crowd and ducking past flailing football players, I followed her. I pretended to pant and limp when we finally reached the table of sodas and chips. Kim made a show of laughing. The music was so loud it reduced talking to gestures.

"Are you having fun?" she screamed into my ear, grabbing my arm.

"Yeah!" I yelled back and handed her a soda. "But I'm going to take a break from the noise! Come with me!"

She nodded, put her hands over her ears, and grimaced.

When we stepped out in the hall, my ears were ringing. We both cracked up at the sound of our voices once the gym doors closed behind us.

"I used to feel like I had to say that I hated that music." Kim laughed. "But, honestly, it is hilarious jumping around to Y-$ugar with a couple of hundred people."

I had to agree with her. For a little while, we talked about songs we were embarrassed to admit that we like, and then I edged us toward talking about the boy with the smile. "The kids from your school are super friendly." I tried to sound as casual as possible. "Who are the guys dancing next to us? There are four of them."

"The basketball players? The ones wearing white high-tops?"

"No, no. To our left. The ones that can actually dance. One of them is wearing a yellow tie. Scruffy hair? Smiles a lot . . ." I stopped myself from commenting on his eyes.

"Oh, that's Topher. He is super nice. You guys would get along really well, actually. I should introduce you to him."

"He goes to school here?"

"Yeah, he's been in my class since we were in kinder-garten. Two of those guys he's with go to school in New Hampshire. They're all in a theater group together."

"Theater, huh? That takes guts, I guess. I can't imagine being on a stage with everyone staring at you. Terrifying." I fished a pretzel from the stash in my pocket. "But you like this guy Topher, huh? Why have I never heard about him? Why aren't you dating him?"

"Ha! I had a crush on Topher in eighth grade. I mean, I *really* liked him to the point where being around him was sort of wonderful and painful all at the same time, you know?"

"I've heard about that kind of thing, yeah."

"But we never dated. And then . . ." She hesitated and glanced at me as if unsure whether she should go on. "And then he told me that he's gay. So, you know, end of story."

I felt like I'd just climbed too high up a tree, the same feeling of terror and joy running through me.

"Oh," I said. "I don't think I would've guessed that."

"No, you wouldn't know about Topher unless he told you. But he's pretty up front about it."

"No kidding," I said. I could see my reflection in the glass of a trophy cabinet. I practiced standing and holding my Coke the way I'd seen a model hold his glass in a scotch ad, his weight back on one leg, the other stretched out slightly in front, as though he wanted to trip a passerby. The picture of nonchalance. "How did he work *that* into a conversation?"

"Topher and I used to walk home from school together all the time. He lives just a few houses away from me. One day I was talking about how much I liked this new boy in school, and Topher let slip, 'Yeah, he's really cute.' And then he went all red."

"Oh, no!" I laughed.

"Yeah, it was adorable. But instead of making excuses for himself—I remember this so clearly—he picked an old crab apple off the road, handed it to me, and said, 'Here. You can have this if you promise to never tell anyone I just said that.' I was sort of sad, because I had such a crush on Topher, too, but I laughed and accepted the apple."

"Well, you better return it now because you just broke your promise," I pointed out.

"Oh, it wasn't a secret for very long. He had a boyfriend, Craig, when we were in ninth grade. One of those guys he's dancing with right now, in fact."

"They're still dating? That's a long time."

"No, no. That one went down in flames after a couple of months. But everyone knew about it. Topher used to complain that Craig laughs and throws like a girl. He said the only thing they had in common was a crush on our soccer team's goalie."

"Sean Gates." I nodded. "Yeah, he's really cute."

Kim gripped my arm and bent forward as she laughed, but then she looked up at me, clearly trying to gauge whether I was being serious.

I shrugged. "There aren't any apples lying around for me to offer you."

The gym doors burst open as though the speakers had exploded. Theresa tottered out in her heels, looking worried and peering down the corridor in the wrong direction. When she turned and saw us, she fixed her smile. "Hi!" she called, hesitantly, and stood staring at us, frozen. I couldn't blame her for misinterpreting the expressions Kim and I must have worn.

"We're regaining our hearing," I called to her, and jangled my plastic cup. "Come have some ice."

Theresa can't walk well in heels. I love that about her. I don't know why she insists on wearing them. "Left, right, left, right," I commanded as she teetered toward us. She gave me the finger, and when she arrived, I put my arm around her. "We were going to go back in when our ears had stopped bleeding," I explained.

"They are in a state of shock," agreed Kim.

I ignored her and hoped Theresa hadn't picked up on her tone. "What's happening after the dance?" I asked. "Is there a party?"

"No one's having a party in the Upper Valley ever again," Theresa replied.

"Don't say that," I groaned.

"James, it's true," Kim agreed. "After the Aaron Foster incident, only a complete idiot would invite a crowd of strangers to his house."

That complete idiot, that hero, turned out to be a kid named Steven, who I never actually met. It took some persuading, but Theresa eventually agreed to go for an hour. Her parents wanted her home by midnight that night, and she was driving. "You're allowed one beer," she told me. Kim rode with us so she could navigate. We had to drive only a couple of miles from Kim's school, but we were on back roads and twenty miles away from where Theresa and I lived.

Cars already lined the muddy road when we arrived at the house of Brave Steve, as I called him for the rest of the night. Or Sucker Steve, as Theresa and Kim said. We entered the house through the garage, where a bunch of shivering kids were playing flip cup on a Ping-Pong table. As I walked past, a kid yelled, "Hey, Liddell! No fisticuffs!" The jokes about our school had begun.

As soon as we walked into the house, I saw Topher perched on the kitchen counter. His pals from the dance stood talking in front of him, but he didn't seem involved in their conversation. When he saw me, he straightened up, raised his beer, and grinned. I smiled and put up a finger. One minute. He nodded and looked pleased.

I sat on the arm of a couch right next to Theresa's friends, so I was excused from being an object of gossip, more or less. My outfit got a thumbs-up. My dancing a thumbs-down. Nothing new.

So it wouldn't be obvious that I was counting the seconds, I glanced at Theresa's watch instead of taking out my phone. I also kept one eye on the garage door, the only door, as far as I could tell, people were coming and going through.

After a little while, Topher walked out of the kitchen and glanced toward us. He saw me sitting with the girls, and he didn't smile or nod or anything. He just walked purposefully to the garage door, jacketless, stuck his head out for a second or two, and then, looking very serious, walked back into the kitchen.

I squeezed Theresa's shoulder and said, "I'm going to go get a beer."

"One," she emphasized.

Kim and I glanced at each other as I left. Her eyebrows furrowed, but she stayed put.

Topher was up on the counter again, but when he saw me, he slid off, stepped away from his friends, and handed me one of the two green bottles he held.

"Thanks," I said. His eyes were deep chestnut, and his

brown hair curled at the ends.

"I'm Topher," he said. At first he was shaking my hand, and then he was just holding it. To distract myself from the warmth of his grip, I sipped from my beer.

"James," I managed. "I'm James." He finally let go of my hand.

"You're friends with Kim, huh?"

"Yup." I was trying to play it cool, but his grin made *me* smile and that made him smile even more. I held the bottle up to the light and pretended to examine it. He was about my height, and he wore a silver ring on the middle finger of his left hand. "So, Kim says you guys are in the theater, huh?"

"Yeah, we're in a production of *Hamlet* this spring. It's an adaptation, not the whole thing. I'm Hamlet, actually. We all agreed not to talk about rehearsals or anything tonight, but now we're running out of things to say, so we've resorted to talking about books. Favorite books. You have one?"

"Steinbeck's *East of Eden*," I said automatically.

"Holy smokes!" He grabbed my arm. "Me, too! I just said that a minute ago! *East of Eden*!"

"No kidding." I laughed. He wore cologne that drew me closer to him than most guys would've considered normal. He talked for a little while about how much he liked Old Sam and Lee, but I wasn't really listening. He was poised like he might do a handspring at any moment, and his skin was perfect. I realized he was watching me watching him, so I looked at the linoleum.

"Have you seen the film?" I heard him ask.

"There's a film?"

He put his hand on my back for a second and said, "James Dean's in it, dude. You probably wouldn't like it as much as I do."

"Never seen it," I admitted, and fixed my gaze on the wallpaper, which was covered in horses and buggies. "Weird wallpaper," I muttered.

"Yup," he agreed. "Then again, I've never been a fan of wallpaper."

I drained my beer, considered the empty bottle for a few seconds, and then asked, "Can I have another one of these?"

He pulled one from the fridge and offered me a lighter to open it, but I popped the cap with my pirate key. I probably shouldn't take such pride in that trick.

"What, do you have buried treasure?" Topher asked, nodding at the key as I returned it to my pocket.

"Yeah, but I can't talk about it. You smoke?" I asked.

"Nah, I just carry the lighter because it comes in handy."

"For real?"

"Yup, yup."

"So helpful."

"Well, you never know when the right person's going to come along asking for a light or an opener."

I gulped from my new bottle. "He hasn't come along yet, huh?"

"Nope." He laughed. He'd caught my use of the pronoun.

"No, *he* hasn't come along yet." He sipped and looked at me sideways. "But sometimes I'm not sure. Sometimes it's hard to tell."

I guzzled nervously again, then reminded myself to slow down, to stop drinking, and rocked back on my heels instead.

"How long have you been dating Theresa?" he asked.

"Well . . ." I stalled. "We've been hanging out for a long time. But it's nothing serious."

"She's pretty," he observed after a moment. "You're a cute couple. And she clearly digs you. I mean, you *could* be dating."

I shrugged. "Sometimes . . ." I paused. "I'm not so sure."

"You're not sure if you could be dating her?"

I glanced at him and then squinted down the neck of my beer, as though I'd dropped something into the bottle. "I'm not sure," I said carefully, "who I should be dating."

"Ah!" He sipped from his bottle to hide his smile. "Maybe you're being too hard on yourself. Maybe you just need to hang out with different people and worry less about whether it counts as a date."

"Any time you spend alone with a girl, everyone counts as a date."

"I'm not a girl." He had his thumb hooked through his belt loop, and he walked in front of me to lean against the refrigerator. "You can hang out with me and be confident that we are absolutely not dating."

"Yeah?" I said.

"Sure," he said quietly. "We're both guys. How could we be dating?"

I rolled my eyes, and he laughed, and then I tried taking a long gulp of beer and spilled it down my shirt. "This is me feeling very nervous," I said, brushing myself clean.

"And this is me asking for your phone number so that we can arrange our first not-date sometime soon."

"What does a not-date involve?"

He shoved his hands in his pockets and shrugged. "I could pick you up at your house *without* bringing you flowers."

I pretended to laugh, but it sounded flat. "What will we do?"

"I don't know. Hang out. What do you and your pals do?"

I thought for a moment. "Sometimes we watch hockey," I offered.

"Well, we could watch hockey."

"What, at your house?"

"Sure, at my house."

"By ourselves?"

"Yeah, by ourselves. Unless you want to bring a chaperone."

"Do you get Great Hockey Television?"

"James, dude, give me your freaking number." When he'd punched it into his phone, he looked up, beaming, and chirped, "I can't believe we're dating."

Just as Topher called my phone to give me his own number, Theresa appeared in the kitchen. "We have to split, James. Hi, Topher."

"I can give him a ride home, Theresa," Topher said. He turned back to me. "Stay. We can give you a ride home later. My pal Jeff isn't drinking."

Theresa looked at me, waiting for my response. I stared at the wallpaper.

"It's a long drive for him," I said to Topher. "All the way over there and back."

"Well, he can give us a ride back to my house. You can stay the night. My parents won't care."

Theresa still hadn't said a word, but she was staring right at me, and I couldn't meet her gaze. I could call my folks, tell them I was crashing at Derek's.

"James, I have to go," Theresa said softly, taking my hand. "I'm going to get in trouble. If you and Topher are going to drink yourselves stupid, just tell me how to get back to the highway from here." She squeezed my fingers.

"I don't drink all that much, but for one night I could be persuaded," Topher said.

"I have to go, too, dude," I said reluctantly. "I'll catch you later."

"Okay, okay. Get home safe."

When I was almost to the other side of the kitchen, I looked back at him. He grinned and raised his bottle good-bye.

Theresa had parked her car right up against some bushes on the side of the road, so I got in the same way I'd climbed out:

through the driver's door and over the gearshift. But when we tried pulling onto the road, the back wheels just spun.

Getting stuck on muddy roads is a rite of spring in Vermont, but somehow it always feels like a surprise. A tow truck driver once told my father that he put his kid through college by yanking cars out of a single muddy stretch up in the hills near our house.

"Don't, don't, don't!" I scolded when Theresa revved the engine. "You're just digging holes!"

"Well, what am I supposed to do?" she asked.

"Do you have any wood or cardboard in the back?"

"I have a snow shovel."

I was still all semiformaled. "Oh, man." I groaned and closed my eyes. "We're going to have to call Henry's Towing. What is their freaking number? I have fifty soccer shirts with it across the front."

"Let me give it another shot." She gunned the engine before I could object. Rocks pinged off the car behind us and the tires screamed like a panicking animal.

A big muddy pickup lumbered past us and stopped just up the road, twangy country music blaring from its cab. Two boys about our age jumped out. Heavy boots. Carhartts. Red Sox hat. NASCAR hat. As one pulled wooden planks from the truck bed, the other stepped into our headlights and made a slashing motion across his throat.

"See? Don't gun it," I said.

Hands in pockets, the kid walked to Theresa's door.

"Stuck?"

"Are you our fairy godmother?" Theresa asked.

"He is," the kid replied, deadpan, jabbing a thumb over his shoulder.

The boys jammed the planks in front of the back tires and then positioned themselves behind the car for the big push. "Go easy!"

The wheels growled instead of shrieked this time and the boys rocked the car as best they could. We went nowhere. "Easy!" they hollered. "Easy!"

"I'm going easy," muttered Theresa.

"Mud's deep!" one shouted when the car came to a rest again.

I rolled up my pant legs and shouted out my open window, "I'll come help!" Theresa had to get out to let me climb out, and one of our rescuers beat his way through bramble along the road to push from my window frame. Two more kids came running down the driveway, and I waved at them without really looking since I was concentrating on not slipping in the mud. The two kids from the house positioned themselves behind the car next to me, and, as we all found our footing, one of them leaned into me so close I looked over in confusion.

Topher.

"Oh hi, James," he said, all smiles.

"Man, you guys are going to get all crazy muddy! You don't have to do this."

"Don't worry about it." His pal laughed. "We're going to be pushing cars out of this ditch all night."

A minute later we were mud-spattered and laughing and slapping backs. Theresa's car idled just behind the pickup. "Thanks, thanks, thanks!" I yelled over my shoulder as I jogged in mud-filled shoes to join her.

"I'll call you!" Topher yelled after me.

CHAPTER 12

My phone buzzed the following afternoon when I was in the car with my dad, driving to a hardware store. If I hadn't been behind the wheel, I would have dug the phone out of my pocket and checked the message right away, but my father would have lost his mind. My parents make a big, big deal out of texting and driving. They both claim to know of about fifty kids who ended up driving into the Grand Canyon or in front of landing planes. So I had to wait until we were walking through the parking lot before I could see what Topher had texted.

But he hadn't texted me anything. The message was from

Kim. *Hey, lunch? Today? Tmrw?*

I didn't want to deal with it. *Sorry. Can't this wkend. Next?* I replied.

She responded nearly instantly. *Dinner during the week?*

Really busy week. Next wkend for sure.

There was a much longer pause this time, then: *Got it.*

That Monday, Lisa Schultz told my English class that she'd visited Aaron over the weekend. He was home and getting better, but he still had headaches and found it difficult to read much. He wasn't coming back to school until the headaches had stopped. I told Derek all this when we were driving home.

"He's been out of school, like, two weeks," I said. "He really got his bell rung. He's really lucky he's not dead. This hockey player died after hitting his head on the ice. Sometimes you crack your head like that and it causes a lot of swelling, which puts a bunch of pressure on your brain, so they get a drill and they—"

"Oh God," Derek interrupted. "No more. No talking about drills."

I made a pistol with one hand. "*Wheee-RRRRR!*" I reached over and put the drill to his head. "*Wheee-RRRRR!* Like that. That's how they do it."

"Where do you want to be buried?" Derek asked.

"I was joking around." I put my hands up in the air. "No more drills. Okay."

"No, for real. I'm asking where you want to be buried. You're going to die one of these days and—"

"Not for a long time."

"Aaron would've said the same thing a couple of weeks ago, but he almost bit it. It makes sense to think about these things. So, when you die, where do you want to be buried?"

"What, are you going to make sure it happens?"

"When you launch your sled off a cliff and you end up on life support, I will announce your final wish."

I stared out the window and thought about it for a little while. We were passing a little farm that sets up a roadside vegetable stand in the summer. The snow had melted from the field, but nothing was growing yet. The muck was probably still too cold.

"I don't think you can just choose where you want to be buried," I said. "Isn't there a cemetery around here where they just drop you in the ground, like it or not?"

"Well, let's say you have a choice. If you could choose where we dig your grave, where do you want it to be?"

"You're a bundle of joy," I mumbled. "Someplace that's quiet and has a good view, I guess. Next to that rock in the meadow way up behind my house."

"The sledding rock?"

"Yeah. Bury me with my plastic orange sled. Like a Viking."

"Done. I'll make sure it happens."

"Thanks. What about you?"

"I'm seventeen and I have the Jesus. I'm going to live forever."

I cracked up, and he started singing some old song we'd heard on a mashup that Hawken played during workouts: *"'I'm going to live forever! I'm going to learn how to fly—high!'* Where is that song? I love that song. It's on here somewhere." He handed me his iPod. "Find it."

"A break from AC/DC? Yes, please." I found the song, and Derek cranked it.

"Hey, how was the dance you went to with Theresa?"

"Fun, yeah!" I hollered.

"Things okay with her?"

I thought about how to respond. "Same! What about Kim?"

He shrugged and shook his head and began to sing along. I thought about Topher and wondered if I'd hear from him that night.

Cell phone reception at my house is terrible because the hills around us block the signal. Poor reception has its advantages, though. When I don't want to talk to someone, I wander to the kitchen, where the call's sure to drop. If I do want to talk to someone, I rush up to the window in Luke's room or out to the driveway, where the reception's best. Derek's the only one who knows this trick, and he doesn't count, since he likes talking on the phone even less than I do.

For four days, I carried my phone with me everywhere,

even on my cross-country runs. I jumped every time it buzzed in my pocket, scrambling to get it out. But it was Theresa calling to tell me she saw a moose on 91 North. Or Coach Greschner to remind me to bring oranges to our next game. Or Kim again, trying to pin me down for lunch. On Tuesday evening, just after supper, when I was supposed to help Rex wash the dishes, my phone rang, and Topher's name blinked on the screen. I mussed up Rex's hair with a soapy hand. "I'll be back down in a minute." As I dashed up to Luke's room, slipping in my socks on the stairs, I could hear Rex yelling incoherently and my mom calming him down. I didn't answer the phone until I was in the top hall.

"How are you, Topher?"

"Hi, James," he responded. His voice seemed unnaturally deep. Was he making fun of me? I tried to sound natural.

"What's been happening?"

"How about Friday?" His voice was back to normal—he *had* been making fun of me. "Do you want to hang out on Friday? Can you?"

"Uh, yeah, sure," I stammered. I was leaning against Luke's window, holding the phone so close to the glass that my hand was cold. "You doing okay?"

"I'm good. I don't do well on the phone, though, so I figured maybe we could just make plans quicky-like. Is that okay? Or do you want to tell me about your week and stuff? You don't seem like a phone talker. I don't have anything to say about the last few days. I went to school today. Also, yesterday. And I just ate dinner. Now I have math home-work."

"No," I assured him, and sat down on Luke's bed. "I don't like talking on the phone."

"Okay, I'll come get you at eight on Friday."

"Sounds good."

"Okay, bye."

"Topher?"

He'd hung up. I sat staring at my phone for a second and then gazed out the window at the sliver of moon through the trees. Patches of snow still clung to the hillside.

The phone rang.

"Yup?"

"Where do you live?"

Stacks of our school's literary magazine, *Sin Qua Non*, appeared in the library and cafeteria. The editors had ded-icated the edition to Aaron, who had a short story in it. I almost never read anything in that rag because it's so preten-tious and melodramatic and often poorly edited. When I was a sophomore, before I knew better, I submitted a short story I'd written for a class. The editors rejected it. They basically only published writing done by themselves or their three friends. One of them dressed like a magician and was trying to grow a goatee. I don't know if Aaron was good friends with them, but sometimes I saw them all talking loudly in the hallway about poets and writers no one had ever heard of.

This time, the journal's cover was a pencil sketch of a genie emerging from a bottle. He looked disoriented and uncomfortable, which I guess makes sense given that he'd been stuffed into such a tiny space. His turban was too small, one ear was bigger than the other, and his eyeglasses were crooked. Hawken asked one of the editors why a genie would need glasses and was told to shut up.

Aaron's piece only ran a couple of pages. The story takes place on a kitchen counter and the characters are a can opener, a roll of paper towels, and a pomegranate. The can opener feels unappreciated and he gets blamed for bad work even though he always does exactly what he's told. He likes the countertop, but he wishes his life could be more exciting. The roll of paper towels is exhausted from being dragged into problems he didn't create. He feels like one day he's going to be used up. He talks about rolling away on an adventure but he doesn't know where to go. And the pomegranate doesn't say anything. The paper towels and can opener call him a "useless red ball," and the pomegranate doesn't try to defend himself. He just sits there quietly, knowing that he has "gems of sweet deliciousness inside him" and that one day he'll disappear from the counter and bring delight to others and his "thousand seed" will sprout into pomegranate trees.

Hawken caught me reading *Sin Qua Non* at lunch.

"Are you reading Aaron's story?" he asked.

"I just finished it."

He squeezed my shoulder and whispered in my ear.

"James, you are that pomegranate. *You*. Are that pomegranate."

Derek overheard him. "Aaron might be filled with sweet deliciousness but one thing he is not going to do is grow a whole bunch of new Aarons by spilling his thousand seed."

Theresa punched him in the arm. "Why would you say that? He got punched in the head. Have some respect."

"All I'm saying is that it's pretty unlikely that he'll be making any new little Aarons. No matter what, he's not going to be planting his thousand seed any place they're likely to grow."

"You are so rude," said Theresa. "Didn't his story make you think for a second, just a second, what it must be like for him at this school?"

"Yeah," answered Derek. "He treats everyone like a can opener and a roll of paper towels. He doesn't talk to anyone because he thinks we're boring and stuck on a counter. He's the brilliant artist who has it all figured out, and he's waiting to leave us all behind and become fabulous. The story's not sweet. It's obnoxious. He's obnoxious."

Theresa was silent for a while. "I don't blame him for wanting to get out of here. He gets treated like crap."

"Well, maybe he wouldn't get treated like crap if he were a little more friendly," snapped Derek.

"Well, maybe he'd be a little more friendly if he weren't treated like crap,"

"You guys are can openers," said Hawken.

"Not me, man. I'm paper towels," Derek said. "Double-Ply. Call me Double-Ply."

"I'm not calling you Double-Ply."

"I'm not answering to anything but Double-Ply."

At the end of English class, Breyer pulled me aside. "Nothing in the literary magazine, Mr. Liddell? How come?"

I thought about telling him how the editors conspired to only publish work by their cape-wearing, thin-mustachioed friends, but I held back. "It's not really my thing. I don't write stories anymore, and I don't like poetry that much."

Breyer screwed up his face as if I'd said something stupid. "Writing isn't really your thing? You should be writing all the time. You're good at it. What else are you doing with yourself? You got kids to raise?" He leaned against his desk with his arms folded and stared at me like he actually expected an answer.

Theresa appeared next to us just then, weaving her arm through mine. "Hi, Mr. Breyer!"

They chatted about his baby, Felix, until I leaned us toward the door.

"Theresa," Breyer called as we left. "Would you make sure that boy does some writing, please?"

"He doesn't listen to anybody, Mr. Breyer. Especially not me."

"What are you talking about?" I said when we were out in the hall. "I listen to you. I got these shoes because you told me to buy them."

Mark called out from behind us. "Hey! I hear you guys went to a dance last weekend without inviting anyone else."

I just stared at him as he walked up to us, but Theresa laughed. "It wasn't our dance to invite you to, Mark, and it was a semiformal."

"Ooh, fancy. So, are you two dating again?"

I changed the subject quickly. "You been running at all? Getting ready for the Big Race?"

I could feel Theresa glance toward me, but she kept up without missing a beat. "That's right!" she gushed, as if Mark and I were six-year-olds with birthdays approaching. "The Mud 10K! When is it again?"

"Not until June," I said. "There's still a long time to get ready."

Mark stretched his arms to the ceiling and leaned back, no doubt to give Theresa a look at every muscle in his body. "Well, yeah, I mean, James will probably win," he said. "He's cheating. He runs, like, every day."

Theresa laughed for real and I pretended to. "Training is cheating? Either way, I'm not training for the race, dude. I just run a lot. I'd run even if there weren't a race."

He rolled his eyes at Theresa, but she pushed him lightly in the shoulder. "I've seen you running after school, Mark."

He grinned and swatted the charge away. "No, you haven't."

"Yes, I have. You're training, so you're cheating, too."

"Nope. You saw someone else. I gotta go to baseball. Because, you know, I'm not a real athlete."

I ignored him. When he was safely down the hall, I turned to her. "Did you really see him running?"

"Yeah, down along the river the other day. It was definitely him."

"Aw, man. He's training. That means I should be training."

"I thought you *were* running."

"Yeah, but, you know, not *training*."

"What are you up to tomorrow night?" she asked out of nowhere.

"Oh. I'm going out to dinner with my folks." I could've come up with something better if I'd prepared ahead of time. I felt bad about the lie for as long as it took me to change the subject. "Hey, what's up with Derek and Kim? Are they talking?" I asked.

And we were on safe ground again.

CHAPTER 13

Topher's car pulled into our driveway at eight o'clock sharp on Friday evening, and I bounded up the stairs for my jacket and keys. While fishing my keys out of the coffee can, I avoided touching the alligator PEZ dispenser, as if it might wake up and bite me. I snatched my woolen hat, raced back down the stairs, shouted good-bye, then shut the front door slowly and strolled, casually, to Topher's car. I'd told my mom I was going to hang out with Derek, and I'd told Derek that I was going to lie low, that I wasn't feeling all that well.

Topher leaned across the passenger seat when I opened the door of his rusting Subaru. He had a green tartan scarf draped over his blue ski jacket, and he pointed at my feet with black leather gloves. "What do you have on your feet, dude?"

"Boots," I shrugged. "It's wet."

"Perfect."

He sat back up and stared at me, smiling, while I climbed in and fought with the seat belt. When I'd won, I looked at him and nervously folded my hands in my lap.

"Hi," I said.

"Hi." There was that cologne again. And that smile. "All buckled up?"

"All buckled up."

I didn't ask where we were going until we hit the highway, and then Topher pulled a pair of headlamps from his jacket pocket and explained that he knew a good little hike. It wasn't too far, and the trail led to a rocky ledge overlooking the Connecticut River. "It turns out we don't get Great Hockey Television," he admitted apologetically. "I did suggest to my mom that we should add it, but she looked at me as if I'd asked for the Playboy Channel."

I laughed. "She'd be surprised, huh?"

"She'd be thrilled. If you and your friends want to come over and watch it at my house, I'm sure she'd consider it a good influence."

"And yet the hockey channel request didn't move her?"

"I think she was suspicious of my motives." He sighed. "She's getting better, but she still isn't totally comfortable with the idea that I'm gay. I told my parents when I was in ninth grade, and my mom made me go to a psychiatrist. She asked him to prescribe me something."

"No kidding. Did he put you on meds?"

"No, that old guy's my hero. He spoke with me for about an hour, and when my mom came to get me, he said to her, 'Mrs. Owens, your son is a happy, articulate young man. He also happens to like other boys. He has a bright future ahead of him, and you should decide now whether you want to be part of it.'"

"Wow, I might need that guy's number."

"For real. I can get it for you. I saw him at Food Safari one time, and we high-fived, He did it reluctantly, but we high-fived."

We pulled into a little dirt parking area just off the road, and Topher reached behind him for his backpack. "I brought snacks," he explained. "Don't forget your headlamp."

The trail was even muddier than I'd expected, and it was tough to avoid stumbling on roots and rocks in our lamps' soft light. Ten minutes in, we had to scramble up a slick, granite face. Topher scurried up first. When he reached the top, he squatted down and stretched out his hand. I didn't need the help, but I put my hand in his anyway, and he pulled me up the rock. Then we walked like that, holding hands—I felt sort of dizzy—until we reached a fallen pine. Again, I let Topher go first, and he ducked under the branches, disappearing for a few seconds beneath a cloak of green needles. "Watch out for sap!" he called, and then started cracking up. "Watch out for sap! The words of a true woodsman."

I tried climbing over the tree instead, but slipped on the wet bark and nearly ended up straddling the trunk. Luckily, I caught myself just in time. "Holy smokes!" I cried. "This was almost a date to the emergency room."

"Nice save." He laughed, and then, "Date, huh? Remember, we're just hiking."

"And nearly emasculating ourselves," I muttered, disentangling myself from the tree.

"We were only holding hands," he joked, reaching out to me as I walked onto the flat, open trail.

"I'll kill you," I whispered, taking his hand in mine.

"You use big words," he whispered back.

The overlook wasn't much farther beyond the downed pine. Standing on a little granite lip, we gazed out at mist rising from the Connecticut as it wound between hills. So many stars packed the sky it was a wonder they didn't make any noise. It's one of the things I miss most about Vermont when I visit a city, the unreal quiet.

Topher squeezed my hand after a minute or two and shrugged off his backpack. "The snacks," he said excitedly. "I almost forgot about the snacks." He pulled out a carefully folded fleece jacket and produced two bottles.

"No way! You carried up beers?"

"Apple thi-der," he gushed. "The *sans* alcohol variety. I don't drink all that often. But I thought this might be a good compromise, since, you know, it's brown and fizzy and comes in a bottle."

"Sure, I didn't really want a beer," I lied.

"Yup. But wait. There's more." I heard paper crinkling and tearing, and then Topher handed me a smaller bottle. "Would you please open this?"

"Are these olives?" I asked as I popped the lid.

"Yeah. I dig olives. And I have smoked Gouda cheese here and some kind of artichoke spread."

"Wow. I was expecting soda and chips."

"I have stone ground wheat crisps. This is all I could find in the fridge." He put his hands on his hips. "We could stop at a gas station for doughnuts on the way home if you'd like, James."

"No, dude," I protested, hands up. "This is great. It's what Derek and Hawken and I usually snack on when we're watching *Hockey Night in Canada*. I like apple juice. Shall we sit?"

"Apple cider. Yes, we shall sit."

Our knees touched as we settled in, stared down the valley, and used Topher's pocketknife to cut ourselves hunks of cheese.

"How do we get these olives out of here?"

"Let me see it," Topher demanded. He emptied the oil onto the ground and handed the bottle back to me. "The thing is, now we have to eat them all."

"We could have speared them with a stick or something."

"Nope. It's better to just go for it, go all the way." He knocked a few olives into his hand, popped them in his mouth, and chewed them thoughtfully. "I'm like that with most things. If I open a gallon of milk, I finish it on the spot. I never have only a slice of cake."

"That's sort of terrifying," I said. "You throw up often?"

"It's how I keep the weight off."

"Mmm. This artichoke dip must help with that."

He shook his head and sipped from his apple cider. "And things had been going so well, dude." He threw a handful of wheat crisps at me. They fluttered in the wind and landed in leaves near our outstretched feet. "Things had been going so well," he repeated over my laughter. "I bait a cute soccer player, a nice guy, all the way up to my favorite spot, and it turns out he doesn't know the difference between juice and cider, dip and spread."

"I know a spot kind of like this one that I'll take you to next time."

"Yeah?"

"Sure, it's up behind my house a ways."

He grinned and popped another olive into his mouth. "I'm glad we've got a second not-date." He knocked my knee with his fist.

It was his idea to race back to the car. I don't normally run down muddy trails in the dark, but I figured I could beat him. It turned out he's really quick, and he's not afraid to cheat. He checked me into a bush right at the bottom and tagged the Subaru. I went home with filthy jeans and a wicked scratch on my face.

"Your mom's going to hate me," he said miserably as he

drove up my driveway.

"She thinks I was out with Derek," I said. "He can do no wrong. You're fine."

"Well," he said, sticking out his hand, "I had fun, James."

We shook hands a few seconds too long.

"I did, too, Topher. Thanks. I'll call you soon."

"Sounds good," and he smiled at the dashboard. I got out, leaned into the car before I shut the door, and said, "Good night, dude. Drive safely."

"Night!" And he threw the car in reverse.

Should I have kissed him? Even just on the cheek? The sound of his car faded down the road. I stood on the driveway for a while longer, hands in my pockets, and stared up at the stars. I'd just gone on a date with another boy. No difference in the heavens.

Kim texted me the next morning to ask if I'd go to lunch with her at the Sleeping Badger Diner. I couldn't avoid her forever, so I agreed to meet up at 1:00 p.m. Just the two of us.

No one knows why the Sleeping Badger is called the Sleeping Badger. I looked up the badger's range one time. It doesn't live in Vermont. Still, the diner's decorated with a few hundred stuffed badgers from the size of mice to bears. None of them are sleeping. We sat in a red pleather booth at the back of the diner, far from any other patrons. Our waitress called me Sugar when she gave us our menus, which made us both crack up.

I didn't open my menu.

"You going to eat?" asked Kim.

"Yeah, I know what I'm getting."

"Me, too. So, listen, Sugar, I'm guessing you've figured out that I want to talk to you about a couple of things."

"Right. I figured." I opened my menu and began reading the breakfast specials.

"James, you have to listen to me."

"I'm listening."

"You just said you know what you want to order. Put the menu down."

I folded it, placed it on the table, grabbed a stack of jelly packets from the condiment rack, and lined them up in front of me. Apricot in the middle of two strawberries. Then strawberry, strawberry, apricot.

"James. For real." She knocked on the table in front of me. "Look at me." She pointed at my eyes with two fingers and then pointed at her own. Her earrings had little strings of blue and yellow beads, and the left one dangled a little lower than the right. "Listen, I never do this, right? But for real, I'm in a very weird spot. You're sort of dating, maybe kind of dating, two of my best friends who are not both girls, and I'm not sure what's okay to say to—"

"Right, right," I interrupted. "Just don't say anything to either of them."

"You want me to stop talking to them both?"

"Not *forever*. But maybe for a little bit if that makes things easier."

She looked at me as if she couldn't tell whether I was joking. "James, I'm not going to stop talking to them. I talk to them both every day. I already spoke to them both this morning."

"What'd they say about me?"

"No, that's not what we're here to discuss. You need to talk to Theresa and tell her what's going on."

"Did you say anything to her?" I whispered quickly. The waitress arrived with glasses of water, and I guzzled from mine. Kim ordered a Greek salad. I ordered a grilled cheese and a milk shake and fries. I waited until the waitress had moved away before asking again, more slowly, but just as quietly, "Did you say anything to Theresa about me?"

"No, of course not. But even if I wanted to, I wouldn't know *what* to say. I don't know what's going on. That's one of the reasons I wanted to see you."

I nodded and stacked the jelly packets in a tower. "I'm not sure what's going on either." I flicked the tower so it tumbled over. "It's sort of confusing."

"Well, let's start at the beginning. First, you told me that you think Sean Gates the goalie is cute."

I looked behind me. The booth between us and the wall was empty. No one was at the table on the other side either. I shrugged and nodded and couldn't help grinning a little.

"And you don't want to date Theresa, right?"

I restacked the jellies. "Not really, no," I admitted. "It's not that I don't like her. She's nice and funny."

"But you're not attracted to her. Not that way. And you like Topher."

I nodded. "He's a good guy."

"And you're attracted to *him.*"

"I like hanging out with him."

"James, you have to tell Theresa that you like boys."

"I like Topher."

"And the goalie of my school's soccer team."

"No, I don't like Sean Gates. He cheats. All I meant was that I recognize that he's a good-looking kid."

"You're being ridiculous. You have to tell Theresa that you're gay. Especially if you and Topher are going to start hooking up—"

"Who said anything about us hooking up?"

"No one, but—"

"Did Topher say that? Did he say—" I dropped my voice. "Did he say that we hooked up? We didn't hook up."

"No! Relax. My God. All I'm saying is that you have to be honest with Theresa so she's not thinking that she could be dating you if she's patient or persistent or whatever. Because at the moment, she thinks that's a possibility. She's always thought you guys would get serious someday as long as she didn't scare you away."

"I know. But I don't know what I'm supposed to do to make it clear that it's not what I want." I balanced the salt shaker on top of the pepper.

"James, you shouldn't be worried about what to do. You should be worried about what to *say*. Talk to her."

"OK. I'll talk to her. I promise. How was the rest of that party last weekend? Did you stay long?"

"*When* are you going to talk to her?"

"Soon. I promise. Don't say anything until then."

"You have one week, James."

"Don't give me a deadline. Nobody likes deadlines. I'll talk to her really soon, I swear."

"Let Topher know what's up, too."

"OK. You got a lot of homework this weekend?"

"So, just to be clear: You *do* or you do *not* like talking about this stuff?"

"I want my lunch. Where's our food?"

"We literally just ordered."

"I gotta pee." I split for the men's room. When I returned to the table, I successfully steered the conversation away from me and kept her talking about sports, past summer vacations, and, in a desperate move, the future of NASA. I'd just read an article about the Mars Rover.

I spent the rest of the afternoon wondering if I should call Theresa and ask her to go for a walk so I could tell her everything. I was still debating the walk when it started to get dark and Derek called to see if I wanted to watch some hockey at his place. Before I left, I scribbled Theresa a letter.

Saturday, May 7th

Theresa,

I don't know how to end our half-cooked relationship. Can I just call it quits casually? "It's not going to work between us. Let's move on." Or do I have to ask you to sit down, stare into your eyes, and get all weepy with you? I'm told that texting is not a good way to say good-bye. But I don't want to say good-bye to you anyway. I guess that's the thing. Everything between us works. Almost. I'd miss the way you fix my collar even when it doesn't need to be fixed. The way you fall asleep against me ten minutes into any movie. That perfume you wear. The way people brighten when they see us together. I wish you could be the one I can't take my eyes off of, the one I can't stop thinking about. I really do. If there were a way to say we're done and know that everything would stay the same between us, I'd do it in a second. I think that's why I keep letting you think there's still a chance that things will work out: if I say it all plainly, you're going to end up in tears, and I'm going to end up looking like a jerk.

There's so much to look forward to.

Love,

James

CHAPTER 14

Monday morning, Derek and I stopped to inspect the little shrine some girls had set up for Aaron just inside the school. Origami birds perched on melted candles in front of a collage of Aaron photos. In most of the shots, he was smiling in a way that he never did in school. Brown wilted carnations were taped to the poster board. "The flowers look terrible," I said, and I started to yank the tape from their stems.

"What are you doing?" a girl yelled from down the hall.

I stood up. "I'm taking down these dead flowers. They're depressing."

She marched toward me. "They're not yours to take down."

Derek imitated a police loudspeaker. "Step away from the shrine. Step away from the shrine, please."

I put up my hands and backed away. "I was trying to help."

"You don't even know him," the girl snapped.

I wanted to scream, *His pink alligator PEZ dispenser stares at me while I sleep!* But I didn't. "He's not dead," I muttered instead.

The girl untaped the flowers as we left.

The same girl was there again the next morning, standing guard. She glared at us. Plastic daisies were now stapled to Aaron's photos. Derek stopped to sniff them. "The flowers are lovely," he whispered to her. "They smell like new inner tube."

That day I kept having these moments when I'd be having a normal conversation, but in my head I was on that hike, holding hands with Topher. Teachers looked right at me and called my name, and it felt like they were talking to someone else. No one but me could see the double image: the kid everyone thought they knew and the kid I really was. I knew what I had to do to pull the two images into one—I had to be honest with everyone—but I didn't know where to begin or even if I should.

Derek and I drove to the library to work on our history projects that afternoon. He was still in his AC/DC phase. Nothing anyone said to him could make it stop. He'd subjected me to this band so much over the previous weeks that I didn't hear them anymore, even as they screamed themselves hoarse from the stereo. Now I was grateful that they provided a cover for my silence.

At some point, I knew, I would have to talk to Derek. But he made jokes about gay people, and I laughed at them. The Jesus he believed in, I was pretty sure, frowned upon gay people. Plus, I wouldn't just be telling Derek that I like boys. I'd be telling him that I'd led him along, persuaded him to be friends with a kid who doesn't exist. And once I told him, I wouldn't be able to take it back, even if I changed my mind. What if I ended up not liking Topher after all? What if I fell in love with some girl? It would be like after that walk with Hawken: I'd wish that I'd just kept my mouth shut. But all I wanted to do right then was talk to Derek about it. I cranked the front seat back as far as it would go and put my feet up on the dashboard. It was as close as I could get to curling up in the car.

Derek glanced at me, turned the radio down just low enough to ask, "What's happening there, Liddell? You about to give birth? You're pregnant?"

"Twins," I groaned. "I don't know how I'm going to tell my parents."

"Your parents are pretty chill. I'm sure they'll be loving grandparents."

"I don't know. I think this news will come as a bit of a shock to them."

"Does Theresa know yet? Have you told her?"

"No. And she's not going to be happy about it either."

"What? She loves babies. And she'll be impressed that you're doing all the work."

"Sure, sure. The thing is, she might not be the mother."

"You're the mommy. She's the daddy."

"I'm the daddy. I'm like a sea horse."

"This is scandalous and strange! Tell me the mother is not Kim."

"It's not Kim. Jesus."

"Gina DeAngelo?"

I punched him. Gina DeAngelo is a Spanish teacher at my school who is widely regarded as hot.

"Dude, there is no reason to punch me. I would've been impressed if Gina DeAngelo were the mother slash father of your twin babies."

"Her husband might be upset."

"Well, you never know," shrugged Derek. "He might be impressed, too. His woman knocking up a good-looking high school boy. He might be into it. He might ask to watch next—"

"This conversation's done," I interrupted. We were pulling into the library parking lot anyway.

"I was just saying," he sang as he slipped the car into a spot between enormous pickup trucks. And then he cranked the emergency brake and turned to look me in the eye.

"For real, dude. Are you sleeping with someone other than Theresa?"

"No," I said honestly.

"Did something happen to turn you into a basket case for the first ten minutes of that drive?"

I slid down in my seat again. I was cold and wanted to go inside, but I wanted to spill it all to Derek, too. "Things have been sort of intense," I began. Here we go, I thought.

"Did Theresa call it quits with you?"

"No. . ."

"Good. Then don't screw it up." And he got out of the car.

Topher and I exchanged a couple of quick notes when I was washing dishes that night. *How's it going? Good, you?* It was weird texting with him right in front of my parents. It's not that I'd never kept a secret from them before, but this time I wasn't just being a little dishonest. I imagined sitting them down and telling them everything that was rattling around in my head. But they were dealing with Rex, who was getting picked on by some kid at school, and they sounded really tired.

At lunch on Thursday, Derek announced that his parents were going back down to Boston that weekend. "We're keeping it very small. Don't tell anyone. I swear I'll turn people away."

My brain began an internal argument with itself. I wanted to hang out with Derek and Hawken, but I wanted to see Topher, too. The thing was, Theresa would be there. I wasn't even dating her, I reminded myself, so why was I worried about it? Because everyone would wonder why I'd invited Topher along—unless I wasn't the one to invite him.

When Derek left the table, I turned to Theresa. "Hey, why don't you invite Kim along to Derek's?" Part of me felt bad about setting this trap.

"Yeah, I was thinking the same thing."

"I don't know why he's so shy about asking her himself. Do you think she'll be able to come?" It all sounded so innocent.

"Sure, if she can get over here. Usually her brother brings her and I don't know if he'll be around."

"Oh, right." I pretended to think hard. "You could invite Topher along, too."

A little gasp. "Smart, James!" She talks to me like I'm a puppy sometimes. "Good boy!" She scratched behind my ear. I smiled and shrugged.

CHAPTER 15

Topher called me later that night. "So, Theresa invited me over to Derek's tomorrow night. You okay with me coming along?"

"Yeah, of course! I was the one who suggested it."

"Oh." He sounded confused. "Why didn't *you* just invite me?"

"Because," I said. I figured it was obvious why and I didn't want to have to spell it out. "Because it's better if she did it. Just come along. I want to hang out."

Silence on the other end. Was he, like me, standing with one hand on his head, eyes closed?

"OK," he said eventually. "OK. I'll see you tomorrow night."

Half an hour later, I got a text from Kim: *Are you kidding me?*

Hawken saw me check my fly and adjust my woolen hat when we heard Kim and Topher climbing the long wooden stairs up to Derek's deck. He tilted his head at me, and I glanced at the others to see if they'd noticed. Hawken and Derek were perched on the railing with beers. Theresa sat in a wooden Adirondack chair with a Diet Coke. To my relief, Mark was working at the restaurant all weekend, so he couldn't make it.

"Topher, right?" Derek shook his hand.

I gave them both hugs of equal length. Two seconds each. I counted.

"What do you think of Derek's haircut?" Hawken demanded. "Don't you think he should grow an Afro? We're deciding tonight."

"You could have a sweet one by next year, right in time for graduation," Topher said.

"That's what *I've* been saying!" cried Hawken.

"Who needs one?" I asked, sliding open the glass door to the kitchen.

Derek put up five fingers.

"Everyone's staying over, right?" Derek asked when I came back out with a six-pack.

"I'm not drinking," announced Kim. "So I can drive Topher home, but I have to leave at ten thirty. Unless, well, Topher, unless you want to stay and someone can give you a ride tomorrow? Or Theresa, are you going to stay? Or are you both staying—?" She looked over at me, and I telepathically told her to shut up. She went silent.

The haircut debates resumed. Hawken defended the mohawk he had when he was eight, and he threatened to bring it back that summer. We all vehemently opposed this plan, and Derek disappeared inside to find a photo of it. He came back with a whole album and a bottle of rum. We had an easy match the next day, I didn't have all that much homework, and I didn't have to worry about getting home. Hawken and Theresa were grinning and flipping through the photos of us all in elementary school, and Topher and Kim were cracking up at one of Derek's stories. The stars were out, and for some reason, for a little while, it seemed like everything would be okay.

I'd never had rum before. After a quarter of the bottle was gone, Derek was making Topher recite lines from *Hamlet* so that we could yell them to the sky in pirate voices. If Derek had neighbors closer by, they would have heard him holler a dozen times *"It harrows me with fear and wonder!"* Pretty soon we were just shouting phrases that sounded vaguely Shakespearean in seadog voices. I hadn't dared to sit next to Topher when he arrived, but now I sat right next to him on the porch rail, our legs touching. Hawken was taking photos of everyone, and I didn't even care.

At one point Derek looked me in the eye and growled, "This is a mud season disquieting and . . ." He frowned, searching for a second word.

I swigged from the bottle, winced, and gasped, "Fine. Disquieting and fine."

After Kim, Topher, and Theresa left in a flurry of hugs and high fives, and while Derek was out on the porch gathering bottles, Hawken and I chugged water in the kitchen. Leaning against the counter with him, the night we'd gone for a walk in the snow seemed long ago, but it'd only been a few weeks earlier.

"Your boy's cute," Hawken whispered.

I smirked at the linoleum and then pounded the rest of my water. "Don't say that," I said, wiping my mouth on my sleeve. "Don't say that out loud. Not around anyone."

"Tell me when you've told Derek," he said, just as Derek slid open the door from the porch, and I banged my glass into the sink.

"You guys can pull the bed out from the couch. You know, the foldy bed or whatever."

"No, it's cool," I said. "Hawken, you take the couch. I'll take the floor."

"Just pull out the bed," cried Derek. "It's a big bed. It takes like thirty seconds to set it up."

"No, it's fine," I insisted.

But he disappeared into the living room, and I heard him pushing aside the coffee table and throwing cushions across the room. Metal hinges squealed as he yanked the bed out of the couch. I glanced at Hawken. He smiled and ruffled my hair. "It's okay, Liddell," he whispered. "I sleep naked, but it's okay."

"There!" Derek yelled from the living room. "It's done! Ten seconds! I timeth't it!"

The next week flew by in a blur of classes. I buried myself in homework, and Topher had play rehearsals every night, so we barely even spoke until the following Friday afternoon, when we went to Wilder Dam to let his dog run. He picked me up at my house, and on our way out to the highway, I saw Theresa's car waiting at an intersection ahead of us. I pulled the seat recliner lever and fell flat on my back.

"Whoa!" Topher yelled. "What's happening there? Was that intentional?"

"Yup, that's Theresa's car up there. Keep your eyes ahead."

"Oh, boy," was all he said.

I watched treetops zip over us for a count of ten. "We're past her, right?"

"We passed her," he confirmed.

I pulled the lever and sat back up. "Sorry. I just don't want to have to answer a whole bunch of questions from her or make up a crazy story if she sees us together. I told her I wasn't feeling well and couldn't hang out."

Topher didn't say anything for a minute or two. "This is a really crazy idea, I know, but you could just tell her the truth."

"I will one day," I promised. "Not today, though."

"Why not just talk to her about everything? Tell her you like boys. It's not your fault, and she might be relieved to hear that she's not the problem."

"It's weird to talk about."

"It'll get easier. *I like boys.* Practice saying it. *I* like *like boys.*" He laughed, and I grinned but shook my head at him. "Sorry, I know this isn't funny for you." He coughed to get serious again. "You have to talk to her."

"Maybe I'll send her a text or something."

"James. Do not send her a text. Are you kidding? Talk to her, for God's sake. She's your friend." We were pulling into the dirt parking lot. It was a nice day, but there were only two other cars. "Awesome. The place is empty." Angus was scrabbling in the back of the old Subaru before Topher had even turned off the engine.

"That dog loves to run, huh?" I said, grateful for the chance to change the subject.

"My dad runs him five or six miles a day. He's out of town on business, so Angus didn't run yesterday." When Topher opened the trunk door, the border collie shot from the back, sprinted along the tree line a hundred yards ahead of us, then bounced into the bushes and disappeared without warning.

"Your dog just ran off the planet, dude."

"He comes back—soaked and salty from the oceans, perfumed from the Orient—but he comes back." He was quiet for a moment, then confessed, "I stole that line from my grandfather. And this." He produced an empty cigarette case from his pocket. "Well, he gave me this before he died. I wish smoking was less deadly."

"I have Aaron Foster's PEZ dispenser. He gave it to me— well, he traded it for my sweater—the day he got punched."

"Yikes. I don't know Aaron. I know *of* Aaron, but I've never met him."

We were walking slowly, the squishy fields still yellow and brown.

"How are things at your school?" Topher ventured. "I mean, since all that happened?"

"No one talks about it all that much," I said, pulling up my hood. "We had small group discussions about 'social choices' one afternoon, and some of our teachers talked with us about it in class, but one of the weirdest parts about the whole thing is how quickly everything has gone back to normal, you know? Now it's almost like it never happened. Like Aaron was a character we saw in a movie once, and he disappeared when the screen went black, and we all went on with real life."

"Yup, I remember that feeling. A kid in my middle school died of leukemia. It was sort of like that."

"And Mark, he acts like nothing happened. He doesn't seem to notice that kids are scared of him."

We were approaching a boat ramp. We'd seen only a few people in the distance across some vast meadows, and there were only a couple of kayakers far upstream.

"Yeah, but Mark's a pal of yours, right?"

"I used to be better friends with him than I am now, but yeah, he still hangs out with us. Hawken looks out for him."

"What about Aaron? How is he?"

"He's not back at school yet. Evidently, he's having nasty headaches."

"Have you talked to him?"

"I tried calling him once. I don't know him all that well," I muttered. I didn't want to get into it.

"Not your type?"

"I feel sorry for him. He's not all that smart in terms of blending in, you know."

"That's what I hear." We stopped where the grass turned to sand and stones near the water's edge. "Do you make a real effort? To blend in, I mean? To make sure no one knows that you like boys?"

"No," I said too quickly. I looked out across the fields and behind me, looked up and down the river. "I mean, I guess I don't have to try all that hard, apart from keeping quiet about it."

"You're just this great without trying, huh?" He put his arm around my back and pulled me close to him.

I didn't answer. I could feel his hand on my waist, his arm around me, feel the rise and fall of his chest next to mine as I held my breath, and I wished the sun would drop out of the sky. My back was as rigid as the old gray jetty posts leading in a sinking line from shore to black water. Chewing the string of my hoodie, I squinted over my shoulder at a trail-head thirty yards behind us, and Topher dropped his arm.

"I'm making you nervous."

"Little bit." I grabbed a flat stone from the ground and tried to skip it across the river. It splashed twice and careened into a post. I shuffled through the sand, searching for another good rock, and Topher walked behind me, kicked my leg.

"Let's go feed the ducks," he suggested. "I know where they hang out."

"You know where the ducks go in the winter?"

He put out his hand, and I tried to smile at him as I took it in my own. "It's freaking broad daylight, dude," I muttered.

He swept his arm across the empty, open fields. "It's not like we're walking down the middle of the street, man. You can keep your hood up if you don't want to be seen with me."

I pulled the hood off, and Topher grinned, mussed up my hair, then leaned over and kissed my cheek.

"That was our first kiss, huh?" I laughed nervously as we headed for the ducks.

"That doesn't count as a kiss, James." He stopped walking, wrapped his arms around me, and really kissed me. Later, I'd wonder and worry about who'd been watching, but for a minute or two, I stopped thinking, stopped fretting, even as his hand slid into my back pocket and I slid mine into his. He tasted like spearmint. He brushed his cheek against mine, kissed my ear and breathed into it, "That was our first kiss."

I put my head on his shoulder and, after a second, said

flatly, "I just kissed a boy."

"Yup," sighed Topher, putting his hand on the back of my head. "You did. And not even very well."

I held him tight and rubbed a knuckle against his ribs.

"No!" He pushed me away, laughing and holding his side. "That's terrible! Never do that again! The ducks are going to hate you."

When we reached the little cove packed with mallards, Topher clapped his hands. "Right where I left them."

"I think they recognize you." Even the ones far out in the river quacked maniacally and raced to the shore.

"Oh, sure, sure. I know them all by name." He pulled half a bag of stale bread from his coat pocket. Within thirty seconds there were as many ducks at our feet, demanding loudly to be fed.

"Topher, feed them quick! They're getting upset." My raised voice made the birds quack louder.

I expected Topher to tear off bits of bread and throw them to individual birds, but he seemed unnerved by all the noise as well. He grabbed the entire loaf, ripped it into four big pieces and threw one in each direction. The nearest ducks and I looked at him, confused, but he shrugged. "They have to learn to share." Ducks fought viciously on three sides of us, and the chunk of bread that had plopped in the river was sinking. A few irritated-looking birds stuck their heads underwater to peck at it, then glared at us.

Topher leaned against me.

"You're really good with animals, huh?" I said, sliding my hand nervously to his waist.

"Just ducks. I'm like the duck whisperer."

Angus bolted out of the trees just then, dripping mud, and the ducks exploded. Five or six of them nearly hit us as they took off in a flapping panic. Topher screamed and tackled me to the ground. We lay there in each other's arms, cackling, as Angus ricocheted around the little clearing, leaping at birds slow to take flight. "Holy smokes!" Topher panted, and then Angus jumped on top of us, sending us into hysterics again. "We nearly got killed by mallards!" Topher gasped. "It was duck apocalypse!"

By the time we got back to the car, the only other two cars in the lot had disappeared along with most of the daylight. "Dude, you are a mess," said Topher. "How did you get mud on your face while going for a walk?"

"Your freaking dog was climbing on my head."

"He has boundary issues." Topher shrugged. He grabbed a napkin from the glove compartment to wipe my face. I felt like I was six years old. "Hold freaking still," he chided. For a second, I thought he was going to lick the napkin the way my grandmother used to, and the thought of it made me start giggling. "Would you quit moving? Your face is filthy. You look like you crawled out of the woods."

"I look tough?"

"Yeah," he snickered. "Dirty is so tough." He put his hand on my waist and reached over me to clean my other cheek. I closed my eyes and felt my heart race when he began to kiss my neck. Ten minutes later we heard tires on the gravel road on the other side of the trees, and we both sat up fast. Topher had his car moving before the ranger's pickup had even reached us.

My parents had gone to visit Luke up at school, and they took Rex with them. I wasn't interested in fending off a party, so I hadn't mentioned this fact to anyone. Topher and I grabbed a sandwich after dropping Angus off at his place, and then we went back to my empty house, where I changed out of my muddy jeans. Topher was pretending to read my palm on the couch when there was a knock on the front door. Derek and Theresa.

"We were driving past, so we figured we'd see what you were up to, see if you're feeling better. Whose car is that?"

Topher came out of the living room. "Hey. Same thing. I was in the neighborhood. Figured I'd stop by to say hi."

Derek and Theresa smiled and nodded. "Nice," Theresa said.

"Come in," I said. It might've been the first time I'd ever had to invite them into my house.

"It's okay. We should go," Theresa said. "We were just stopping by to say hi."

"No!" I yelped, although I wanted them to leave so very badly. "You don't have to go!" I made it sound like a crazy idea. "My parents are out of town, so, you know, we were just hanging out. Who are you calling?"

"Hawken and Mark," Derek said. "Hawken has some beers. Can we have a fire out back?"

We kept it to just us six. There were enough stumps around the old fire ring for everyone to have a seat. Derek took charge of building the fire, and the rest of us stared up through black branches at the stars while big trees creaked and clattered in the wind. When Theresa leaned against me, I glanced over at Topher. Looking down, he scratched the back of his head. I knelt on the ground to offer Derek help. "I got it," he muttered, balling tiny twigs and birch bark into kindling. Theresa walked away, back toward the house. Soon flames crackled, and Derek blew the base of the fire to a roar.

"Look at how fast that plane's going!" Hawken cried. "Way up there. That little dot. It's booking!"

"Are you sure that's a plane? Could be a satellite, right?" Mark asked. "Derek? Plane or satellite?"

Derek stood up from the fire. It took some pointing and directing, but eventually he saw it. "Oh, satellite. It's way, way too small to be a plane."

"Maybe it's a UFO," said Hawken.

"It's not an Unidentified Flying Object because I just identified it as a satellite."

"MFO," suggested Hawken. "Misidentified Flying Object. Last time we had the telescope out, Derek told us that there is definitely intelligent life on other planets. Without a doubt, a hundred percent certainty, there is another civilization out there among all those stars, and when they find us, they will enslave us."

"I did not say they would enslave us." Derek laughed.

"It's a good bet, though, right? Why wouldn't they shackle us and sell us to an intergalactic mining company?"

"Maybe it's a whole 'nother civilization of black people, Derek," said Mark.

Just the crackle of the fire.

"But maybe," continued Hawken, "when they get here, they'll just die from common colds or, I don't know, pollen allergies or something like that, so our horrific ordeal won't last all that long."

"Gluten might be fatal to them." Mark nodded. "Sulfites. The good thing is, we'll be safe up here in Vermont. They won't be able to find us in the hills. It'll just be in the major cities where people get rounded up and shipped off to, you know, work to death in cobalt factories or what have you."

"Cobalt?" asked Derek.

"Or any kind of factory."

"Mark?" Derek asked, breaking sticks and feeding them to the flames. "Are you planning to stay here forever?"

"Where? America?"

"No, here. In this town. You don't want to go explore a big city sometime?"

"I like it here. Why would I want to leave?"

"Sure. I mean, I guess you got everything you need," said Derek. "Plenty of fresh water." He fell in to a Southern accent. "Critters to chase and chew on. Leaves for good bedding. Maybe when you *de*-cease your restaurant will mount your head on the wall."

"They put up real art," Mark pointed out. "Paintings and crap like that."

Theresa reappeared. She was wearing a hoodie that was too big for her.

"Hey," I barked. "Is that my hoodie?"

"Yup. I'm borrowing it."

"Where'd you find it?"

"In your room. On the chair."

I just shook my head.

The wind shifted and blew smoke right into her face. "I hate white rabbits I hate white rabbits I hate white rabbits," she hollered. The smoke changed directions again. "See?" She grinned. "It does work. It's magic."

"Just like James's Magic Soccer Socks," said Hawken.

"You have Magic Socks?" Topher asked. "What, they help you score?"

"They help him cripple his enemies," explained Hawken. "Like that goalie." He laughed. "James has a little goalie friend on another team."

"My school's goalie? Sean Gates?" asked Topher, grinning.

I stared at him, wide-eyed. "Different goalie," I said quickly. "I don't know his name. We got in a shoving match a few weeks ago, but I was wearing my Magic Socks, so, you know, he was vanquished."

"The socks layeth him on the plastic grass," Hawken said solemnly. "In the manner of the departed."

"I didn't know you were a fighter," said Topher. He didn't sound impressed.

"He's not," said Mark, smirking. "Who needs another one?" He counted all the raised hands—Derek and I raised both—and wandered into the woods to pee.

"Isn't he supposed to be *not* drinking?" whispered Derek.

"Yeah," Hawken whispered back. "You try telling him that."

We hung out around the fire for an hour or so, mostly listening to Mark talk about girls. At one point he disappeared into my house to fetch a yearbook from my room so he could remind us of who these girls were. Mark asked Topher his opinion about each one.

"Sure, she's pretty," Topher would say.

"She's not pretty. She's hot! Right?"

"Sure," said Topher.

Hawken and I tried hard to change the subject, but Mark always brought it back to girls. Eventually, Topher announced he had to go.

Derek waggled his bottle and asked, "You're *driving* home?"

"I haven't had a drop," said Topher. "And I have an early-morning rehearsal. So I should split."

"I'll walk back to the house with you. I'm going to grab

my water bottle," I said.

In the dark by his car, we kissed good night. "Maybe you should just stay over?" I whispered. He laughed. He couldn't. He'd see me soon.

When I came back into the house, Derek was standing in the middle of the kitchen, arms folded. "Hey. I want to ask you something," he said. He coughed and stared hard at the floor.

I dug my hands in my pockets and waited for him to speak. He looked up again, pointed a finger toward the front door and said, "That dude. Topher—"

I interrupted him. "He's a good guy, right? It's nice making friends at other schools. Instead of the same old crowd—"

Derek flinched. "What, you're *bored* with us?"

"No, I'm not *bored* with you," I began, but Theresa, Mark, and Hawken barged in through the back door just then. Derek looked at the ceiling and turned away from me, placing his hands on the counter and leaning forward as if he were being sick.

"Last call!" shouted Mark. "It's time to go home! Last call! Last call!"

"I just hit my exhaustion wall, and you guys are out of beer, anyway," said Theresa. "So it's past last call and your designated driver is on the way out the door."

Derek walked past me without a word.

"Hey, where's my hoodie?" I asked as all four of them went down the front steps.

"Derek already put it back up there. Right?"

"Is she lying, Derek?" I called after him.

He yelled over his shoulder. "I put it back!"

I waved from the porch as they reversed down the driveway, and then I walked up to the Guaranteed Cell Phone Reception Zone in Luke's room and sent Topher a good night text. I fell asleep on Luke's bed waiting for a reply.

CHAPTER 16

I shuffled into my own room the next morning and stopped dead in my tracks. My keys were lying on a notebook. I had not put them there. I never put them there. Not ever. I put them in the coffee can full of coins. Always. It's why I don't lose them. I remembered distinctly putting them in there the night before because I had growled at Aaron's alligator PEZ dispenser when I did so. Someone had been handling my keys.

Cursing, I fumbled with the keys and opened my top desk drawer. They were still there. My letters. "Thank you," I sighed as I picked up the whole pile. What was the last one I wrote? That letter to Theresa.

It wasn't on top. A letter to my soccer coach was first.

I broke into a prickly sweat and flipped through the dozens of handwritten pages. Nothing. It wasn't on the bottom of the stack either. I checked the drawer again. Empty. I closed my eyes and thought back to the night I wrote it. Did I remember putting it in the drawer? Could I have put it in another notebook or somewhere else? Maybe it got mixed up with my schoolwork? I rifled through my backpack, through all the papers on my desk, through my recycling box, through my stack of blank printer paper. Nothing. Twice more through everything. One by one through the letters, front and back. It wasn't there. Was I sure I wrote it? I could picture it. I'd drawn a little swirly coil in the top corner.

Someone had it. And if they took that one, they probably took others, too. Someone knew everything about me. My whole story.

Collapsing on my bed, I shoved my head under my pillow and thought back to the previous night. Who had been up in my room? Almost everyone. Mark had gone up at least twice—once to get a yearbook so he could point out girls he liked and once, obeying my command, to put the yearbook back. Theresa had wandered in to borrow my hoodie. Derek had returned it. Even Topher had been up there on a self-guided tour of the house. He hung out in my room long enough to be able to comment on photographs, books, and random stuff on my shelves, but he had no motive to go digging.

I rolled off my bed and picked up the letters again. Was the one to Theresa the only one missing? There was one I'd written to Hawken back in the fall that complained about his laziness during one of our games. Found it. Were there more? A letter to my mom, my dad, Luke, Derek, Aaron, my soccer coach, my chemistry teacher, the weatherman from Vermont Public Radio's *Eye on the Sky*. I couldn't remember all the letters I'd written since freshman year, but I spent the next couple of hours trying. I'd think of a single line I'd scrawled, and then I'd shuffle through the pages until I found it. I found nearly every memorable phrase I looked for. For the few I couldn't find, I couldn't remember if I'd actually written them down or just thought them. Eventually, I'd read so many pages that I could barely recall what I'd written over the past few weeks, let alone years.

I decided the best way to deal with it was to wait and see whether anyone said anything. There was no point in stirring things up before I even knew what had happened. Maybe I'd just misplaced the letter or overlooked it. Maybe it would turn up in a notebook or pocket. Stuff presumed stolen has a way of turning up and making you feel like a jackass.

I was under my bed with a flashlight doing another scan for the letter when the front doorbell rang. On my way to the stairs, I peeked out a window in the top hall and spotted Theresa's car in the driveway. "Oh, man," I sighed.

"The doorbell?" I said as I let her in. "That's a first."

"Well, why is it locked?" No hug or anything, which was weird. "What's with the flashlight? And why are you covered in dust?"

"I'm looking for something," I muttered, leading her into the kitchen. "What's up?"

"Are you super hungover?" she asked, wincing.

"I had, like, *two* beers last night. That's why you came over here? To give me a hard time about drinking?"

She sat down without taking off her jacket and didn't look up at me. "I came over to ask you about something, and I want you to be honest with me, James."

I folded my arms. If she was going to drop in unannounced and force the issue, I wasn't going to make it easy for her. "Is this talk going to take all day?"

"Do you want to sit down in case it does?"

"Not really."

She got to the point much more quickly than I'd expected. "What's going on with you and Topher?" she asked quietly.

I dodged the question. "Did you steal letters out of my desk last night?"

She just stared at me, not denying it. Her silence screamed guilt. I banged my flashlight on the counter. "Do you have them here?"

She looked at me as though I'd just thrown up on myself. "I don't know what you're talking about. And you haven't answered my question. What's going on between you and Topher?"

"He's a good guy, and I like hanging out with him. Is that a crime? Why is it your business?"

She stood up, her hands in fists. "You must be *joking* me." She seethed. I'm not sure I'd ever seen her so angry. "Why is this my business? You've been lying to me for years, leading me on and making me think we might get serious someday, and now you want to know why it's my business when I find out you're gay?"

"Whoa, whoa!" I yelled, hands up. "Slow down. Who told you that?"

"Oh, please. I'm not an idiot, James. But Kim confirmed it, anyway—by accident. I kept asking her what she thought was going on, and she kept saying 'talk to James, talk to James' until she slipped and said 'I promised I'd let him tell you.'"

That seemed like more than a slip to me, but all I could do was shake my head. I had no way out. "This isn't how I wanted this conversation to go," I muttered.

"Oh, because you wanted to lie to me some more? String me along for another year or two?" She wasn't backing down.

"I wasn't trying to lie," I said angrily.

"No, clearly lying comes very easily to you."

"Oh my God." I bent double, head in my hands, then stood back up. "Way to be melodramatic. Did you rehearse your lines before coming over here or what? Sometimes you are such a freaking—"

She cut me off by stepping forward, her hand raised as if she were going to slap me, but she caught herself and just shoved her finger in my face instead. "The only thing you should be saying to me right now is 'I'm sorry.' You should be *begging* me for forgiveness."

I put my hands in my pockets and glared at the floor. She was waiting for my apology, but she wasn't getting one. Not yet, anyway. After a long, painful silence, I shifted my feet and mumbled, "Let me be the one to talk to my friends."

"Oh, right," she gasped. "Because all of this is about you and your friends. You are *such* a selfish little boy."

She stalked out of the kitchen as I rolled my eyes to the ceiling. When I heard her opening the front door, I yelled, "Cuz threatening to hit people is so mature, right?"

The door slammed behind her.

That went well. I stood staring out the window for a while, but no easy solutions presented themselves. Groaning in frustration, I grabbed my running shoes.

Usually running helps me sort things out, gain some perspective on problems. Not this time. When I came in from my five-mile loop, my parents and Rex were back, but no one had left an apology message on my phone, my letter or letters were still stolen, and the culprit was still one of my best friends.

The next day, Sunday, my father and I worked in the yard. We cleaned the gutters, yanked dead plants from flower beds, and cut down a pine out back that had lost limbs during a heavy wet snow. I raked the entire backyard once and had started on round two when my dad came over, put his hand on my shoulder, and said, "That's probably good." So I went inside and buried myself in homework for the rest of the day.

At the dinner table, I barely spoke. Rex dominated the conversation, as he'll do when given the chance, by recounting six or seven *Calvin and Hobbes* comic strips. Evidently, my parents were caught up in their own heads, too, because no one tried to change the subject. I think Rex figured out that no one was listening, because when I looked up, he was quietly stabbing his cauliflower.

As I finished washing the dishes, my mom asked, "You okay?"

"Lot of homework."

"Is it Theresa?"

"We're just friends." I'd said it so often that it sounded robotic. Although I wasn't sure if she still *was* my friend anymore.

She nodded. "Is that the problem?"

"Not for me it isn't."

"But maybe for her it is?"

"It's not Theresa." A bad slip—now she knew something was up.

"Then what is it?"

"Chemistry," I lied. "I'm terrible at it."

"Well, if there's anything else going on—"

"Nope." I disappeared into my room for the rest of the night. I typed *coming out to parents* into Google and read a dozen articles that gave advice about how to start the conversation. I would have to talk to them soon.

Topher had also given me a few tips, and I included some of them in the letter I scribbled that night. To be honest, I thought twice about writing it—what if it disappeared, too?—but I had decided that no one was coming into my room ever again, and my pirate key was never going to leave my pocket.

Sunday, May 22nd
Dear Mom and Dad,
Next Sunday's the day I'm going to tell you I like boys. It's a long drive home from my soccer game in Grantham, and I'll ask Hawken to drive himself, so we'll be alone in the car. When we hit the highway, I'll take a deep breath and say the magic words. Unlike me, the road is straight there, so if I tell you on that stretch, you probably won't drive off into a ditch. I've read a couple of "coming out to parents" tips online and my friend Topher—my friend who is a boy who I've kissed and so I suppose is maybe my boyfriend—gave me some good advice, so I'm prepared to tell you that, no, this isn't just a phase, that I don't need to see a psychologist, that it's not your fault, that I wasn't molested as a kid, and that I'm aware of the HIV risks. (I'm debating whether to say, "I'm wearing a condom right now." Is that over the line? That's probably over the line.) I'm ready to answer your questions and to tell you where you can go to read respectable, authoritative, non-pornographic information

about all this stuff. I'm even going to pack some cookies in
case your blood pressure drops or skyrockets upon hearing my
news. If the conversation gets out of control, if there's yelling
and screaming, there are a bunch of exits between the one for
Grantham and the one for 91. You can drop me at any of them
and I'll call Topher to come get me. I'll pack my toothbrush and
a towel—thanks for the tip, Douglas Adams. At least I'll have
that much and my soccer gear if you disown me.

Your loving, not-straight son,
James

CHAPTER 17

It crossed my mind in the morning to play sick, to take a day at home to figure out how to deal with everything. I wouldn't have had to do anything desperate, like when I held a thermometer to a lightbulb in sixth grade. "James, you have a 112-degree fever," my mother had sighed. "We'll bury you out back." This time I could've honestly said I felt too ill and tired to concentrate—my eyes burned from lack of sleep, and I felt wired and exhausted all at the same time—but I wanted to act as if everything were normal. And if I got the chance, I wanted to beg Theresa again to keep her mouth shut.

I got a lift to school with my dad that morning to avoid having to drive in with Derek. A kid in a white parka with the hood pulled up walked into the building just ahead of me. Aaron's shrine greets students who enter through that door. It's the first thing you see. The boy in front of me stopped short and his bag fell from his hands.

"OMG," I heard him gasp. It wasn't clear whether he was impressed or horrified. He took his hood off just as I passed, but I'd already recognized the voice. Aaron Foster.

"Hey!" I slapped his arm. "You're back from the dead!"

"James, who did this?" he hissed. "This is so incredibly embarrassing. Where did they find that photo of me?" He pointed to one that showed him laughing with his eyes half closed and his mouth wide open. "Did they call my dentist or what?"

"Aaron!" a girl squealed from down the hall. Others picked up her shrill cry. I backed away as four girls hugged him and cooed and stroked his head.

"Um, are you responsible for this?" Aaron asked, twirling a finger at the photos and flowers, candles and quotes.

"We didn't want anyone to forget about you or what happened," one of them explained.

"That's so incredibly nice of you," Aaron gushed. "And I'm going to take it all down now because I'm back"—he knelt and began tearing photos off the poster board—"and it is time we all just move on." He handed them each a plastic daisy. "These are gorgeous. And who found this quote?" It was written in white ink on black paper:

I will not leave South Africa, nor will I surrender.
Only through hardship, sacrifice,
and militant action can freedom be won.
The struggle is my life. I will continue fighting for freedom
until the end of my days.
—Nelson Mandela

No one knew who'd found the quote or put it on the poster. "Well, it doesn't really matter," sighed Aaron. "I'm just overwhelmed. Thank you."

Aaron got a lot of attention during first period—we had English first thing and Breyer made a big deal of him—but by second period it was as if he'd never been gone. The same people who had ignored him before the incident ignored him once again, but that afternoon he stopped me in the hall.

"James, I'll bring back your sweater. My mom had it dry-cleaned." He hesitated. "Thank you for calling that day. My mom is really sorry for what she said on the phone. I yelled at her when she told me about it, and she's super embarrassed."

I waved it away, but I was glad his mom felt bad about it.

"She was just upset, you know?" Aaron shrugged.

"Totally. I get it." But his mother was not forgiven. "Thanks for taking care of my sweater. I've missed it. And I have your PEZ dispenser."

"It's a gift from me to you." Aaron laughed.

Hawken interrupted us. "Where were you at lunch, Liddell?"

"The library. I had a bunch to do." I acted as if that were normal. "I wasn't hungry," I added, which was true.

Hawken frowned and poked my chest. "You look terrible, man. You really didn't eat lunch?"

"I ate some coffee earlier."

"You ate coffee."

"Yeah," I mumbled, walking away. I didn't feel like talking. "I'll catch up with you later."

Later turned out to be right after school. I got a text from Hawken: *U home can i come over?* This was not like him. Hawken usually just showed up.

Yup! I replied. Sure enough, when he arrived, he looked worried. He tried to smile at me, but it was the kind of smile that accompanies bad news. "You here alone? Your parents home?"

"Just Rex. He's out back somewhere."

"Cool. Can we talk up in your room?"

I felt a hole opening in my gut and numbly led the way upstairs. Before he sat down next to me on my bed, Hawken pulled a folded envelope from his jeans' pocket. That bad news smile again. "This was waiting for me in the mail when I came home from school today." He handed me the envelope. His name and address were in type, not handwriting, and there was no return address.

I coughed nervously. "I didn't send this to you," I whispered.

"I know."

I slipped the letter out of the envelope's ragged end and unfolded it. Sure enough, what I saw confirmed my worst fears—more than one letter had been taken. There was my handwriting. Date: *December 22*. Greeting: *Hey, Hawken*. I skimmed it and went red. *No one makes me happier . . . I just like sitting next to you . . . Your eyes . . . Your smile . . .*

"I didn't write this," I said.

Hawken looked pained.

"I mean, no, obviously I *did* write this. But I didn't *send* this. I never would've sent this to you. I'm really, really sorry." I held my breath. I hated crying around Hawken. I'd done it before, and I hated it.

"Hey, Liddell, relax, okay? You already told me that you liked me, remember? None of this was news. And everything you wrote was super nice."

I nodded, my elbows on my knees, my fingers laced behind my head. Hawken put his arm around me. Back in December, we were going to watch some zombie movie up in his room, and we were trying to find a place to put his laptop so we could both see it. I persuaded him that we could both easily fit in this big comfy chair and the laptop could go on the table right by it. So he settled in next to me, cracking up a little, and fifteen minutes later he fell asleep with his head on my shoulder. I put my arm around him, and his head slid onto my chest. He slept curled against me for nearly the whole flick. Zombies tore off children's heads and ate their innards, and I smiled through it all. When Hawken woke and sat up, I thought he was about to kiss me. Instead, he just rubbed the side of his face, grinned, and groaned, "I fell asleep!" Like it was all totally normal. If it had been Derek—well, it never would've been Derek because he never would have agreed that there was plenty of room for two in that chair. And I never would've wanted to squeeze into it with him in the first place. I had written about all this in the letter Hawken had received, but mercifully, he didn't bring it up.

"I'm sorry you got this, Tim," I snuffled. "I'm really sorry."

"I take it this is why you look like you haven't slept in two days."

I nodded.

"What happened?" he whispered. "Who sent it?"

"Someone got into my desk drawer the other night. They used the pirate key and took all this stuff I wrote. I don't know who. Theresa or Derek or Mark? Topher was up here, too." I looked at the envelope and pointed to the postmark: Saturday, May 21. "They stole it on Friday night and mailed it out the next day."

"You sure that's what happened? Maybe this letter got mixed up in your other papers? Maybe you dropped it by accident or left it somewhere?"

"I don't think so."

"Well, you should just ask everyone. 'Did you take a bunch of letters from my desk?'"

"Why would they own up to doing it?"

"I don't know, maybe they were out of their mind for a little bit and now they're thinking clearly again."

I thought about that possibility. "No, that would make sense if they just *stole* the letters. But they made the decision to *mail* one of them. They want to ruin me."

"Or they legitimately wanted to set us up."

I pretended to laugh. "Who would think you'd be interested in that, dude?" He raised his eyebrows. "Other than me," I admitted. "No one. Anyway, this would be a really weird way to go about that, right? That's not what's going on." I got up and looked out the window. "Did I tell you Theresa confronted me about Topher?"

"Then why aren't we talking to her about all this right now? I thought we had to figure this all out in secret."

He had a good point. He texted her and found out she was home. On the way to her place, I filled him in about our fight the morning I discovered the letters were gone. "I already asked her about the letters, and she was like, 'I don't know what you're talking about.'"

"Maybe she wasn't ready to admit it," Hawken suggested. "Maybe she'll just come clean."

When we arrived, Theresa seemed totally normal with me. I hadn't seen her at school all day, but she wasn't shooting me glares or slamming the door in my face now. Unfortunately, her mom was home, and we had to spend twenty minutes talking to her in the kitchen about school and college plans and how our parents were doing. I thought I was going to go crazy, until finally Theresa announced that we were going upstairs to work on something for school. She could've said that fifteen minutes earlier.

When the door to her room closed, I got right into it. "Remember I mentioned to you that someone stole letters from me the other night, when you guys were over and we hung out around the fire?"

"You said something about that, yeah." Theresa nodded, sitting down on her bed.

"Well, Hawken got one in the mail today."

He pulled it from his pocket, held it up. She reached out for it, and I put my hand on Hawken's arm. "You don't need to read it. But I don't know, maybe you already have. That's what I want to know. Do you have my letters? Did you send this one to Hawken?"

Theresa shook her head.

"Yes or no?"

"No."

"You're positive?"

"James, I didn't even know you wrote letters." She sat up and leaned back. "And the only thing I want to steal from you is your hoodie. One day I will succeed."

Hawken pretended to laugh.

"Why haven't you mailed those letters yourself, anyway?" she asked.

"Because I didn't write them to be read by anyone," I

mumbled. I looked around her room. Would it be wrong to dump out all her drawers? I rubbed my eyes. I was losing my mind. "OK. I need to go home. Hawken, can we go?"

On the way back to my place, Hawken suggested we talk to Derek. "I'm too angry right now," I said. "Or I don't even know what. Just worked up. I feel like I drank two pots of coffee and I'm crawling out of my skin."

He thumped my thigh with his fist when he dropped me off. "Hang in there, Liddell. When you want to talk to Derek, let me know."

That night, as I lay in the dark listening to branches claw the side of our house, I tried to figure out who was more likely to have committed the crime: Derek or Mark. I couldn't see Mark going through the trouble of looking up addresses, printing out envelopes, and buying stamps. But then again, I couldn't see Derek deciding to torture me just because I'm gay.

That phrase thudded in my gut. *I'm gay. Gay kids get killed.*

Years ago, Derek had said that gay people were "an abomination." I remembered it clearly because I'd asked my mom what *abomination* meant. Around the same time, he told me that gay people were "an American disease." I related this fact to my parents, and I remember them looking at each other sideways. "That's not true," my mom said gently. "Derek's parents are very nice, very smart people, but not everything they believe is true." Derek didn't believe everything his parents believed anymore—I knew that—but he still believed a lot of it. I didn't know if he still believed in a hell that would punish *me*.

The next day in English, we did a "quick-write," where you can write about whatever you want for ten minutes and then Breyer asks for volunteers to read aloud what they wrote. This boy who never volunteers put his hand up and, with the brim of his Carhartt hat pulled down over his face, he told us about his older brother and how they go hunting together and he can tell him anything and how even when he thinks his brother will be disappointed in him he's not ever—he's the best brother a guy could hope for and sometimes he lets him ride his snowmobile but not all that often now that he thinks about it, the end.

That piece got me thinking about Luke the rest of the afternoon. Maybe I'd underestimated him. If I told him about everything that was going on, he might back me up when I told our parents and make sure they didn't flip out. When I got home, I took a deep breath, made myself walk up to his room, and dialed his number. He answered right away.

"Oh, perfect. I'm hanging out with your secret admirer." I could hear a girl laughing and yelling at him to shut up. "Claire saw a photograph of you and declared it was love at first sight. You two have to talk. She's a little unhinged but otherwise a good person."

Was she hitting him with a pillow? He yelped, and the

phone thumped onto the floor. Sighing, I put my hand over my eyes, cleared my throat.

He picked the phone back up. "You still there?" He giggled.

"Yeah. I was just calling to say hi. But you're busy."

"Hi. I am a little busy, yes."

"Okay. When are you coming home?"

"Like the second weekend of June. I got this internship up here."

"Right, right. I'll talk to you soon."

"God bless you, James Liddell. God bless you and this country we love."

"Right, God bless you, too," I repeated flatly. "Thanks." And I hung up.

Kim and I chatted online that night while I was trying to study. I would've ignored her first message, but it sort of demanded attention.

Kim: Hey, I drove past you in the Food Safari parking lot the other day. I'm telling Topher that you were with another boy.
Me: What?? That was my brother. And he's ten.
Kim: Yeah, but he's a hot ten.
Me: You're going to prison.
Kim: Hey, I held Theresa off as long as I could. Sorry it turned out the way it did.

Me: Not your fault. But thanks. Different topic, please . . .

Kim: Umm, how are things with Topher?

Me: Good. I like him a lot. I don't know why, but I do.

Kim: Maybe because he's cool and honest and super cute?

Me: All true. Also, it's like he's untouchable. He has this crazy confidence. He's totally out, and no one gives him a hard time.

Kim: He used to get picked on. He got the crap kicked out of him in ninth grade.

"What?" I whispered.

Me: He's never said anything about that.

Kim: Have you noticed his chipped front tooth?

Me: I figured he fell off his bike or something.

Kim: Some kid banged his head into the water fountain while he was drinking. And he stopped playing hockey. He's a beautiful skater, but he stopped playing after he fell on the ice during a practice and a kid kicked him a bunch of times, cracked his ribs.

I stared at the blinking cursor.

Me: I talk about watching hockey all the time. He's never said a word about playing.

Kim: He doesn't like talking about it. He really loved it.

Me: Then how does he pull off the 'no one can touch me' attitude now? Why does everything seem so easy for him?

Kim: He got into acting, for one thing. I think that gave him confidence and a supportive group. But also, I remember him telling me that he just decided he had to make a choice. He could either be who everyone wanted him to be—and be miserable—or he could just ignore people who hated him, be himself, and be happy.

I drummed a pencil on my desk.

Kim: There is a moral in that story.

Me: Yeah, yeah. Talk to you soon.

Kim: XXOO.

CHAPTER 18

I had checked out completely by second period on Friday. Glancing up from my desk in Breyer's class, I found everyone staring at me. "Can you repeat the question?" I asked, sitting back up straight. A few kids laughed.

"There wasn't any question," Breyer said softly, smiling a little. "I said you looked tired. Do you want to get a drink of water, go for a little walk?"

"Yeah, I do, thanks." I started to get up. Then I remembered that Mark had history class two doors down. What if I ran into him alone in the hall? "Wait, no," I said, sitting back down. "I don't. I'm good."

Breyer raised his eyebrow but went on with the lesson. At

the end of class, I waited until another student had Breyer's attention, then shot past him, out the door before he could corner me. Hawken grabbed me by the arm in the hall. "Dude, you're wearing your shirt back to front. You are a mess."

Topher texted me later on. *Hey, 18 & under show tonite. Come with me?*

Concerts weren't really my thing and I was worried I might fall asleep on my feet, but I couldn't face staring at the wall worrying about everything for another night, and being around Topher would make feel better. Without even asking what kind of music it was, I texted: *Great. What time?*

He texted back a minute later. *It's Neil Diamond, okay?*

I thought I recognized the name, but I wasn't sure. *OK, cool,* I replied.

Ten seconds later: *I like you when you're clueless.*

Topher picked me up in his old Subaru and waited until we were on the highway before leaning over to kiss me on the ear. He sort of missed my cheek because he didn't want to take his eyes off the road.

"You have to be anywhere tomorrow morning?" he asked.

"Nope, I don't think so."

"Good. My parents are gone. Stay at my place tonight."

"Cool, sure," I said nonchalantly, but I felt myself go tense. Did I care what Derek would say about me? Or Luke?

I imagined my father finding out. My mom.

Topher put his hand on my thigh. "Hey, how would you feel about me filming you?"

"What?!"

"I'm joking, joking," he said. "But in all seriousness," and he glanced at me with a look of concern. "What size hand-cuffs do you wear?"

"Stop it!" I laughed.

My phone rang in my pocket, and when I fished it out, Derek's name flashed on the screen.

"Derek!" chirped Topher. "You want to invite him along?"

Frowning, I turned the phone off.

Topher was quiet for a few seconds, then said, "You could've answered that. I don't mind."

"It's all right. I don't feel like talking to him right now."

The show turned out to be in a little student theater at Dart-mouth College, not too far from where I live. As we crossed the campus green, I kept glancing over at Topher, his easy smile, the curves in his arms. He's not at all a big guy, but he's the kind of kid who makes pull-ups look easy. Part of me wished that everyone we passed knew that I was with him, that he was mine. I looked up at the sky, grinning at the thought, and nearly walked right into this guy and girl hold-ing hands. Topher and I kept ours in our pockets.

The theater's walls were painted black and all the pipes

and air ducts on the ceiling were exposed. Topher and I stood at the back for a while. I didn't recognize anyone—no one from my school was there—but Topher nodded at a few scruffy kids and they wandered over to say hi. Near us, a bearded guy had sleeves of tattoos and wore a fluorescent orange woolen hat. A lot of people up here use those bright orange hats when they're out in the woods during hunting season. But we were not outside, and it was not deer season. The first time I saw a city guy wearing a hat like that was when Derek's cousin visited from Los Angeles. He also wore a John Deere shirt, which Mark complimented. The kid seemed confused, which confused Mark, and the subject was dropped. I didn't know if the clown next to us was a Dartmouth student or what, but it felt like he was making fun of us locals somehow. I sort of hated him.

The band climbed on stage at nine fifteen, even though there were only a couple dozen people milling around. The guy in the orange hat turned out to be the bassist. The lead singer was a skinny guy with a mop of brown hair, a big smile, and a hint of a lisp that a girl Topher knew declared "so adorable." A lot of his songs were about breakups or death, but most of them ended on happy notes. Everyone else seemed a lot more lost in the music than I was, their heads nodding, shoulders moving. Some people were even singing along.

When the singer panted "We have one more for you!", I cheered loudly. Then they played four more.

After we got to leave, we huddled in the parking lot with

Topher's friends. "Where to next?" was the big question.

"Why don't we head back to Topher's place?" someone suggested. "Aren't your folks gone for the weekend?

Topher sighed. "Let's keep it very small."

About ten kids showed up, but it didn't get out of hand. Everyone just stood around talking, very mellow, and Topher made sure the drivers were drinking Cokes or water.

A guy wearing a striped scarf had appointed himself DJ for the night. Every once in a while, Topher would walk past the stereo and turn the volume down, and the kid in the scarf would turn it back up. I didn't recognize a single song he played. Some of it had acoustic guitar and harmonica. I'd been avoiding him, but as I walked by him and two other guys to get a beer from the fridge, he insisted on introducing himself.

"I'm Michael, and you're Topher's . . ."—he paused dramatically—"new friend?"

"Yup. Who are we listening to? Bob Dylan?"

"Earlier it was Dylan. This is Lou Reed."

"Who the hell is this Lou Reed character?" a kid named Ronan asked. He had both ears pierced with little black squares. His pal, Glenn, had startling green eyes. "Whoever he is, he needs to cheer up."

"You don't know who Lou Reed is?" Michael asked, flipping his scarf over his shoulder. "He was, like, an American poet slash rock star. He played in The Velvet Underground.

He was friends with Andy Warhol."

"Oh, he was friends with Andy Warhol." Ronan laughed, fiddling with one of his earrings. "Well, in that case . . ."

Michael rolled his eyes. "Andy Warhol. Pop art? Campbell's Soup paintings?"

The other boys laughed harder. I edged my way past them and opened the fridge.

"James, you'd like Lou Reed," Michael insisted. "He was bisexual."

Their laughter turned to coughs. They were all staring at me when I turned around. I told myself to relax.

"Oh, yeah?" I said. "He doesn't sound bisexual."

Michael just shook his head, but Ronan and Glenn smiled.

"They did electroshock therapy on him when he was a teenager," Michael said.

"Electro-*what*?" said Glenn. "They electrocuted people?"

"Kind of. They zapped their brains to alter their personalities. That's how they tried to make gay people straight back then."

They all looked at me for a response.

I shrugged. "So, he was bisexual? It worked halfway?"

The boys cracked up, and Michael sipped from a big bottle of sparkling water. "We are very lucky is all I'm saying. No electroshock therapy for our generation."

"Just Ritalin," Glenn said happily.

"Ritalin makes you not gay?" asked Ronan.

"I guess so. It's been working for me, anyway. Maybe

that's just if you snort it."

Topher came into the kitchen just then. "Hey, no snorting anything. No snorting anything in my house."

"Nobody's snorting nothing," Ronan said, hands up. "But it might help pick things up more than this Lou Reed's doing. Come on, put on something that makes everyone want to wear their pants on their heads."

An upbeat hip-hop song kicked in.

"This does make you want to dance," said Glenn. "Or at least jump up and down. Get it started, Topher! Ditch those jeans and hop up on that table!"

"My house is not your jungle gym!" Topher hollered, and then he pointed at Michael. "No more we-are-all-going-to-die-slowly songs," he warned. "And keep it down." He took me by the hand and led me out of the kitchen. Ronan and Glenn clinked my bottle and nodded as we passed.

"You ever date one of those guys?" I whispered to Topher.

"Who? Ronan? Glenn?"

"I don't know. Either one."

"No, they're straight. They're both straight. That's Glenn's girlfriend over there. Wait, are you jealous?" He punched my arm. "Very cute."

By one thirty, Michael was the only one left other than Topher and me. Topher must have walked through the place six times before he announced that there wasn't any major damage. Someone had dribbled beer on the living room carpet, but he'd get carpet cleaner in the morning.

"After you use it, get rid of the container," Michael advised. "Sure way to get busted is to put new cleaning products under the kitchen sink." He yawned. "I don't know why I'm so tired!"

"Because it's one thirty in the morning," Topher said, pouring a glass of water. He handed me the glass, clapped Michael on the back, and walked him to the door. I padded upstairs to find Topher's bedroom.

His room smelled like the cologne he wore. Two big windows looked out over the backyard. Burgundy walls. Wood floor. Tidy desk. Curious George and an orangutan slouched next to trophies and family photos on top of the bookcase. A framed poster of muddy cyclists passing a cigarette between them dominated one wall. His neatly made bed was the same size as mine, just for one person. I picked up one of his hockey trophies to read the date. He won it when he was thirteen.

"Hey." Topher stood in the doorway, grinning. "There's a boy in my room. Weird. Did you find the bathroom okay?"

"Yeah, thanks, I'm good." I'd brushed my teeth with toothpaste on my finger and gargled blue mouthwash earlier, figuring this point in the night was near.

"Back in a minute. Don't steal nothing."

Topher's closet door was open, and a sleeping bag was rolled up on the top shelf. I looked at the bed, looked back at the sleeping bag, and pulled off my socks and my shirt. Curious George and I made eye contact. I picked him up and turned him around so that he faced the wall. Then I did the same to his orangutan friend.

When I crawled under the covers, I could hear Topher brushing his teeth. He spat. The faucet went on. The faucet went off. Part of a radio ad for a local mechanic was whistled. The bathroom door opened. Footsteps down the hall.

He stopped in the doorway. "You okay in there?" he whispered.

"Yup, I'm good."

He walked to his closet, and, standing on one leg to pull off a sock, observed, "That bed is not made for two."

"I know. Get out of here."

He laughed, tossed his socks into his closet, pulled off his shirt, and dropped it on the floor. For a moment, he stood still, as if unsure about what to do next.

"How can you be that fit," I whispered, "when you don't even play any sports?"

"My mom and I do Jazzercise."

"No. Not true."

"But you would still like me if it *were* true, right?"

"Not really, nope."

He sat on the bed and his belt buckle jingled as he unclasped it. I put my hand on his back, feeling his warmth. For a little while, like me, he was holding his breath. He wriggled out of his pants as he leaned in to kiss me, resting his hand over my heart, as if trying to slow it down. I skimmed my hand up to his shoulder as he curled his leg across my waist. I resisted the urge to peek at the door to make sure it was closed.

He broke the kiss and laughed. "Why are you still wearing jeans, dude?"

"I don't know. I didn't want to make any, you know, bad assumptions."

He cracked up again.

I began to unbuckle my belt.

"No, it's cool," he said, slipping his hand over my stomach and wrapping his fingers over my own. "I got 'em."

But first he reached over to the bedside table and switched off the light.

When I woke up, Topher was sleeping with his head on my chest, an arm and leg wrapped around me. The clock said 7:42. I wondered where my parents thought I was right then. I'd called home the night before to tell them I was crashing at Derek's, but it had probably crossed their minds that I might be lying, that I might be in a bed or on a couch somewhere with Theresa. I thought of all the people I knew, all the awkward conversations ahead, all the stuff that would be said about me behind my back. I closed my eyes again, and we slept until ten, when a huge truck snored and rattled past the house.

Topher insisted on bringing me coffee in bed, and we stayed there until noon.

★ ★ ★

My dad was fixing the lawnmower on the driveway when Topher dropped me off. "Is he going to be weirded out when I climb into your lap to kiss you good-bye?" Topher asked.

"Keep that seat belt buckled," I answered sternly.

We made a show of shaking hands. Topher waved at my dad. My dad waved back.

"Who was that?" he called to me as Topher's car reversed onto the road. "I don't recognize him."

"Kim's pal. He stayed over at Derek's last night, too. Dropped me off on his way past." That seemed to satisfy him. He went back to fixing the lawnmower, totally oblivious to who Topher was, to who I was, to the fact that I'd woken with a boy in my arms that morning. The guilt that seeped through me was physical, a heaviness in my legs and arms. I was wading through cold water. I wondered if I looked pale when I said hello to my mom in the kitchen.

CHAPTER 19

My parents couldn't drive to my game that Sunday, which sunk my plans for coming out to them on the ride home. I told myself that I really would've done it, but the plan was destroyed, and now I would just have to wait for a better opportunity.

We beat Miracle Tire, 9–6, and Hawken scored a hat trick. Coach yelled at me for falling out of position a lot, but the guy playing right wing was dogging it. He would not get into the corners fast enough, so I'd get in there first and shout for Hawken to cover the center. That's why he got a hat trick, to be honest, because I kept winning the ball and feeding him crosses.

The only problem with playing someone else's position well is that, eventually, you get reassigned to it. I try to avoid playing goalie for that reason. I'm actually terrible at goalie—I don't like getting the ball kicked at my face—but my fear is that I'll have a strangely brilliant day in net during practice and find myself wearing gloves and long sleeves at the next game. I've seen our goalie dive headfirst into the post. It's just not for me.

As I was setting up Hawken's third goal, someone began slapping the glass and hollering at me. I glanced up to see the goalie I'd pushed down a few weeks earlier. He was standing with a pack of guys from his team, watching us play. Their game must've been right after ours. Turning away, I just ignored them. I'd get my chance to destroy them soon enough.

I spent all Monday, Memorial Day, working on my history paper. After school on Tuesday, Theresa arrived at my house just as I was about to go for a run. She caught me doing hurdlers' stretches on the front lawn, gritting my teeth through counts of twenty.

"Those are bad for you," she called as she got out of the car.

"Everything's bad for you," I called back. "I read that kale is bad for you."

She dropped onto the grass next to me. "We have to talk," she said. "Is here okay?" No one else was home.

"Sure," I said hesitantly. "Here's okay."

She gave me a pitying smile, reached into her jacket pocket, and pulled out a folded-up piece of notebook paper. A letter. Somewhere, deep inside my head, I could hear someone or something cry out, long and high and desperate, like a dying dog. This was misery. This wasn't how my life was meant to go. But I stayed quiet, kept my face straight.

"It came in the mail today," she said. "It's actually really sweet in some ways. So, thank you, I guess."

"Can I see it?"

She handed it to me.

"And the envelope?"

She looked confused. "I don't have the envelope. I threw it out."

"Was it handwritten? I want to see the handwriting. And the postmark."

She shook her head. "It was typed," she almost whispered. "And I didn't look at the postmark."

"Hawken's was typed, too." I unfolded the letter and skimmed my sentences. The words looked different in the light of the day. They sounded so stupid. *I'd miss the way you fix my collar even when it doesn't need to be fixed. . . .* Oh, man. *That perfume you wear. The way people brighten when they see us together.*

I crumpled the paper into a tight ball.

"James!"

And then I unfolded it enough to rip it into pieces.

"That's mine!" Instantly, she was crying.

"No, it's not yours!" I snapped. "It's mine. You got it in the mail, but that doesn't make it yours. Someone steals my stuff and mails it to you, doesn't make it yours."

"You wrote it to me!" she sobbed.

"But I didn't send it! You were never supposed to read it!"

She was crying really hard, her hands over her face. The earrings I'd given her for her birthday the year before dangled from her ears. Kim had picked them out. Theresa said she'd wear them on special occasions. I wasn't sure this qualified. I ran my hand through my hair and sighed. If I let her go away this upset, who knew who she'd talk to, what she'd say. "Theresa," I said softly. "Hey, I'm sorry. This is just really hard. I'm in a terrible spot."

She snorted. "Oh, yeah. *You're* in a terrible spot. It's all about *you*. As usual."

What I wanted to say at that point was that if she honestly believed that her bad spot was anywhere near as bad as mine, just because she liked someone who didn't like her back, she was out of her mind. But I had to calm her down. I had to calm us both down. "OK, right. We're *both* in a terrible spot. I'm really sorry. I've been trying to figure everything out."

"You *had* figured it all out," she choked. "You wrote it all down."

"That was then. For that little while that night. You wake up the next morning and all the confusion's back again. It's not like you figure this kind of thing out, and it stays figured out. It's not like a math problem."

"You wrote it *down*."

"Yeah, but the problem doesn't stay solved. Even when you write it down."

She didn't say anything.

"Why would he do this?" I asked.

"Who?" she snuffled.

"Derek. Why would he mail my letters?"

"Why are you blaming Derek? What makes you so certain it's him?"

"It's either him or Mark. They were the only ones up in my room that night other than Topher. And this isn't the kind of thing Mark would do. He'd photocopy them and post them around school or hand them out at lunch. This is too, I don't know, *patient* to be his work. It's too cruel."

"You really have a lot of respect for your friends, huh?" She got up and walked back to her car.

"When they do this kind of thing?" I called after her.

She was getting good at slamming doors, and somehow she even managed to start the car so that it sounded angry.

Five minutes after Theresa left, my phone rang. I was still sitting on the lawn, staring at the sky, and I didn't recognize the number. Normally I don't get calls from numbers I don't know, so I answered prepared to say, *You dialed the wrong number, dude.*

"Hi, it's Aaron."

It took me a few seconds to connect the Aaron at my school with the idea that he'd call me.

"Hey," I said hesitantly. "What's, uh, what's going on?"

"James, oh my God—I don't even know where to start. Just, well, thank you so much!"

I stood up.

"Hello? Are you still there?"

"Yup," I said. If I walked too far, I risked losing reception, so I paced in a circle. "Um, you're welcome." I hoped that hadn't sounded like a question.

"Everything you wrote was just so nice. So honest. It's really the nicest letter I've ever received. I mean, of the three I have ever gotten, it's the nicest." He cracked up. "And I never would've guessed it about you."

I sat back down. This was way out of hand. Who else had gotten a letter? Who else was reading stuff right now they were never meant to read? "Listen, please don't—" I started, and then I caught myself. "I mean, I'm glad it was okay you got that letter—"

"It was more than okay! And listen, I'm so sorry I didn't thank you earlier but I literally just got it. We don't get our mail delivered way out here, you know? My mom only goes to the post office to pick it up, like, once a week because usually it's just catalogs and junk mail and stuff, you know? But I saw you mailed it last Saturday."

Last Saturday. The same day Hawken's letter was sent out.

The day I discovered the letters were missing.

"So, I'm really sorry I didn't say anything earlier," Aaron continued. "You must've been wondering."

"No, it's cool," I said, stalling while I thought about what this all meant. "I'm, um, just glad you got it. That's great. But listen, I can't remember if I wrote this, but I'd really like to keep all of this on the down low, you know? Like, don't tell anyone. Not anyone. Not a single person."

There was silence on the other end.

"The thing is," I went on, "I'm dealing with a lot of other stuff right now, all of a sudden, sort of unexpectedly, and I'd rather handle one thing at a time. If you don't mind just keeping everything I wrote between the two of us, I'd really—"

"Oh, okay. Of course. I won't say anything to anyone, James. None of your story is mine to tell anyway."

"Thanks." I sighed. I almost felt like smiling. "Thank you. I hope I didn't write anything that made you feel bad. Or angry."

"No! Not at all. It was very sweet. You're so sweet. The part about you feeling threatened by me made so much sense. I get it."

I remembered this letter. I'd written it late at night, from deep in my head.

"How long have you *known*?" he asked.

"A while," I mumbled.

"Listen, I thought maybe we could—if you're not too busy in the next few days and have the time and all—maybe hang out? For a little while? Tonight, even? There's a lot I want to ask you about, talk to you about."

"Yeah, sure. Sure. Soon, okay? Tonight I have a bunch of things going on." He interrupted with a string of apologies, and my mom's car pulled up the driveway. "It's okay, but listen, real quick: Would you mind if I swing by and take another look at that letter? I just want to . . . I forget how I worded something, and I want to say the same kind of thing to someone else . . ."

"Of course! The thing is, though, I have to go out in five minutes."

"Can you just leave it for me? Like, do you have a door-mat or something you can tuck it under?"

"Yeah, I guess I can put it under the mat. If you think it'll be safe there."

"I'll be right over."

I found my mom in the kitchen. "Can I borrow the car?"

"Hi, how was your day?"

"Hi, how was your day can I borrow the car? I have to grab a book for school from Derek. I totally forgot about this project, and Derek just texted to remind me."

I passed Aaron driving in the opposite direction. He honked and waved. My letter was waiting for me under the mat. His name and address were in anonymous type on the envelope, just like Hawken's, but scrawled across the back was *Thank you! XXOO.* In purple gel pen.

When I arrived home, my mom met me at the garage

door in her coat. "I have an evening meeting, your father's working late, and Rex is at a friend's house. I'll see you around nine!" And she was gone. I read the letter up in my room, just as it was getting dark.

April 18th

Dear Aaron,

I'm sorry I invited you to that party. Being a nice guy has all sorts of unintended consequences. Ha ha. But for real, I really am sorry for everything. I wish life at school were easier for you, man. If people knew me better, I'd probably have a much tougher time, too. I know I used to be one of the guys who made things hard for you, and I don't have any good excuses for myself. I think I've been scared of you. It sounds stupid, I know, but it's true. I guess I knew you were gay and, somewhere, at some level, I knew I wasn't straight either, even a couple of years ago, back when we were freshmen. But I didn't want to deal with it, and just being around you made me have to think about it. So, that's why I was such a jerk. You had already figured yourself out, and being around you sort of reminded me that I hadn't yet, and I didn't even really want to. You were this reminder that I was hiding. You made it harder to avoid it all.

No one knows you're actually the toughest kid at school. Maybe some time I'll be able to say all this in person.

Later,

James

Why was I so stupid? Why hadn't I burned each letter after writing it instead of accumulating a nightmare in my desk drawer? Why hadn't I seen any of this coming? I fell asleep clutching Aaron's letter.

My phone buzzed me awake. A text. I reached for it, imagining the possibilities:

Derek: *Thanks for your letter. Keep in touch.*

Mark: *Got ur lettr. U r ded met.*

Luke: *Thanks for your letter. . . ha ha?*

Topher: *We're done.*

I pulled my hand away from the phone as it buzzed again. Burying my head under my pillow, I ignored it. Again. Three times. Six. Eight. I stopped counting. All these people opening letters I'd never sent, texting me to say, *Wow, what a surprise*, and not bothering to mention that things would never be the same between us again.

I slept until what felt like the middle of the night. With one hand I felt around my bed for my phone, found it, and squinted at the clock. It was only 9:15 p.m. And I had sixteen messages. Reluctantly, I clicked open the first one, saw the words and all the exclamation points and bolted off my bed, raced down the stairs out onto the back porch, and looked up into the sky.

Just stars. I pulled my hands into the sleeves of my wool sweater.

"Are they out again?" my mom asked, stepping out onto the porch.

"I slept through them," I said. "I missed them all."

"Oh, James. I'm sorry. It really was spectacular."

I didn't answer. Spring peepers, those tiny frogs, were going bonkers in the woods.

"There's some dinner for you," my mom said softly.

"Thanks." I didn't take my eyes off the sky.

Sixteen messages and I'd ignored them all. Sixteen attempts to get me to wake up and run outside and I had my head under a pillow. The next day, the *Valley News* called it a once in a lifetime display of the northern lights. Once in a lifetime.

First thing the next morning, I got a text from Aaron. *Hi James! Would you bring my letter back today? Thank you!* Going into my room, I put the letter in my top desk drawer and then locked it tight with the pirate key. I'd give him the letter back . . . eventually. Not yet.

A couple of hours later, Aaron caught me in the hall and hugged me. "Thank you!" he said.

I patted his back, whispering, "Sure, sure," and disentangled myself from him.

"I have something for you," he said, reaching into his bag. Out came my green sweater.

"Hey, no kidding! Thanks! That's great." I might've hugged it like a stuffed animal. I hope not, but I might've.

"I was so happy to get that letter, James." He really looked like he might cry.

"Don't worry about it, man. Listen, I'm late for class."

"No, we still have a few minutes."

Dumb excuse. He's in most of my classes. "Right, but I have to go to my locker first."

"First can you give me my letter back?"

"Oh, right!" I slid my backpack off and went through it. "Man," I said, flipping through papers and peering between books. "Where did I put that?" I unzipped the front pocket. Nothing. What a surprise.

"I hope you didn't lose it." Aaron laughed nervously.

"No," I said. "I bet I just forgot it. I swear I remember putting it in here, though. Weird."

"OK." He shrugged. "Tomorrow, I guess."

"Right. Tomorrow." I put my hand on his shoulder. "Hey, thanks again for staying quiet."

He smiled and pretended to zip his mouth shut. "Let me know when you have time to hang out."

Now whenever I left class to go to the boys' room, I worried that I would end up on the blue tiled floor in a puddle of piss and blood. I didn't know who knew what, so I was being pretty careful about where I went alone. Most guys I could handle—my dad had taught me how to throw a punch at least—but if I met two guys at once, or three, or the whole baseball team, I'd be in big trouble.

So I had my fists clenched in the pockets of my hoodie, and I was trying to figure out whether I'd be charged with murder or manslaughter if I banged someone's head hard on the sink as I walked into the bathroom. It was empty, except for one person. Mark stood at a urinal with his back to me.

It's sort of amazing how much can go through your head in a couple of seconds, how many scenarios your brain can process in a heartbeat without even trying. I imagined myself shutting the door and hurrying back down the hall. I pictured walking up to the urinal and unzipping my fly next to him— leaving the requisite empty spot between us—and standing there calmly, willing myself to pee, then feeling his fist, like the head of a ram, slam into my kidney. I envisioned walking up casually behind him and making a preemptive strike, hitting him as hard as I could in the small of his back and then breaking his ribs with rapid-fire kicks.

But before I could set any of those plans in motion, Mark glanced over his shoulder and flicked his head in what passes as a hello among the gorilla set. I tried to play it cool, but I couldn't even muster a *hi* as I walked to the urinal farthest from him. I heard him zip, flush, and shuffle to the sink, clear his throat, and spit. I still hadn't managed to start peeing when he spoke over the sound of the faucet and his impressively thorough handwashing. "You running today?"

I jumped a little at the sound of his voice, but relaxed when I realized he wouldn't ask me about running right before he decked me. "Yeah, I'm running the river road."

Mark grunted and hit the hand dryer as though he wanted to bust it. "I guess that race is in a few weeks, huh? You registered?"

"Yup. You?"

"Hawken made me do it, the jerk. It was, like, twenty-five bucks! He even drove me to the post office to mail in the form, since he knew I didn't even know where it was."

He left without saying good-bye.

What a clutzy moron, I thought. Only Mark would incriminate himself by insisting, for no reason at all, that he had never been to the post office. I had to hand it to him—sending out my letters was an imaginative way to torture me. Now I just had to get back whatever ones he still had.

CHAPTER 20

I wish I could say that the stupidest things I've done in my life were all impulsive, but, unfortunately, a few of them were carefully planned. I asked Hawken, casually, which nights Mark worked up at the restaurant. I knew from stories Mark told that his dad usually worked late.

My mom agreed to lend me the car to go up to the library that evening. Digging around in a box of camping gear, I found a headlamp and checked to make sure the batteries worked. I left as the sun threatened to set.

I slowed as I drove past Mark's house, a small ranch with a satellite dish on the roof that's so big it looks like it might tip the house over. I'd been inside a few times and knew the layout.

All the windows were dark and no cars sat in the driveway or out front. The nearest neighboring house was dark, too. Luckily, Mark lives on a dirt road that isn't frequently traveled by anyone who would recognize my parents' car, so I parked down a ways without worrying about it. After reaching the border of Mark's yard, I crept along the woods' edge and peeked at the house from behind a big maple. His dad shouldn't be home, and despite Mark's dog-walking business, he didn't have a dog of his own.

Still, I waited five minutes.

Quiet and dark.

The ground was soft and wet as I ran at a crouch the thirty yards from the woods to Mark's back door. I was counting on a stubborn Vermont habit of leaving your doors unlocked. With my hand on the doorknob, I listened for canine panting, counted to ten, and turned the knob. Unlocked.

Another deep breath, and I pushed open the door. A cat bolted out of the house, straight across the yard, and into the woods. I imagined a coyote snatching it up just inside the trees. First casualty.

I stepped inside quickly, closed the door behind me, and removed my wet sneakers. The whole place smelled like cat litter. There hadn't been any cats last time I'd been there, years earlier. I crept down the hall toward Mark's bedroom and froze after five feet. Still no sounds. Another five feet and I stopped. In three more steps I'd be between the open bedroom doors: Mark's on the right, his dad's on the left. I crept the remaining few feet and peered into Mark's father's room.

In the dim light, I could see the bed was unmade and empty. I flicked on the headlamp, casting a beam of blue light around the room. A white cat rose from the blankets, stretched, and jumped off the bed with a thump.

"Hey," I whispered as it curled around my legs, purring. Another cat, black and white, arrived, and they both followed me into Mark's room. Papers littered his desk: Notes from history and English class, an A– math test. Impressive. But no letters. None in the desk drawers. I stuck my head under the bed. Nothing but dust bunnies. I lifted up his mattress. Nothing. I opened every drawer in the room. No letters. I spent the next ten minutes rifling through all the stuff in his closet, his bookcase, even, in desperation, his hamper. Discouraged, I slumped on his bed. His running shoes caught my eye. Maybe if I stole them he'd have to forfeit the Mud 10K. I hated myself for agreeing to run that race.

Suddenly, the whole room glowed as a car turned into the driveway. The hair on my arms stood on end. Did I have time to race down the hall? What if whoever it was entered through the back door, though? I'd run right into him. A car door slammed. I lay flat and scooted under the bed. *Please don't be Mark,* I thought over and over. He'd hear my heartbeat beneath the bed for sure.

Then my pulse skipped. My sneakers. I'd left them next to the door. I heard someone enter the house.

The cats trotted away to greet my murderer.

A cough from the kitchen. The *trk-phhffft* of a can of beer opening? Footsteps down the hall. I held my breath. Something dropped to the floor of the bedroom across the hall. It was his father. Thank God. Should I escape out the bedroom window, abandon my shoes? Movement back down the hallway. TV on. Noises from the kitchen. A long beep from a microwave. Would I go to jail if Mark's dad caught me? What if he had a gun? My God, of course he had a gun. Many guns and crossbows. I tried to steady my breathing. If Mark came home, could I just crawl out and pretend everything was totally normal? At what point would my parents start wondering where I was and call the police? I closed my eyes. *Stay calm.*

Twenty minutes must have passed before the phone rang. Mark's dad's voice was soft. Talking to his girlfriend or sister, maybe? He asked about a kid, mumbled about work. Lots of *uh-huh*s and *mmm*s. I could hear the scrape of a fork or spoon on a plate. "You know"—he cleared his throat—"I can't find one of the cats. He always comes running into the kitchen when I get home. . . . He's probably dead under a bed. . . . Right. . . . I mean, I wouldn't mind if he's dead. That cat's Mark's favorite, but it was his mother's favorite, too. . . . No, Mark still tries though. Emails, phone calls, but he never hears back from her."

I'd never asked Mark about his mom.

"Good to talk to you, too. Will do. G'night." A dish dropped in the sink and he came back down the hall. If he decided to check under Mark's bed for the cat, should I just play dead? Should I make a run for it right now? Dash through the house and out the back door? Maybe throw a lamp to knock the uzi out of his hands? He turned into his bedroom and clicked the TV on, and then came the sound of the shower. Was it the shower? Definitely the shower.

I scooted out from under the bed and squinted in the light from the hall. After two deep breaths, I crept out of Mark's room. The cats dropped from the kitchen counters as I passed, so I kicked them back as I edged out the door, closing it with a gentle click behind me. The runaway cat appeared, meowing at my feet. Letting out a pent-up breath, I opened the door a few inches so it could slip back inside.

When I got home, my mom asked me how the research had gone.

"Fine," I said, pouring myself some orange juice. "Some interesting stuff but not what I was looking for."

Ten minutes later, I got a text from Topher. *Hey, I ran into Mark getting gas.*

He ran into Mark? Just by chance? Or was Mark following him? Was he going to beat Topher up? I told myself to calm down. *What did he say?* I texted back.

I asked him what he was up to and he said, "Going home, lots of reading to do." That's it. He is not a warm person.

Lots of reading to do? Maybe he had the letters with him? I wanted to tell Topher not to leave his house until I'd figured everything out. I wanted to write back, *Please watch your back.*

Look out for his car. But I didn't. I just wrote back, *Do Not Approach Wildlife*, and changed the subject.

Hawken and I worked at the library after school the next day. He tried to talk about the letter situation but I waved it away. "I don't want to even think about it, man. I have to get this history paper done." It was nearly dark by the time he dropped me off at my house.

Hadn't there been a light on inside when we pulled up the driveway? The garage door was open. My parents cars weren't in there. Was Rex home by himself but off playing in the woods? Or was someone else in the house? I shuffled into the garage.

"Hello?"

Not a sound.

I slipped off my backpack—I was ready to throw or swing it—and climbed the three brick steps to the door. It creaked as I opened it.

"Hello?" I called again.

No answer.

Stepping into the dark, I felt along the wall for the light switch. Nothing happened when I flicked it. Was the lamp unplugged or was the bulb dead?

I'd only taken two steps toward the kitchen when a shadow leaped over the couch toward me. I swung my backpack as hard as I could, knocking the figure into the wall with such a crash that my mom's treasured cuckoo clock flew from its nail and broke into pieces.

It wasn't until my assailant scrambled to his feet and fled that I saw how short he was.

When he'd reached safety on the other side of the kitchen, he flicked on the lights. Rex squinted in the sudden brightness and rubbed the side of his head. "That really hurt!" he shouted. "And you broke mom's clock. Why did you do that?"

"You jumped me in the dark!"

"Who else did you think it would be? A real ninja?"

We both stared at the busted wood and tangle of chains and weights.

"Where's Mom? Why are you here by yourself?"

"She went to the store."

"Well, come here and give me a hand with this," I said.

"I'm not helping! You did it, you faggot!"

I stood frozen as Rex dashed through the living room. "What did you just call me?" I yelled, but he was already thumping up the stairs. His bedroom door slammed just as my mom's car pulled into the garage.

She was surprisingly calm about the cuckoo clock considering she'd bought it in Zurich with my father twenty years earlier. "Rex has got to stop the sneak attacks," she said as she watched me put leftovers in the microwave. "He dropped out of the garage rafters in front of me the other day. I swear I nearly kicked him in the face. I don't know how he got up there." She sounded really tired. "He'll grow out of it. You'll both grow out of it."

"Me? Grow out of what?"

She just looked at me for a few seconds, and then sighed, "This weird, dark, silent phase, James. You haven't been yourself for weeks. Months. It's like you're in eighth grade all over again. What's wrong?"

The microwave droned, and I watched the clock tick down fifteen seconds. Rex slipped into the kitchen. "The ninja stuff," my mom said firmly, "is going to stop. No more!"

Hawken caught me in the hall before English class on Friday afternoon and said quietly but firmly, "So, we're going to Derek's tonight. It'll be just the three of us. You two need to talk things through, and—"

"No way," I interrupted. "I have plans." A lie.

"Cancel. You guys need to kiss and make up."

I shook my head.

"Poor choice of words. But actually, that might be a good icebreaker. We could play spin the bottle." He cracked up. "It would be a nice gesture of acceptance on Derek's part."

"Please keep your voice down. I'm not going."

Aaron walked past, smiling. I smiled back weakly and then frowned again at Hawken.

"You have to go," he said.

"You don't know what's going on. You don't know half the story."

"Derek doesn't know the full story either."

Breyer strolled by. "Let's go, gentlemen."

"You're going. We'll put everything on the table. It'll be good."

Before Hawken arrived to pick me up that night, I double-checked that my drawer full of letters was locked and looked around my room as if I might find an excuse to stay home. Hawken beeped from the driveway just then, so I dragged myself downstairs and out the door.

Derek was watching cartoons when we arrived. We exchanged brief hellos. Hawken pulled a tall bottle from his backpack, Derek fetched three glasses, and Hawken sloshed liquor into two of them as if it were apple juice. "I'm driving," he explained. "And I don't really like the stuff."

Derek and I clinked without a word. I tried to down mine and came close, but started coughing.

"Oh, dude!" Hawken cried. "That is rum! What are you doing?"

Derek had taken only a sip of his. He looked at his glass, looked at me, and placed it back on the table. "You going to be okay?" he asked.

"I need some water," I croaked. *Do not throw up, do not throw up*, I repeated to myself as I went to the kitchen. As I returned to the living room with water for everyone, Derek asked casually, "What's Topher up to tonight?"

"I don't know," I lied. "Probably in rehearsal." I slurped from my glass.

"Would you take it easy with that?" said Hawken.

"So, listen," sighed Derek. "I know what's up between you two—"

"Yeah, I know you do," I interrupted quickly and a little loudly. "And I know how you know."

Derek stared at me. "Because I'm not an idiot? Because I'm not blind?"

"Because you like to pry into other people's lives? Invade their privacy?"

"What?" Derek looked at Hawken, pointed at me. "What is he talking about?"

"No more rum," said Hawken. "No, do not fill that glass again." He took the bottle out of my hands.

"You are a cruel bastard, Derek," I nearly shouted. "You don't think of anyone but yourself, and you get off on making other people squirm!"

"What?"

"And now I'm supposed to pretend like it's all okay? Like we can just be friends again?"

"You've got to be kidding me. You've been lying to me for—how many years? And now *I'm* a cruel bastard?"

"And a liar."

Derek walked backward away from the table, hands up in front of him. "You should get out of here. Right now. Or I'm going to lose it."

I was already headed to the front door. I clambered into Hawken's car without even waiting for him. He came out five minutes later and leaned into the driver's-side door to talk to me. "You know how long we were in Derek's house? Less than fifteen minutes. You drank, like, six shots' worth of rum and started a fight with one of your best friends all in less than fifteen minutes."

"We were already in a fight," I said.

"No, you weren't," he said. "You *thought* you were in a fight, but you weren't. Now you are. And you have to get out of my car because I guarantee you're going to throw up."

I didn't move. "Come on, man," I moaned. "Just take me home."

"Come back up to the house and talk."

He really wasn't going to drive me home. Fine. I unbuckled my seat belt, opened the door, and climbed out a little unsteadily. I rose and fell on a wave of rum. "I am going to be sick."

"Away from the car and the driveway," Hawken ordered, pointing.

I stumbled through some shrubs and fell down onto wet ground, vomited for what seemed like a lifetime. When I stood back up, spitting, Hawken asked, "You ready to talk now?"

"Aw, dude," I whined. "I've just been puking. No, I'm not ready to talk. Another night." I spat. "Just." I spat again. "Take me home. Please?"

He shook his head, got in the car, and started it up.

We didn't talk most of the way, but as he pulled up my

driveway, Hawken asked, "Have you told your folks yet?"

"No. And not tonight. Tomorrow. On the way home from the game."

"Good. Remember, I can't play tomorrow. Good luck out there." And then as he watched me trying to get out of the car, he added, "And good luck in *there*."

CHAPTER 21

My parents still weren't speaking to me when we got home from the game the next day. I disappeared into my room and wrote a long email to Topher, explaining that I wasn't allowed out of the house until they'd calmed down, which might be tomorrow or might be next year.

> Hi, Topher,
> Today did not go well. My parents aren't really talking to me anymore.
> I had a little rum with Derek last night. Hawken dropped me back home, and I managed to open the front door and yell "I'm home" pretty convincingly.

Just by terrible luck, though, my dad started coming down the stairs just as I started going up. I thought I'd fall if I tried stepping down backward, so I turned around really carefully, hands on the wall and railing, and by this time my dad was right behind me. Suddenly, his hand was on my shoulder. "Up," he said. "Upstairs." So I walked up the stairs, my dad guiding me along the way and then he steered me into the bathroom. I put two hands on the sink counter and my father, not even sounding angry, said, "You going to be sick?"

I remember nodding and kneeling next to the toilet, and I heard him close the door behind him as he left. He came back with water and made sure I got in bed, told me to sleep on my stomach. He put the trash basket next to me. It was a good thing he did. I'm pretty sure he ruffled my hair before he left the room.

But then he woke me up at 6:00 a.m. It was barely light out. "Get up. Now. And meet me in the garage." He handed me a jug of water and a bagel when I shuffled out there. "Take everything out of the garage and line it up neatly on the driveway. Everything. Then sweep it. Then come get me so I can check your work."

"I have a soccer game at ten."

"You've got three hours. This is Project Number

One." And then he turned and left. Two minutes later, I was still just standing there shivering, feeling like I might be sick when he stuck his head back out and said, "Get moving." No slamming doors or anything, to his credit.

It took less time than I thought, but I felt like I was going to puke six or seven times. At 9:00 a.m., I wheeled in the lawnmower, the last item.

Back inside, my mom just glared at me and we drove to my game in silence. My dad took my coach aside as soon as we got there, and coach came back all serious and said to me, "How you feeling now?"

"Terrible," I muttered.

"Loosen up with a trot down the road to the gas station and back."

So while the rest of the team kicked the ball around and did keep-away drills, I ran outside in the cold. It's half a mile to the gas station. And then he had me do push-ups and sit-ups. Everyone in the facility was watching all this. After all that, Coach said, "We're going to give you a rest today. Alan's starting."

I felt so crummy that sitting out the game was a relief. I just walked away and slumped on the edge of the bench in my socks.

"What the hell did you do?" our backup goalie asked. I ended up telling most of the story to him. At the end of it, he sighed. "That sucks. I'm high as hell right now. I get stoned before every game." Which explains why we lose when he's in the net.

So now I'm grounded for a month. Supposedly.

And I never even got the chance to tell them about you.

I hate rum,

James

"I'm sure that wasn't your first drink, James," my mom said sharply. We were sitting at the kitchen table, me in the interrogation chair, after they'd sent Rex to bed. "But as far as I know, it's the first time you drank yourself stupid."

She was mistaken, of course, but I nodded in agreement.

"And it's the first time, as far as I know," my dad picked up, "that you drank the night before you had a soccer game. What the hell were you thinking?"

There was a lot that I was thinking about, I wanted to say. But I wasn't going to get into it that night. If I was going to tell them about Topher and all that, I wanted to talk about it when I was feeling good, when I could come across as confident and strong. Not when I felt about as bad as I'd ever felt. All I wanted to do was curl up somewhere warm. But they were staring at me, waiting for a response.

"It was stupid, I know," I finally said. "I won't do it again. Does it help that now I hate rum?"

"No," they answered in unison. My dad had his arms

folded, while my mom was perched on the edge of her seat as if she might launch herself across the table at me.

"Didn't you learn anything from Mark getting drunk and putting Aaron Foster in the hospital?" she asked.

She actually wanted an answer. "Don't punch people?" I tried.

"Don't drink like that. Ever. The night can end in an ambulance. Or a police car." She was on a tear.

"Please stop. I just want to sleep," I moaned.

"First, you're folding that laundry," my mother said, getting up and pointing to a basket overflowing with socks. "Your father's working up a list of more things that need to be done around the house and in the yard. And Rex is free from dishwashing duty for the next week." Suddenly, she was stabbing the air in front of me. "And if your brother, who worships the ground you walk on, ever sees you drinking, you'll be sleeping in the garage. Do you understand me?"

I glanced at my father, hoping for some sympathy, but he looked even angrier than she did. "Okay," I sighed, slithering out of my chair. I had to appear sorry and worried, though I knew my parents would either forget all those punishments or, after a couple of days, just tire of following through on them. They always did. I started for the stairs, but my mother called me back.

"N-n-no, young man," and she laughed the sarcastic laugh that makes me want to scream. "What did I just say? Laundry."

"In the morning," I moaned.

"Now." She stood there, hands on her hips, until I walked back into the kitchen and collapsed into the chair next to the hamper.

"And this conversation isn't over," she said.

I folded the first few socks, boxers, and T-shirts as though I were murdering them. But the rest of them would've won in a fight.

I woke up at 3:00 a.m. and could not get back to sleep. Was Derek ever going to speak to me again? Theresa? Even Hawken was angry at me now. I got up, took my notebook and a pen, and went downstairs to the kitchen. I made a sandwich, drank some water, and wrote a letter to my parents at the kitchen table. Part of me was hoping one of them would come down to investigate and I could just tell them everything that was going on. But that didn't happen.

> Sunday, June 5th
> Dear Mom & Dad,
> I know I'm behaving miserably at the moment, but trust me—there's nothing you can do to solve my problems. If I'm cool and quiet about it, things might get better on their own. Even if this problem won't fix itself completely, maybe I'll just get used to things being broken. Last time Luke asked you whether we could have someone come in to tune the piano, you told him that he needed to get used to it sounding out of key.

"It's only out of tune if you accept someone else's definition of what's in tune," you said, Dad. I know you were joking, but you still didn't get the thing fixed. And maybe that's the attitude I need to adopt. I'm only not okay by someone else's standards. If I can get all this anxiety back down to the lower-level worry it was before, everything will be fine. At least by my standards.

Love,

James

I felt fine on Sunday. Rex and I ran into each other on the stairs, and we karate fought long enough to earn a yell from the kitchen. I could hear Rex quietly continuing the fight against invisible assassins as I shuffled into the kitchen. The promised list of jobs waited for me on the table.

"How do you feel today?" my father asked, peering over his glasses.

"Great," I chirped.

He exchanged a disappointed glance with my mom, and then muttered into his coffee, "Wait until you hit twenty-five."

I was cleaning the upstairs "boys' bathroom," as we call it, when my mom stuck her head in and announced, "Tim Hawken's here. He thinks you're going for a run with him."

I put down my sponge. "May I?" I overplay the model prisoner for the first thirty-six hours of any grounding.

My mother shook her head. "I suppose I should be encouraging you to find better ways to spend your time than drinking. I'll tell him you'll be down in a minute."

Hawken thumped my back when I bounced into the kitchen. "I'll have him home in an hour, Mrs. Liddell. He's looking a little pale, you know?"

"Well, you should have seen him yesterday, Tim. Better pale than green."

"Let's go!" I shouted, and pushed Hawken to the front door.

"Thanks for getting me home the other night," I said once we were outside.

"Yeah, you were a real mess. Who do they think brought you home?"

"Theresa."

"Oh, that's good of you. Let the lies just pile up."

What's great is that Hawken and I run at exactly the same pace, so that neither of us has to slow down or speed up to accommodate the other. Within a half mile of leaving my house, our feet had fallen into that easy, gentle rhythm that I never find when we're just running laps around the soccer field. For a mile and a half, all the way to the river trail, we just ran in silence, listening to our feet on the road's gray grit, listening to our deep breaths. "Summertime!" Hawken yelled without breaking pace, and then without any attempt at a segue, he said, "So, I take it you haven't talked to your folks yet, huh?"

"The timing didn't seem right yesterday."

We splashed through a sprawling puddle. "Talk to Derek again."

"I will."

Just the sound of our feet hitting sand for a few yards. "He's a little fired up," Hawken continued. "Derek, I mean. I had to explain the letter situation to him. He doesn't understand why you think he was the one to do that. And he doesn't care that you're gay, you know."

I couldn't help wincing. That word just bothered me. "When did he figure it out anyway?"

"That night at your house, the fire ring, and Topher. It wasn't hard to do the math. He asked me about you guys. He was surprised, but he doesn't hate you because of it."

"His church doesn't like gay people."

"He's not brainwashed, dude. Give him some credit. He wants to talk to you about it, but he doesn't know how. Well, neither of you knows how."

"And you don't think he cares," I ventured, not knowing what else to say but not wanting the conversation to die.

"I know he doesn't care, dude. He's furious that you accused him of being a liar and a thief, but that doesn't have anything to do with the fact that you like boys."

"That I like Topher," I said.

"Right, Topher, who you like because he's a great *guy*, a good-looking *boy*. Who cares? You like boys. It's not that big of a deal."

"To some people it is."

"No doubt, but not to Derek. Not to me."

"My parents? The soccer team?"

"Who *cares* about the soccer team?" And Hawken stopped running, stood with his hands on his hips. I walked back toward him. "I don't know your parents all that well," Hawken panted, "but it's not like they're abusive. They'll get over it. My father didn't sleep for a while after my brother came out to him and my mom cried a lot. But that was years ago. Now Patrick's boyfriend comes to our place for Thanksgiving. They sleep in the same bed when they visit. My parents love him."

"That's your parents. And maybe I'm not like that. Maybe I just like Topher, and later I'll meet the right girl and end up marrying her and having kids and living a totally normal life. I don't want to cause all sorts of confusion for nothing."

"Really? You really think you'll meet a girl who you'll like enough to marry? Do you like Theresa at all in the way you like Topher?"

I just stood there, breathing hard and sweating and staring off to the river.

"Have you ever wrapped your arm around a girl's shoulders and walked her down a dark road to confess your love to her? Honestly?"

I looked up at him, embarrassed and little hurt that he'd bring up that night.

"Come on, man, that didn't bother me, you know that.

But you're being totally dishonest with yourself. And dishonest with your friends. You're not giving Derek any credit, and Theresa got completely jerked around. Neither of them understands why you've dumped them."

"I didn't dump anyone," I muttered.

"They feel like you've dumped them. You should set things straight with them. Even if you find being straight difficult."

"Ha ha," I said. I wiped my face on my sleeve and nodded. "Okay. I'll talk to Derek. Maybe tonight."

"He's in Boston with his folks. They don't get back until late."

"Aw, that's right. Well, I guess tomorrow. And I'll figure out what to say to Theresa. But, well, one more thing." I took a deep breath. "What about Mark?"

"He won't care. He gets along fine with my brother."

"I mean, the letters. He's the only one—"

"No. No." Hawken looked off into the trees. "He doesn't do crap like that. No. Seriously, he's okay around my brother."

"But does Mark even know your brother's gay? You've laid it out for him? I didn't know until you told me."

"Mark's been around my brother more than you have. He's met his boyfriend."

"I've met him, too. I always figured they were just friends."

"I'm sure he's figured it out." He hit my back and we started to run again.

We ran the rest of the route in near silence. When the stop sign that marks the finish line came into view, I was actually disappointed. Normally, I can't wait to reach it. We walked slowly up my driveway, dripping sweat, happy to be hot in the cool of a spring evening.

"Hey! I have something for you," said Hawken, ducking into his car.

When he came out, he handed me a black-and-white photograph. It was from Pirate Shakespeare Night, as Derek referred to it. Topher and I sat on the porch railing, his arm around my shoulders. My smile was cloudless.

"I like this photo a lot. You look really happy."

"Yeah, that is a good shot. I was hammered."

"Naw, it was before you were hammered. Anyway, I have to split."

I tried to hand the photo back to him. "Thanks for showing it to me."

"No, it's yours."

"Oh."

"Unless you're uncomfortable having photographic evidence of your gayism lying around."

"Yeah, maybe." I tried to hand him the photo again.

"James, I was joking. It's yours. Frame it."

"Right. I'll hang it in the living room. That won't make anyone uncomfortable or anything."

Hawken grabbed a towel from his car and pulled off his shirt.

"Does this make you uncomfortable?" he asked, stepping close to me, trying but failing to keep a straight face.

"Does this?" And I stomped on his foot.

He howled, then limped to the driver's door, laughing, wished me luck, and left.

I was just out of the shower when my mom knocked on my door and called from outside.

"Are you telling your friends to just show up, knowing that I won't have the heart to send them away?"

"Derek's here?"

"No, it's a young man named Topher."

I think I actually jumped a little. I rubbed my chin, wondering what he'd said to her. *Hi,* all casual, *I'm James's boyfriend.*

I stuck my head out the door, "So it's okay if he stays for a while?"

"Is he a friend from school? I don't remember you ever mentioning him."

"Yeah," I started to lie, and then realized I'd never be able to sustain it. "I mean no, he goes to another school. We just know each other. From, like, around."

"Well, he's very charming and polite. I'd been thinking that some new friends might do you good, so I'm not going to send him away. But don't leave this house."

She'd been thinking I needed new friends.

I did a quick survey of my room. Clothes covered the floor and my schoolbooks were scattered across my bed. The place was a disaster. And I knew that if I told my mom to send him up here, she'd listen from the hallway.

"Tell him I'll be right there," I said, shutting my door. I tried to fix my hair and put on cologne at the same time, but I wound up spraying on too much. Grabbing the nearest sock, I wiped my neck, then stuck two sticks of gum in my mouth, thumped down the stairs, and tried to stroll casually into the kitchen.

"Hey, man," I said when I shuffled in. Topher was sipping a glass of water. I attempted to fist bump him, which we'd never done before. He tried shaking my hand and then realized what was happening and sort of slapped my knuckles instead.

I saw him glance toward my mom, who was glancing toward us, and then he coughed nervously, and said in a voice he probably had when he was ten, "Hi, James."

Could my mom read me? Could she see that I couldn't control my smile around this kid? I wanted to get him out of my kitchen as fast as possible, but if I'd immediately suggested that we go outside, my mom would've wondered if he was selling me drugs. I hoped he had a plan.

He didn't. He just sat there grinning with his head tucked into his shoulders. "How was your weekend?" I asked, and sauntered to the fridge, hoping that slow movements would disguise my panic.

"Good, good. Nothing big. I had play practice and then some homework."

"Oh, you're in a play?" my mom asked enthusiastically.

This is good, I thought. Neutral conversation. This is okay.

"Yes," he replied, and smiled. Not *yeah* or *uh-huh* or *yup*. *Yes*. "I'm Hamlet in, well, *Hamlet*."

"Oh my God, your school is putting on *Hamlet*?"

"Not my school, it's a nearby community group, and it's just an adaptation," he explained, and he told her about how the director has rewritten a bunch of Shakespeare's tragedies for the high school stage. While he was talking, I came up with a plan to get us out of earshot of my mom. Before she could ask him to recite his lines, I interrupted.

"Hey, Mom, Topher is friends with Theresa's friend, Kim. She sent him over to give me some advice about that whole thing."

"What whole thing?" she asked. "Your drinking?"

There was silence for a moment.

"The whole Theresa thing," I said.

"Oh." She looked surprised.

"Yeah. So, is it okay for us to hang out on the front step or something?" Before she could answer, I turned to Topher and pretended to explain, "I'm under house arrest. I threw up in my room."

"While Topher's memorizing Hamlet's soliloquies, you're vomiting rum. That's lovely," sighed my mother. "You may talk on the front steps. Or in the living room, where it's not buggy. Topher, please talk some sense into James. It's too bad you're not rehearsing the part of Polonius."

Evidently, that was hilarious. I went to grab my sneakers,

and Topher's laughter followed me up the stairs. He is a good actor.

I led us out through the garage door. In the window of my mom's car, I could see the reflection of my worried eyes when Topher wrapped his arms around me and kissed my cheek. "Good to see you," he whispered.

"We should go out front before my mom gets curious."

We were two steps from the driveway when Rex leaped from behind my mom's car, spun in the air, and landed in his favorite ninja pose. Topher made a weird little barking yelp, but Rex didn't say anything—he was just breathing heavy, nearly panting. Not knowing what he'd seen or what he might say, I couldn't ignore him. I had to handle him carefully. Crouching, I circled him, drawing him out onto the driveway. Topher backed away.

"You want to fight?" I challenged.

"You going to die," he whispered, and then he launched himself at me. I ducked low, and he landed with his chest on my back, his legs over my shoulders, his arms wrapped around my stomach. I stood up, grabbing his legs, and walked him upside down onto the lawn. He was half cracking up, half wailing. "Where should we put him?" I called to Topher. "In that puddle or in the bramble?" I started to spin.

"No!" yelled Rex, and he squirmed so much I really nearly dropped him.

"The bramble? Is that where we're going?" I set off across the lawn.

He went berserk, screaming and laughing, punching and kicking.

"Stop! I'm letting you down, dude. You're really heavy. Stop squirming and put your hands out so you don't drop on your head!"

Rex managed an awkward handstand landing. He was still cracking up as he stood. I got on my knees in front of him and took him by the shoulders. "How long were you hiding in the garage, you weirdo?"

"I hid behind the car when I heard the door open," he panted. "Why? What were you doing?"

"Nothing." I stood up. "Topher," I announced, relieved. "This is my brother, Rex. Go shake, Rex."

Rex charged Topher obediently and tackled him. It was tough to tell whether Topher's fall to the pavement was staged or real.

"Down, Rex! Heel! Heel!"

Rex stood and, placing his boot on Topher's chest, pumped his arms in the air. Topher looked stunned.

"Dude, don't put your dirty paws on him!"

Rex removed the foot. "Sorry!" he said down at Topher.

He is a good kid. I do like him.

Topher stood, brushed himself off, laughed less convincingly than he had earlier.

"You have to go inside," I said. "Mom said she has something for you."

"What? What does she have for me?"

"I don't know. You have to go find out."

He sprinted to the house.

"Your brother's named *Rex*?" Topher asked as we walked to the front step.

"My older brother, Luke, and I wanted a dog. His real name's Daniel." As I leaned back against the railing of the stone steps, I felt good for the first time all week. I'd missed Topher's eyes and smile.

"It's been a crazy few days," I began, stretching my legs out so that my foot hit his. "Crazy, crazy." I apologized for not being in touch more often and started to give him a brief version of recent events: "Someone stole a bunch of letters I wrote but never meant to mail out."

The front storm door swung open just then. Rex banged both fists against the glass. "She had nothing!" he shouted at me. "She had nothing for me!"

My mother appeared, looking apologetic, swept him away, and shut the door again.

"So, yeah, I wrote all these letters to people just to get my thoughts out on paper, like an escape valve for steam, you know?" I paused and scraped the front steps with a stick. I hadn't even reached the weird part yet, and I was already embarrassed. I just kept going. "And then Hawken and Theresa and Aaron Foster all got these really personal letters in the mail that were humiliating for me, as the author of them, although they were all pretty cool about it. I don't know what other letters are missing. I thought it was Derek who stole them, but Hawken asked him about it, and, apparently, it wasn't him. And Hawken says Mark wouldn't do that kind of thing, but I'm not sure—"

"Why didn't you say anything about all of this, James? It's crazy. Are you kidding?"

"I mean, what could you have done? What can anyone do? I figured I might be able to find out who it was and that would sort of be the end of it."

"You keep way too much to yourself, dude. Way too much. You're going to go off like a gun one of these days." He shook his head. "And you're not going to be able to figure out who stole those letters just by sitting around thinking about it. Talk to everyone involved. Be honest with them."

"You think I should interrogate Mark?"

"Maybe, but first you should tell him that you're gay. Steal that from *him*. He's probably waiting to use it against you. And you have to talk to your parents."

"I want to wait until they're over Rumscapade."

"Well, man, you have to talk to someone about all of this. If you're not going to talk to your parents, go talk to someone at school. Guidance counselors are paid to listen to this kind of stuff. And think about it—it'd be a career highlight for them, helping a kid like you come out of the closet."

I'd been peeling bark from a stick, but I forced myself to smile. He kicked my foot.

"Honestly. You have to talk to someone before this gets any uglier. And if this jerk mails your letters to people who aren't cool about it, you're going to regret not having had the guts to beat him to it. You'll want that moment back."

The sun had dipped below the hill, and the black flies were out.

"I don't want to talk about any of this with someone I don't know."

"Then what's your plan?"

"What's my *plan*?" I said *plan* as though he were an idiot for using the word.

He looked away, rubbed his eyes, and then stood up.

"Sorry, no. I don't have a plan. I don't know what I'm going to do. Please sit back down, Topher. I'm sorry." I stood up.

"I should go, actually," he said quietly. "I've got to help work on sets at the theater."

"Tonight? On a Sunday night?"

"I'm supposed to be there already."

"Don't go yet, Topher. I'm sorry. Please stay."

My mom opened the front door just then. She peeked her head out and grimaced. "Aren't you boys getting eaten alive? Come inside!"

"Thanks, but I actually have to go," Topher said. "It was really nice to meet you, Mrs. Liddell."

"It was nice to meet you, too, Topher," my mom said. "Good luck with *Hamlet*."

"Thanks."

I stood up, willing her to shut the door so I could walk

him back over to the garage and say sorry a hundred times over again out of sight, but she didn't move.

"You sure you can't hang out for a little bit longer?" I said.

"Yeah, really. I have to split." He didn't seem angry, and he put out his hand. "I'll give you a buzz soon."

"I'll walk you to your car."

"It's cool. I'll talk to you soon."

Why wouldn't she go inside and close the door? "Thanks for the advice, man," I said robotically, shaking his hand and making myself smile. "I'll let you know when I'm ungrounded."

Turning as he walked across the lawn, Topher gave us a little wave.

"What a nice young man," my mom said as she shut the door behind us.

"Yup," I agreed, and I disappeared upstairs to Luke's room to text Topher. *Thx 4 coming over!! Hope u r not mad. Love, James.*

I stared at the *Love, James* for a few seconds, deleted it, and hit Send.

No response.

CHAPTER 22

Still not ready to deal with any messy conversations, I avoided everyone in school the next day. I sat on the opposite side of classrooms from friends and dodged down hallways to avoid talking. I did think about going to my school counselor that afternoon—I could've made an appointment for last period during my study hall. Instead, I decided to skip out and go running. The Mud 10K was less than a week away. Tomorrow I would talk to someone, I told myself.

In the locker room, I fumbled and dropped my combination lock trying to get out of there as quickly as possible. I had a sneaker on one foot and a sock on the other when I heard the locker room door open. Squeaky footsteps on the tiles, and then Derek peered around the corner of the lockers.

"I figured you were here," he said, his hands in his pockets. He took a seat on the wooden bench.

"Yeah?"

"I don't even get invited to go running anymore?"

"You want to go running?" I offered.

"Nope. I'm beat. No running for me."

I just stood there. I'd managed to avoid him all day, and now he had me cornered. Should I talk to him here? Should I tell him I'd meet him later? Before I could decide, he said, "Hawken talked to you yesterday, huh?"

"Yeah. Yeah, he did. And you spoke to Hawken."

"Right. It's almost like we spoke to each other, but not quite."

"Ha." One shoe still hung limp from its laces in my hand. "I'm sorry I called you a liar, man. There's a whole bunch going on and—"

He held up a hand. "Hawken told me about it. I'm sorry that's happening. But I don't know why you'd think I'd do that to you. I was so upset about that I couldn't even call you. I've *never* been cruel to you. Not once." He looked away from me and bit his lip, held his breath.

"Derek, come on, man. I know."

He took a deep breath, calmed down. "I'm sorry whoever it is has you thinking so crazy," he said.

"Yeah," I replied. "It has me thinking crazy."

"Anyway, he's a nice dude," Derek said. "Topher, I mean."

I nodded for what was probably ten seconds and then whispered, "Thanks. He is a nice dude."

"But you knew before you met him?"

It took me a moment to figure out what he meant, and then I nodded again, hoping that'd be the end of it. Derek was speaking too loudly. We were in one small section of a big locker room. There were showers at one end, a couple of offices for coaches at the other. Anyone could have been in there listening.

"It doesn't make a difference to me, James," Derek continued before I could stop him. "You could've told me that you were gay and—"

Mark stepped around the corner of the lockers, grinning.

"What's going on? You two running away together?"

Derek stood up. "Mark, would you take off?"

"Whoa, whoa! I'm sorry! I didn't mean to interrupt anything between you two."

"Well, you did," I said, and I wished my voice had been steadier. "We're talking." Suddenly, I was cold and sweating.

"My bad, my bad." Mark pretended to apologize again, his hands up. "But let me ask you one question: Who's the man in this relationship and who's the—"

Derek's punch cut him off. He hit him square in the jaw. Hard. Mark staggered backward two steps and put his hand to his mouth, then looked at his fingers, checking for blood.

I froze, my shoe still dangling by its laces in my hand. As Derek crouched, fists clenched, ready to fight, Mark stepped forward and landed a punch with all his weight behind it . . . right in my eye. The clang I heard must have been the back of my head hitting the metal lockers when I fell, but at the time, I thought it was the bone cracking around my eye socket.

I remember being on the ground, then back on my feet, and I remember Coach Williams, the baseball coach, pinning Mark to a locker with both hands while yelling "Hey! Hey! Hey!" in rhythm with my throbbing skull. I remember Derek and Mark screaming curses at each other. I remember Derek walking ahead of me to the principal's office, and Mark howling at his coach behind me, "That queer just made a move on his friend." I kept walking. *One foot shod*, I remember thinking, *one foot and one eye socked*. And I remember somehow wanting to grin, not only because of the dumb pun, but also because it felt like something was over. Something was finished.

As ordered, Derek and I sat on the wooden bench outside Ms. Reed's—the principal's—office. I was holding an ice pack against my eye, when suddenly Derek put his arm around me. I turned to see him with my good eye, but he was looking past me at Mark, who was being escorted toward us.

"Oh, I know," said Mark as he passed us on his way in to see Ms. Reed. "Believe me, I know. You don't have to make a show of it."

Even though I hadn't hit anyone, the school insisted on calling my father to let him know that I'd been in a fight. "We're not sending you home with a black eye and no explanation," Ms. Reed said as she dialed my father's cell phone. Of course he wanted to immediately come pick me up, and Derek and I were back on the bench when he arrived. Ms. Reed tried to reassure him by saying, "James didn't actually throw a punch." I did my best to glare at her with one eye and an ice pack.

"What was this all about?" my dad asked. "I thought you two were friends with Mark."

Derek pretended to laugh.

"It's complicated," I said, standing up. "I'll explain it all when we get home." I looked at Derek, who was opening and closing his bruised hand, and turned back to my father. "I'll catch up with you, Dad."

After he left, I kicked Derek's foot lightly, twice. "Dude. Thanks for the black eye."

He laughed.

"Come over later," I said.

"I'll try. I might not be allowed out of my house."

"Will I be allowed in?"

"Yeah." He looked confused and then caught on. "Yeah. Are you kidding?"

"You can explain everything to your folks if you want. I'm about to do the same, and they'll probably end up calling your parents anyway. I'll see you later on."

"I'm not sure I know enough to explain anything, but, yeah, come over—unless they keep me here forever." He turned to the woman who ran the office. "Maggie, seriously, when can I go?"

My dad was ten yards ahead of me on the way to the parking lot. Three baseball players, Mark's teammates, were standing outside the gym.

"Liddell!" one of them called.

I didn't know who had heard what, so I waved.

"You faggot!" the kid yelled back.

Ducking my head, I walked faster, but my father had stopped in his tracks. He stared at them as I caught up to him.

"Let's go," I muttered, and grabbed his elbow. "Let's go, let's go, let's go."

I was glad we lived so close to the school. It meant a short, silent drive home. My mom's car was in the garage when we pulled up the driveway. My dad must have phoned when he got the call from school, and she'd left work early.

We calmed her down about my eye. "He does not need to go to the hospital," my dad reassured her as he opened the freezer. He tossed me a bag of frozen peas, which I tried to catch with one hand and one eye and missed. "He just needs to sit down and explain what happened," my father continued. "I still haven't heard the whole story."

"You guys might want to fix yourselves some drinks," I said quietly.

My mom now looked even more tense, and she lowered

herself into a chair at the kitchen table. I think she had suddenly connected some dots.

My father slapped my shoulder as he walked past. "James, I'm sure we can handle whatever it is you have to tell us." He squeezed between my mom and the wall to get to the chair by the window. She looked frozen. She didn't even scoot in to give him room. "And we are not fixing drinks at this time in the afternoon."

"Well, can I have one?"

My dad shot me a look. "Sit down and relax. What happened?"

I slumped into a chair and with a shaky hand held the frozen peas against my punched eye. I closed the other. "That kid after school, Dad," I began. I took a deep breath and opened my good eye. My father looked puzzled. "That kid after school," I tried again. "The one who yelled that stuff at me. That didn't come out of nowhere."

My father stared at me for a moment, then crossed his arms and leaned back in his chair. It creaked beneath his weight.

"What did he yell?" my mom asked weakly.

Neither of us answered her. I pushed the pack of frozen peas so hard against my eye it hurt.

"What did he yell?"

"He called James a—" My father leaned forward, put his elbows on his knees, then his hands on his head. "He said James is gay."

I had the pack of frozen peas over both eyes now and

heard my dad ask, "And you think it's true?"

I nodded.

"James, answer me."

"Yeah," I said, letting my hand holding the ice pack drop to my leg. "It's true." And then I said it, as if it weren't already clear. Two words if you count the *I am* as one mumbled contraction.

My dad looked up at me, and then he winced and gazed off out the window.

"Excuse me?" said my mom quietly. I thought at first she was talking to my father. I thought she might've seen the disgusted look on his face and was challenging him: "Excuse me? How dare you react to our son that way?"

But she wasn't. She was talking to me. *She wants you to repeat it,* I told myself. You just made the most painful admission of your life, and she wants you to repeat it.

I rocked back in my chair, which drives my mom crazy, and cleared my throat as if I were about to speak, but I didn't say anything. I looked to my father for help. He rubbed his jaw as if he were making sure he was awake, making sure this was real, and then he rocked back in his own chair, too.

"How long have you thought this?" he asked quietly.

I shrugged. They were supposed to be saying it was okay.

"Months?" my dad offered.

I closed my eyes and shook my head.

"Years?"

I didn't move. When I opened my eyes again, he was

looking at my mother. Her jaw was tense, as if she were clenching her teeth, and she stared at the kitchen table.

"Why didn't you say something?"

The front legs of my chair banged onto the kitchen floor.

"I just did," I said, much more loudly than I'd meant to.

My mother's head snapped up, and I thought she might scream at me.

"I just did," I repeated more quietly. "And I don't know what else you want me to say. Look at my eye. This is why I didn't say anything to anyone. People find out and this happens and you guys look like you don't want me for a son." Somehow I was managing to speak coherently while tears poured down my face.

"We don't look like that," said my dad, "We don't think that, James. My God . . ."

"Yes, you do look like that."

"James, please, stop." My dad had his hands over his face, his elbows on the table. Sliding his hands down across his jaw, he gazed out the window.

I turned to my mother, but she didn't say a word. She didn't even look at me.

I stood up and walked out of the kitchen, down the hall, and up the stairs to my room, waiting for one of them to call me back. Neither of them did.

My eye, as I inspected it in the mirror of my bedroom, felt like a throbbing golf ball, and it was so red and purple that it might have been turned inside out. I couldn't see out of it anyway, but the tears made it doubly blurry. I'd been up in my room only five minutes or so, first examining my reflection in the mirror, then sitting at my desk, staring out the window, imagining following moose tracks over the hill and disappearing into the forest forever, when my father knocked and opened the door at the same time, as he does. He didn't say a word as he walked in and sat on the bed. I turned back toward my window, and the index card I'd stuck above my desk caught my eye:

> *IF YOU AIN'T SCARED STANDING UP*
> *FOR WHAT'S RIGHT,*
> *THEN YOU AIN'T STANDING UP FOR MUCH.*
> *—NOT MARK TWAIN*

"You took us by surprise, James," my dad began. "You know your mom and I love you no matter—"

"Then where is she?" I said without looking at him.

"Listen, it's a lot—it's a lot for her to digest. For us to digest. I mean, we've both always thought of you as one way, thought of your life as going one way, and now, all of a sudden, out of nowhere—"

"I'm someone else."

"You're not someone else. Obviously. We know that. But we thought we knew you better than we did. It's alarming. It's unsettling to find out that—"

"Disappointing?"

"I didn't say disappointing. I said unsettling."

"It's not like I'm coming home with a mohawk and tattoos and a pierced lip. It's not like I made a bad choice."

"You're sure about that? You're sure you're not making a choice? Sometimes we make choices without realizing that we're making them."

I turned from the window and looked straight at him. "Believe me," I said. "Believe me, I didn't make a choice."

"At seventeen? You're sure of this at seventeen? I just don't know if you can be sure of these things when you're your age."

"You met mom in high school and *married* her. Did you make a choice to like her?"

"It's not the same."

"How is it not the same?"

My mom appeared in my bedroom doorway. She'd been crying. "Is it the boy who was over here the other day? What was his name? Topher?"

I nodded. "Yeah, Topher."

"He's very polite," she started to say, but her voice cracked, and she stared at the ceiling. "You wore cologne for him," she managed when she'd regained her composure. She walked into my room and dropped next to my dad on the edge of my bed. "How did you meet him? On the internet?"

I stared at her. "At a dance. I met him at a dance."

"Are you—" She repositioned herself on the bed. "Are

you sleeping with this boy? With this young man? With Topher?"

"What?" I whispered. My dad looked as stunned as I felt.

"I think it's a reasonable question to ask after your seventeen-year-old son comes home from school with a black eye and announces that he's gay," my mom said in a hurry.

"No, it's not a reasonable question. You never once asked me that when you thought I was dating Theresa."

"I never worried about you contracting HIV when I thought you were dating Theresa."

I looked for help from my dad, but he just gazed back at me.

"This is a nightmare," I said.

No response from either of them. They were waiting for me to answer the question. "I mean, I know to use condoms. That's what you want to know, right?"

"Don't raise your voice at me."

"I didn't raise my voice."

"I asked you a question."

I sprang out of my chair. My dad stood up, too, but I stalked past him out of my own room, down the stairs, out the front door. I made it halfway down the driveway, planning to walk to Derek's, when I realized that I'd have to hike along the main road with my black eye. People I knew would pull over, and I didn't want to talk. Or fight. I crossed the lawn. Rex had left a soccer ball outside, and I booted it hard at one of my mother's azaleas. Pink blossoms exploded like fireworks. I walked faster before anyone could scream from the house, and when I reached the woods, I disappeared.

There's a narrow deer trail a few feet into the woods. It's not easy walking, especially when you have only one eye. Thorny branches and vines caught my shirt, scratched my arms, drew blood. Black flies bit my ears and ankles. Swatting them away, I pushed through a green tangle, and a thorn ripped a long stinging streak across my neck. Then I tripped on a root and cracked my shin against a log. Cursing Mark and my mother, I stumbled into a little sunny clearing.

Beech and ash trees surrounded tall grass and a carpet of moss. There was the old oak cradling the rotting deer stand. I hadn't been in that stretch of woods in a couple of years, at least. I looked around and took a deep breath.

Kicking through leaves, I headed to the stream.

Rex had dammed it with big, smooth granite stones. I recognized some of them from when I was younger—I remembered their size and shape and color, their cold weight in my arms as Derek and I stacked them in walls and towers. Some of the frogs along those wet banks had spent so much time cupped in my muddy hands that they didn't bother to jump away when I crawled close. I didn't remember there being so many fish, though. Tiny trout darted into the shadows beneath overhanging roots. Ankle-deep stretches of stream would've reached my knees now, but the air was the same—that mossy smell you can taste when you close your eyes in winter and remember green light and birdsong.

I knelt on a sunny stretch of pebbles and splashed water on my cuts and swollen eye. Once when I was ten, I slurped from the stream—it was so hot, the water so cold, I couldn't resist. Somehow I didn't get sick.

I lay down on the sunny stones and closed my good eye.

When shadows fell across me, I stood and followed my old path up to the meadow with the boulder on the hillside. I hadn't been up there since the beginning of April, our last sledding day of the winter. Rex's sneaker prints led the way through muddy stretches of trail. I wondered if my parents were looking for me. Or if they were crying into the phone to their friends. Maybe they were figuring out how to apologize. Maybe they'd take me to dinner. Or buy me something out of guilt. My eye still ached, and I didn't have any ice.

The field, when I stepped out of the woods, was gold in late afternoon light. Crows called back and forth as I crossed the dry grass. I climbed onto the big rock, warm from the afternoon sun. I'd told Topher that I'd bring him here to see this—the view across the valley, Mount Cube and the long slope of Smarts, and in the winter through the trees, the hunch of Ascutney. I'll bring him here in the summer, I thought. We'll watch the stars and my parents can go—

A stone cracked the rock next to me and landed in the grass. I spun, squinting.

Derek was trudging toward me, hands in his pockets.

"I thought I'd find you here. Second time in a single afternoon I get to say that."

"You see my folks?"

"Your dad answered the door. He said you'd split for the hills."

"Yeah, I'm on my way. Just resting up. Maybe my mother will have moved out by the time I get back."

"Yikes. The conversation went well, huh?"

"She punched me. In the same eye, luckily. So you can't tell."

"Seriously, she kicked you out?"

"She didn't kick me out. I just left. She asked me whether I was sleeping with Topher."

"Huh. I was going to ask you the same thing. What's the big deal?"

"You're not my mom."

"True." He picked a grass stalk and stuck it in his mouth. "But. So . . . are you sleeping with Topher?"

I cracked up and ignored the question. "I still don't get how you're so calm about all this. I thought you hated gay people. You used to say some nasty stuff about them."

"So did you."

"Yeah." I shrugged. "I was scared. It's confusing."

He threw a rock out toward the hills. "It's definitely confusing," he said.

"So, you don't think I'm an abomination, huh? And you're not going to go to hell for hanging out with me?"

Derek shot me a glance and lobbed another rock. "You know, a few years ago a kid at my church told me I was damned because I'm black. Something about Noah cursing the descendants of Ham. He showed me the Bible passage. I was sort of scared, so I asked my parents about it, and they just laughed at the idea. I remember my father rolling his eyes and saying, 'Of course you're not going to hell.' But then I asked him whether gay people were going to burn, and my dad stopped laughing. He just goes, 'Are you gay? No? Then don't worry about it.' Since then, the whole 'God hates you and you're going to hell' idea has seemed sort of stupid. I don't know. Seems like Jesus probably likes you and Topher more than He likes the Christians who kill people."

"Why didn't you tell me?" I asked.

"Why didn't *I* tell *you*? We've been talking about girls since we were twelve and you've been gay this whole time and you ask me why *I* didn't tell *you*?"

"Okay, okay. You've said that already."

"Yeah, that's right. Now climb down off your rock. I have to go home and take all sorts of heat for being a hero."

"You just got here."

"I wasn't factoring in the hike."

I jumped to the ground, and we started back toward my house. We'd just left the bright meadow and stepped into the forest's shade when Derek stopped short and grabbed my arm. "Look," he gasped. I followed his gaze and there, not twenty yards away, stood a moose. His gangly legs were white up past his knees, as if frosted by deep snow, and his stubby antlers ended in fists.

"Whoa," I barely whispered.

The moose stared back at us. We all stood frozen for ten, maybe fifteen seconds.

And then Derek sang just a little too loudly, "Heeere, moosey moosey moosey . . ."

"Don't scare him," I started to say, but the moose was already galumphing into the woods.

"Whoops," said Derek. "Should we follow him?"

I considered it for a moment. "No, let's leave him alone. Maybe he'll come back around later." This is his place after all, I thought. He should be able to be where he belongs without being scared.

"That was crazy!" Derek laughed, back to full volume. "I've never seen a moose around here."

"You said you saw one on your way to pick me up one morning."

"Oh, yeah? I didn't. I must've been lying."

"Why would you do that?"

"Again, you used to talk about girls as if you liked them. That turns out to be false."

"Well, now we can talk about them much more honestly."

"Oh, that's generous."

"Which girl should we talk about?"

"Kim. We're supposed to hang out this weekend."

"No way."

"Yup. It's true."

"Well, that's great. What else can I say?"

"Nothing. It is great. And guess who Hawken's been talking to?"

"Tell me Theresa."

"Genius."

As we emerged from the woods onto my lawn, Derek asked, "You going to school tomorrow?"

I shrugged. "I don't want to fall behind in my learning. So, you know, yeah, I'll be there, I think. I might sleep out here, though."

My phone rang. Hawken.

"Hi, Tim Hawken."

"I'm sorry he hit you." No hello or anything. "What's wrong with that kid? Why would he hit you?"

Derek patted my shoulder and jabbed his thumb at his car.

"Hawken, hold on a second." Derek ignored my out-stretched hand and hugged me good-bye. I hoped my parents were watching from the window.

"Sorry, Hawken," I said as Derek got in his car. "So, I thought you said Mark was okay with your brother."

"I thought he *was* okay with Patrick. In fact, I called Patrick a little bit ago to tell him about all of this and I said, 'Mark's been fine around you, right?' And he goes, 'I don't know. We've never had that much to say to each other.'"

"It's easy to misjudge people, I'm learning."

"I told my mom what happened, and she said she won't let him back in the house. She also offered to call your parents to, you know, talk about, uh, what to do with a gay son and all." And then he started laughing that scratchy laugh of his. "Sorry. For real. She offered to call. You want her to?"

I hesitated. "You're a jackass. Let me get a read on the situation, but tell your mom I said thank you. I'll let you know. My mom didn't take the news all that well today, and I sort of bolted out of my house."

"Holy smokes! You ran away? Where are you?"

"On my driveway."

He laughed harder this time.

"I'll see you tomorrow, dude. Thanks again."

He hung up, still laughing, but I pretended to still be on the phone as I walked into my house. Rex and my parents were in the kitchen.

"Yeah, yup," I said into the dead receiver as I walked past them all.

"What happened to your eye?" shouted Rex.

"I got in a fight," I said over my shoulder as I grabbed a package of mixed vegetables from the freezer.

"Did you win?" he gasped.

"Nobody won," shot my mother.

Letting the comment slide, I walked out of the kitchen, up to Luke's room, and called Topher. My dad peeked in, where I lay on the bed relating the day's events, and gave a little nod and wave.

I didn't come down for dinner that night, and nobody came up to get me. I don't know if it was my mom or my dad or Rex who opened my door around 9:30, but I'd already crawled into bed and pretended to be asleep. I got up in the middle of the night and scribbled Derek a letter.

Tuesday, June 7th

Derek,

It's 2:15 a.m. I was thinking back to our conversation earlier, when you pointed out that we've been talking about girls since we were twelve and I've known the whole time that I'm gay. And you were sort of right, sort of wrong. I knew I liked boys. But somehow I managed to convince myself that liking boys didn't mean I was gay. I know it doesn't make much sense, but I believed it.

I guess it was in middle school that I started figuring out that I like boys. Remember that kid Charlie? I can't think of his last name, but he was in our eighth-grade class for a few months, and he had brilliant blue eyes. I'm sure that helps you out. Anyway, I remember Charlie standing near my locker after school talking to Julie Taber, a girl I knew I should like because she was hot, and I couldn't stop staring at him. Man, he had great eyes. I remember it really clearly. He was wearing a blue and black rugby shirt. He was chatting away with Julie, and I felt all sorts of jealous, and then I suddenly realized that my jealousy was toward her, not him. I wasn't jealous that he was going to get the girl; I was jealous that she was going to get the boy. I remember that dawning on me and feeling sort of sick to my stomach. I turned away and stared down the hallway in the other direction, my books scattered around my feet. I think I probably started drinking heavily right about then. Aaahaha . . . no wait, actually, that's probably true. Hmm. Interesting. Then again, you were drinking with me, so what's your excuse?

Anyway, I didn't have any trouble knowing which girls to like. It's not as though I couldn't tell who was pretty. So it hasn't been tough hiding. I don't feel like I've been lying to anyone, though. I mean, since I was little, everyone's told me that I like girls. Think about it—even when you're in kindergarten, there are all sorts of messages that eventually you'll grow up to like girls. Man, when you're barely able to walk people make these cutesy comments about your girlfriends and how you're going to be a lady killer and all sorts of crap like that. You were an ugly little kid, Derek, so perhaps you didn't get that sort of attention, but I've always been told that I'm straight. And that's the story I was trying to make happen. I didn't come up with the lie. It wasn't mine. They handed the lie to me, and I tried like hell to make it work for a while.

No one meant any harm, but I've spent some long nights unable to sleep, worrying about how it's all going to work out and blaming myself for being some sort of pervert. You know, I was lying in bed at night worrying when I was in, like, eighth grade. That ain't right.

Okay. It's now 3:30. There was a lot of choosing words and staring out the window. No moose out there tonight, by the way. I should probably actually send this letter. Hate to break the streak, though.

Nighty night.

James

CHAPTER 23

The next morning I stayed up in my room until I heard Derek's *beep-beep* from the driveway, then I ran down the stairs and shouted "later" back at the kitchen as I flew out the front door. Derek had in-school suspension for punching Mark, so I promised to get him a couple of books in case they let him read. In the library, I grabbed him a couple by Vonnegut, his new favorite, and found him in the main office, waiting to hear where he'd be spending the day. Mark was slouched not far away, arms folded, half-asleep.

"Hey, man," I said.

No response from Mark.

"Hey, Mark!" I called.

He raised his eyebrows and turned slowly toward me.

"Hey, can you give me the other letters back now?"

He just stared at me blankly.

"Whatever letters you still have. Can I have them back? It's not like they're going to surprise anyone at this point, right?"

He squinted at me, shook his head, and turned away again.

"He's wicked hungover," whispered Derek.

Of course he was. I'd have to come back and ask him again later.

I went straight to English, my first-period class that day. Breyer was reading the *New York Times* on his laptop, and he grinned as I came in. "Hey, it's your fifteen minutes of fame, James!" He rapped the screen with a pencil. "Front page of the paper." Four other kids were already in the room, none of them my good friends. One of them managed a weak "hey" and a smile.

Without even throwing my backpack on a chair, I crouched next to Breyer to see my story. It was a photograph of the star center for the Boston Bruins, his arms raised after scoring in overtime, his eye blackened. I smiled and shook my head.

"He has more teeth than you, but still. There's a resemblance. Wait, there's more." He toggled screens to a blank document and typed:

A few things:

(1) I'm sorry you got punched. But the black eye does sort of suit you.

(B) If anyone gives you trouble today, I will pick up where Derek left off.

I chuckled nervously.

A group of kids walked in loudly and then fell silent when they saw me.

Breyer typed, *Come by for ten minutes during lunch?*

I nodded and muttered, "Yeah, yeah."

Hawken waltzed in just then. "Hi, Breyer." He ruffled my hair as he passed. "Looking good, Liddell!" Everyone cracked up and started to breathe normally.

I don't know if kids had warmed up or woken up or calmed down or what by the end of first period, but they started to speak to me in the halls between classes. Kids on my soccer team stopped to ask questions I knew they knew the answer to. A couple just patted me on the back without a word. The baseball team's best pitcher grabbed my arm as I passed him. "That's messed up, James. Mark hitting you. It's messed up. I've never liked that kid. No offense, Hawken. I got a black eye once when I was a freshman. Took like two weeks to get better."

Farther down the hall, two sophomore girls stopped us and insisted on inspecting the damage. They offered to put glitter makeup on my black eye. "It'll make you feel better."

"It'll make me get hit again."

Hawken asked to see the glitter options. They dug five or six bottles out of their purses, all with ridiculous names. "This one's called No Nonsense and this one's called So Maintenance."

"See, this has always been a big question for me," Hawken sighed. "Am I more No Nonsense or am I So Maintenance? I can never decide."

Theresa appeared just then. "This one," she said, pointing to the blue glitter. "It'll bring out your eyes."

"You think?" Hawken inspected the bottle. "Liddell? Second opinion?"

"Yes. The blue."

"OK. Ladies, next time, when I have more time, I will take the blue. Thank you." The girls looked disappointed but they laughed, packed up their bottles, and took off.

"Listen, James," Theresa said, putting a hand on my arm. "Can you come over to my house after school? Kim's going to be there."

"Yeah, sure, I guess so."

"Perfect." And she started down the hall.

"What about me?" called Hawken. "I get no invite?"

Theresa turned. "I thought we were hanging out later on, like, at seven?"

Hawken shrugged. "Yeah. But I want to hang out, like, now."

Theresa continued down the hall, waving over her shoulder.

"You guys are going to talk about me, huh? That's why I'm not invited."

"Yeah, probably. Can you give me a ride over there?"

Breyer was scribbling on student essays when I found him during lunch. "Oh, good," he gasped when I walked in, and he slumped in his chair. "Rescue me from these. How you feeling?"

"Fine." I closed the door behind me and sat on a desk in the front row. "But you knew that I got hit before you saw me. How did you hear about it?"

"Facebook." He laughed when he saw my mouth fall open. "No, the copier. It's an amazing contraption: it spits out double-sided, stapled, hole-punched copies and enough corrosive gossip to make you never want to work here again."

"Word travels fast," I said lamely.

"Small school in a small town." He shrugged. "Tough place to keep secrets. When I first moved here, an old timer gave me some sound advice." He dropped into a Vermont accent. "You might as well tell everyone everything 'bout yourself right now, because what we don't know, Christ, we'll just make up."

"Yeah." I laughed. "It's true."

"And is what I heard true?" He inspected his pen as he spoke. "Did Mark punch you because he suspects you're gay?"

"Yeah."

"Has he explained what's given him that"—he hesitated—"impression?"

I shifted on the desk and stared out the window. "I started hanging out with this kid a few weeks ago. Dating, I guess, this kid. And this kid is a boy. He goes to another school."

Breyer laughed in relief and looked genuinely happy. "I'm not laughing at your predicament. I just thought we were going to have to tiptoe around the big question. I'm glad you feel okay talking about it."

"I'm getting there."

We talked for a bit about how Derek and Hawken were handling it.

"And you're okay at home? You spoke to your folks?"

"My mom's upset, I think. I mean I know she's upset. My dad—better. Surprised and all, I guess, but I don't know why, he was a little less shaken up by the news. It's funny. As much as I was scared to come out, part of me figured that everything would get better when I told the truth. But now that some of what I feared is actually happening, now that I'm actually getting hit and cursed at, I keep thinking: it was supposed to get easier. Coming out was supposed to make life easier."

"Well, you can always count on some people to be human and others to be monsters, right? That'll never change. That should never surprise you. So practice the smile that you're going to flash when other kids insult you. Arm yourself with a few clever one-liners. Remember Atticus Finch from freshman year? Carry a handkerchief in your back pocket so you can wipe the spit from your eye."

I smirked.

"I'm serious. This is the big fight you've been reading about. It's going on all around you. Right now. It doesn't matter whether you feel courageous. Make them believe you are. You win this one by acting like you're a happy, calm, strong kid, even when you don't feel that way."

The bell to change classes rang.

"Have you spoken to Aaron?" he asked.

"Yeah. Well, no. Not really. I need to talk to him, I guess."

"And listen to him. It would do you both good."

Hawken dropped me off at Theresa's after school. Kim was already sitting at the kitchen table when I walked in the front door.

"Whoa," I said. "You got here fast."

"Last period free," she explained. She gave me the kind of tight-lipped, nervous smile that I'd seen a lot over the past few weeks.

I checked my messages. Nothing from Topher. "How's Topher?" I heard myself ask. "I mean, everything's okay with Topher? With Topher and me, I mean? If something's up . . ."

Kim got up and hugged me. "You are ridiculous. Topher is fine. You guys are fine. But look at your poor eye." She kissed me on the cheek.

Theresa came into the kitchen behind us. "This isn't about Topher." She put her hands on my shoulders and gently pushed me down into a chair. "It's about you and me, and I asked Kim along because I know you guys get along, and she'll be able to keep everyone cool and . . ." Theresa waved her hands, trying to find the words.

"Well, cool and on the path to a good friendship again," said Kim. "That's all this is about. You and Theresa were such good friends for so long, and it would be terrible if all that ended over some . . . misunderstandings."

"Oh," I said, brightening. "I thought you had awful news. Yeah, I'm all for staying friends. I know I haven't handled everything great recently, but it's been pretty confusing and stressful. I never wanted us to stop being friends."

"Exactly." Theresa put a glass of water in front of me and sat down across the table. "It's been confusing and stressful for me, too, James."

I nodded emphatically. "Totally. I can imagine."

"And you know, you do stupid things when you're confused and stressed. You think you're doing the right thing—"

"Oh, believe me. I hear you. I know." I was about to list half a dozen examples from my own life over the past six months, but Theresa kept talking.

"Sometimes you do something stupid, and . . . and you can't take it back, and there's nothing you can do about it, and even saying sorry sounds just completely inadequate."

I stopped nodding.

She reached into a bag looped over the chair, pulled out six sheets of paper, and placed them in front of me. My handwriting. "I'm so sorry, James." She turned away from me.

My phone dropped from my hand onto the ground. I wanted to be sick. "You said you didn't do it," I whispered, and then a little louder, "You *swore* you didn't do it."

No response.

I stood up. "Why couldn't you come clean when I asked you the first two times? Why didn't you just tell the truth when I asked you point-blank?"

"Okay," Kim interjected. "I think this is where I come in to help you both stay on the sunny path back to friendship."

"Screw that, Kim," I said, without turning from Theresa. "Do you have any idea what the last few weeks have been like for me?"

"I said that I'm sorry."

"Why aren't you crying this time? There have been tears every time I handle something badly, and now when you tell me that you went out of your way to humiliate me and hurt me—"

"I was trying to help you!" she yelled.

"No yelling," said Kim.

"Help me? Are you out of your mind?"

"The only two people I mailed letters to were Hawken and Aaron. No one else." She tapped the stack of letters. "I actually thought you and Hawken would be great together. And Aaron, I figured you could at least be friends. He needed to hear what you wrote, anyway."

She had lost her mind. "Theresa, you broke into my desk and stole the most personal things I've ever written. And you probably read a lot more than what you took. What kind of twisted logic makes you think that's okay?"

"Because I knew you were lying to me. It was the only way I could know for sure that what I knew was true *was* true."

"Oh, that makes a ton of sense," I scoffed. I pictured myself lying under Mark's bed in the dark, listening to his dad's phone call. I slouched in my chair, crossed my arms. "Are there more? Do you have any others?"

No, she didn't. She promised. No one spoke for a while. There's a clock in Theresa's kitchen that actually ticks. I'd never noticed it before.

"Well, look," Kim said. "A lot's been shared much more quickly than I think anyone was prepared for. Maybe it'd be good if I just summarize the concerns I've heard from each of you."

I couldn't help smirking. "Kim, have you taken a class in this?"

She giggled. "I watched a YouTube video on mediation last night."

When she finished reviewing our points, she asked if either of us had anything to add.

"I just want to be friends again," said Theresa.

Kim looked at me for a response.

I let out a long breath. "Can you give me a ride home?" I asked.

As we reversed down Theresa's driveway, Kim said, "You know, she really does just want to be friends again, James."

"If you'd read my letter to Hawken, you'd understand where I'm coming from. It was a crazy thing for her to do. Totally crazy."

"Agreed. But she *was* a little crazy at the time. She's back to normal Theresa now, right?"

I shook my head. "Remains to be seen," I muttered, flipping through the letters Theresa had returned. One to a cute boy in my tenth-grade math class. One to Mark from last summer, forecasting prison in his future. Four more to teammates and classmates, filled with nasty abuse that I'd never have been able to take back. It could've been worse—Theresa could have royally screwed me—but I wasn't about to thank her.

When I arrived home, my mom was sitting at the kitchen table, typing on her laptop. "Hello!" she sang without looking at me. Clearly she was trying to be cheerful. "How was your day?" I'd prepared myself to grab an apple and head straight up to my room without speaking to her, but instead, I guess we were just going to pretend that nothing had happened.

"Good," I replied, scratching beneath my black eye. "My day was fine. You?"

"Busy. You?"

"Sure, busy, I guess."

"They're still assigning you a lot of homework?"

"Yeah," I lied. "I'm going to go get started on it."

"Did you ice your eye today? It looks better," she claimed, even though she still hadn't looked at me.

"I did, yeah," I lied again. I stood there for a few seconds, then went up to my room and slept until dinner.

Conversation at dinner was equally polite and stiff.

"James, would you pass your brother the kale?"

"I didn't ask for the kale. I can't handle any more kale."

And thirty silent seconds later, "James, did you submit your history term paper yet?"

"Yup. It's all done. I turned it in last week."

"Well, that must be a relief."

"Yeah, what a weight off my mind."

It was as if we were new colleagues in an office.

"Why'd Mark hit you?" Rex asked suddenly.

"Because he's a . . ." I reconsidered. I tried answering exactly as my mom would have done. "Because he's a very confused young man."

Rex furrowed his brow. My mother chewed with raised eyebrows.

"He's got a lot of anger and he likes to punch people," my father explained.

Rex was satisfied.

Later on that night, my dad leaned against my bedroom

doorframe. "How you feeling?"

"It still hurts."

"Yeah, I bet it does. I'm sorry. And how's your eye feeling?"

I swallowed hard. "Hurts."

"You want ice? I'm not sure it will do you any good at this point, but do you want some?"

"I'm good."

The championship game of the indoor season was on Thursday evening against Done Right Plumbing, the team with the goalie I'd scuffled with earlier in the season. I invited Topher, even though my dad would probably recognize him on the sidelines and feel obligated to say hello, and it would be very awkward for everyone. But Topher had a rehearsal that he couldn't miss. I was kind of relieved. *No fightin',* he texted me that evening.

When Hawken and I arrived at the field, Coach Greschner did a double take. Hawken saw him coming and stepped in front of me. "Tell him everything," he whispered. "Now's your chance to stop worrying about that conversation. Tell him. If you don't, I will."

"No," I whispered fiercely. "How am I going to bring that up?"

"I got punched in the eye because I'm gay. Done."

Greschner reached us. "What in the world happened to you, Liddell?" he cried. He was smiling but looked concerned.

"I'd prepared my Leave-that-Goalie-Alone speech and here you are, beaten up before the whistle."

"Coach, let's talk over here," Hawken said, nodding toward an empty corner near a drink machine. I followed them over and leaned against the wall.

Greschner wasn't smiling anymore, and he looked so worried that I had to take a deep breath to keep it together. He put his hand on my shoulder. "What happened?"

"I got hit," I said. "I got punched by this kid at school." I looked at Hawken, and he frowned just enough to remind me of his threat. "And he hit me because I'm gay. So that's what happened. I got punched because this kid found out that I'm gay."

"What?" whispered Greschner.

Oh God, I thought. *Here we go.*

"What?" he repeated. "He punched you? Did you annihilate him? Hawken, did you and Derek find and kill the son of—"

Hawken hugged him, cutting him off. "Perfect," I heard him say into our coach's shirt. I laughed nervously, and Greschner looked uncomfortable but patted Hawken on the back. When Hawken let go, he didn't even look at me. He just walked away to join the guys warming up on the field.

"So that's it," I said, my hands on my head as if I were under arrest. "I can see okay to play and all. I hope it doesn't, you know, change anything."

"If you can see okay, it doesn't change anything, right?"

"No, I meant, you know, the other—"

"Don't insult me," he interrupted. And then he grabbed the back of my neck in one hand, the way I do to Rex, and started walking me to the field. "You think the guys on the school team know?"

"Oh. Dude." My laugh came out like a sob. "They all know. Believe me, everybody knows."

"Excellent." He pushed me in the back. "So go score some goals."

I felt jittery with relief and excitement, like a newborn colt anxious to try out its legs. When I jogged onto the field, kids on Done Right Plumbing yelled to their goalie, pointing at me and my black eye, and laughed. At the coin toss, their captain shook his head at me and said, "What up, thug?"

The ref put up his finger. "No nonsense between you boys tonight, you hear me? Clean playing and have fun."

And we did. At least, my team did. There are games when it seems like you and your teammates are telepathic. Every pass connects like there's metal in the ball leather and magnets in your boots. One person's magic seems to cast a spell on everybody else. Four minutes into the game, Hawken beat three kids along the boards and drilled the ball into the top left corner of the goal. Two minutes later, a normally flat-footed kid on our defense spun his way around a couple of players and fed me a perfect ball, which I tucked beneath the diving goalie. I hadn't had so much fun on the field in a long, long time. The best moment came when the goalie shoved me after my second goal, and I stumbled, but walked away, never even looking at him. He got a yellow card, and his coach yanked him from the game. Our own goalie lived up to his nickname, Señor Fuego, and Hawken and I each scored twice. We won 6–2. On the way home, we cranked Queen and sang out the car windows, cracking up each time we missed the high notes.

We ate dinner late that night after I came home from the game. My mom distracted herself by talking about her plans for Rex's summer. "I'm going to see if I can still get you into a soccer camp"—she twirled her fork in the air—"or a baseball camp. Wouldn't you like that?"

"Baseball? I don't play baseball. I just want to hang out."

She wasn't listening, though, and she wasn't actually going to sign him up for baseball. She was just making noise.

I tried to redirect the conversation. "Luke comes home this weekend, huh?"

Rex heard only the word *weekend*. "Can my friend Jack come over this weekend?" he asked. "I want to show him the fort."

"You have a fort?" I asked. I wanted to see the fort.

"Can he come over?" he asked again, ignoring me.

"Of course," my mother replied. "You have a soccer game on Saturday, so Sunday's better. Do we need to pick him up?"

"His mom can drop him off, I think. He doesn't have a dad. And his brother is, you know—got hit in the head."

"Jack Foster," my mother said.

"Yeah, Jack Foster."

Aaron Foster's younger brother. Small school, small town.

My mom nodded slowly at her plate while she chewed. "Would you mind if I invited Jack's mother for lunch?" she asked after a minute.

Rex looked from her to our dad to me, clearly unsure who she was asking. "Sure," he said finally. "I don't care."

My mom looked at me. "We should invite Aaron, too."

I couldn't imagine what my mother thought she was going to say to the Fosters, but I nodded. "Yeah, sure. Talk to his mom."

When I came down to the kitchen later that evening, my mom was crying silently while folding laundry with my father. She left as I walked in. My dad tried to smile at me. "Hey, Champ," he said. He never called me Champ, but it was nice of him anyway. I leaned against the doorframe.

"When Luke comes home this weekend," he began, "why don't you two go hike Camel's Hump while your mom and I take Rex down to his soccer game in Springfield. You know how Luke gets when he has to watch you guys play soccer."

It's true. Luke always ends up in a crummy mood when he has to stand bored on the sidelines. But that's not why my dad was suggesting the hike.

"It's been a while since either of you went up there," he continued. "And, well, we haven't said a word to Luke yet.

We figured you'd want to talk to him yourself."

"Yeah. Cool. I do. Thanks."

"And maybe you two can figure out how to break the news to Rex."

I nodded, turned quickly, and walked back down the hall to the stairs.

"I didn't mean *break the news*," my dad said behind me. "Explain things to Rex. That's all I meant."

CHAPTER 24

The last half day of school, a Friday, was a scorcher. In most of my classes, we just sort of hung out, panting and sweating. But Breyer made us write. I used the time to write the letter I'd composed while lying sleepless in bed the night before.

> *Friday, June 10th*
>
> *Theresa,*
>
> *We walked past each other without a word a little while ago, and now I'm in English class, scribbling my final "quick-write" of junior year. We're supposed to be writing about what we learned this year. In fifteen minutes.*

One thing I learned: It turns out that a black eye hurts
a hell of a lot less than being betrayed. Than being lied to.
Manipulated. Whatever you want to call it.

I suppose in your head, we're even on that score. I'm
sorry you felt like you had to do something so desperate
to deal with the situation. I'm sorry I left you feeling that
crazy. Although I'll never understand how you could think
it was okay to do what you did to me, I guess you'll never
understand why I let you believe that things between us might
work out one day. All I can say is that part of me thought it
was true. I should've been more honest with you about the
part of me that knew it wasn't.

I wish I could take credit for being mature enough to look
at all of this from your perspective, but Topher's the one who
talked me through it. We spoke on the phone for a long time
last night. I should've listened to him weeks ago, as he pointed
out several times, and explained everything to you.

I told Topher that I was trying to figure out how to tell
Hawken that he should have nothing to do with you, but
Topher argued that you're probably not as rotten as the past
few weeks suggest. You probably only temporarily have a rancid
soul. His words, by the way. He reminded me that I used to
think you were great and that I had good reasons to think so,
and he made me admit that there's a chance you'll turn back
into a real person sometime soon, especially if you're given some
encouragement. He suggested I say nothing to Hawken and
instead say all this to you.

So here you have it. I hope it helps bring the real Theresa back.

Happy Summer Vacation,
James

When Breyer called time, I tore the letter from my notebook and folded it into quarters. On my way to my next class, I slipped it into Theresa's locker.

Topher came to my house that afternoon. I'd sent him a photo of my black eye, but we hadn't hung out since the day before I got punched. I was counting on my parents working late and Rex going to a friend's house.

I led Topher up to my bedroom, shut the door, and tackled him onto my bed. "Congrats, James Liddell." He laughed. "You made it!"

I broke our kiss. "Made it where?" I whispered, running my hands up his arms.

"Wherever we are. This place without secrets. It feels good, right?"

I put my chin on his chest. "I have never, ever felt this free."

The sun was still a new thing, so we went outside, took off our shirts, and lounged on the back porch. Twenty minutes later I heard my mom's car pulling into the garage and Rex tearing into the house.

"Oh, man, are you kidding me?" I groaned.

Topher put his shirt back on.

"Dude, don't," I whispered. "We're just lying here."

I could see my mom enter the kitchen, glance outside, and freeze. I waved. She fixed her hair and put on a tight smile as she walked to the porch door.

"You remember Topher, Mom."

Topher stood. "Hello, Mrs. Liddell. Good to see you."

"Hi," she managed. "James, put your shirt on please, dear." She smiled at me as though she expected me to agree that she was being perfectly reasonable.

"What? Mom, no. It's like a hundred degrees."

She stood there for a moment, carefully choosing her next words.

Just then, Rex pushed past her wearing only bright green shorts and sunglasses with fluorescent blue frames. He pulled his chair right up next to Topher's and sprawled in it. Topher had to shift his leg so their feet wouldn't touch.

"Rex," my mother began, uncertainly.

"He's fine, Mom. Leave him alone."

She looked at the sky. "Wear sunscreen," she said finally, and shut the door.

Topher and I took off a little while after that. Normally, my mom wants to know where I'm going and when I'll be home. This time, I just shouted toward the kitchen, "See you later!" She looked up from her laptop to watch us leave, but didn't say a word. We drove to a swimming hole over in New Hampshire. Thankfully, we didn't know any of the other kids leaping from the cliffs and splashing around. We sprawled on a high rock and basked in the sun until Topher looked at his watch and yelped. He was supposed to go to dinner with his parents, and I knew I should be home to greet Luke.

That evening, before Luke arrived, I was inspecting my black eye in the bathroom mirror when Rex appeared in the doorway. "How come Mark punched you?" he asked.

I answered without looking at him. "We already talked about this, remember? Why are you bringing it up?"

"Because when Dad got home tonight, I heard him telling Mom about how he talked to Mark's dad."

I turned and stared at him. "And what did Dad say?"

"He said that he told Mark's father to teach Mark how to control his temper or something like that, and Mark's dad said, 'You aren't in any position to tell anyone how to raise a son.'"

My mouth felt dry. "And then what?"

"And then Mom noticed me under the kitchen table and got all mad and told me to go outside."

"That's all you heard?"

"That's all I heard."

I shook my head. Why would my dad do that? He'd just set me up for more trouble.

Rex gripped the sides of the bathroom door and leaned forward, arms at full length. "Are you scared?" he asked.

"Of what?"

"Of getting punched in the face again?"

"No," I lied.

He was still leaning in, and now he squinted at me.

"Rex, don't worry. I'm not going to get into any more fights. Mark's not going to hit me again."

"How do you know?"

"Because he's not allowed to," I said.

He pulled himself back to standing up. "That doesn't make any sense," he said as he disappeared down the hall.

Camel's Hump rises about halfway between Montpelier and Burlington. The best time I'd ever had up on that mountain was on a Friday in October during my freshman year, when Luke was a junior. For some reason, my father decided to take us hiking instead of sending us to school. My mom wasn't so pleased, but we were ecstatic—until my dad announced that we were leaving at four thirty in the morning. We started climbing in the frozen dark, up through endless switchbacks. When we scrambled up the rock and ice of that last few hundred yards, that last steep pitch where any bad step could send you tumbling headfirst down the granite, the sun had just peeked above the horizon and golden light seeped across frosted, fiery maples and green spruce. No one spoke once we were above tree line. There wasn't even much wind that day. We were the only ones up there, crunching granola bars and apples, enjoying the cold, inhaling that long view across impossibly colored hills.

That's the kind of morning I looked forward to: alone with Luke on the summit and the whole world feeling so right that my words couldn't break a thing.

I underestimated how important my dad's four thirty departure time was to the success of that previous expedition. The morning Luke and I hiked, we didn't leave the house until after 9:00 a.m., when the first hordes were probably already climbing back down the trail. Conversation in the car was one-sided. I asked questions to keep him talking about his own life over the past few months instead of him asking me about mine. When he'd arrived home the night before, at almost midnight, I told him I got the black eye from soccer. My parents must've understood that I didn't want to get into it right then. All the way up 89 North, during the drive to the mountain, I was building up my courage.

When we had to park in the overflow lot, I should have abandoned my plan. I should have known it was a crummy idea. But I'd spent so much energy gathering the guts, and I remember thinking, *Screw it, I'm telling him anyway.*

On the way up the trail, Luke was practically panting, so we couldn't talk much about anything until the first time we stopped for water. "Did they make this mountain steeper?" he managed.

At the top, there must have been thirty people perched on those rocks. Clouds ripped past in the north, but it was sunny and clear in the southeast, back toward our home. I hardly looked at the views, though. I was searching for a space to hide from the wind, eat my sandwich, and possibly ruin my relationship with my brother forever.

Half-sheltered from the gusts by a couple of big rocks, we ate in a little hollow. Luke was chewing his sandwich with his eyes closed, when I thought, *Just start talking.* As Topher had promised, starting the conversation had become easier with practice.

"Dude," I began formally, and pulled my fleece collar up against the deafening wind. "I have to talk to you about something."

"What?" he shouted back, cupping a hand to his ear without opening his eyes.

"I have to talk to you about something!"

He opened his eyes and must have seen that I looked all serious. "Oh, yeah?" he shouted, taking another bite of his sandwich. "Did I do something wrong or did you?"

I shook my head and laughed. My legs were pulled against my chest and I wrapped my arms around my shins. Dropping my head against my knees, I took a deep breath and peeked up at him.

He'd been lying across a slab of granite, but now he sat up, looking very concerned. "Hey. What's up?"

I tried to smile. "So," I started, "there's a reason that I don't want to go out with Theresa."

A big gust of wind picked up right then, but I could see Luke say, "Yeah?"

I could hear Topher urging me, "Just say it." The wind fell silent just as I yelled, "Because I'm gay!"

Feet scuffled on the rock behind me, and I hugged my legs a little tighter.

Luke looked stunned for a moment, then shifted on his rock, rubbed his black woolen hat so that his eyes disappeared beneath it. He wasn't exactly frowning, but I was waiting for him to start smiling a little, and he didn't.

"For real?" he finally asked, pushing his hat back from his eyes.

I nodded and put my forehead on my knees.

"No, seriously, man. For *real* for real?"

I didn't say anything.

"What, you and Derek?"

"Really?" I said, looking up again. "You think me and Derek? He's like my third brother, Luke. No, not me and Derek."

It wasn't the way I'd expected the conversation to go, but then again I shouldn't have been surprised. No one has ever called Luke predictable.

"Tim Hawken. It's Tim Hawken."

"What? No." My voice sounded a little desperate, and I stood up.

"Dude, sit back down." Now he smiled, but barely. "Come on. I'm trying to make sense of this. You, it never even crossed my mind. Rich, I always figured. You've met my pal Rich up at school. He never talked about girls, but he didn't actually tell me he was gay until one night when we were skinny-dipping. At least you managed to find a moment when we're both wearing pants to tell me that you like naked boys."

I looked over my shoulder. The wind had died completely, and a family of four was eating lunch on the other side of our rock. The parents did not look up, but their sons stared at us, their apples arrested at chin level. Neither of them was much younger than me. I motioned for Luke to drop his voice.

"How long have you known?" he asked, just as loudly as before.

I didn't answer. I was stuffing trail mix and a half-eaten sandwich back in my pack.

"Dude, how long have you known?"

I hoisted my pack on my shoulders.

"Come on, James," he spoke softly now. "Sit back down."

I started for the trail.

"James!"

I took long strides across the granite, but he still caught up quickly and put his hand on my shoulder.

"Dude, stop."

He put his arms around me as I turned toward him, and I buried my face in his shoulder.

"I don't give a shit," Luke whispered. "You freaking moron."

I nodded into his jacket. I couldn't see them, so it was easier to ignore the dozens of people who must have been watching us stand in that embrace. We stood like that for a long time. Eventually, I took a deep breath and rubbed my runny nose into Luke's fleece collar until he pushed me away.

"I cannot freaking believe you just did that," he said, inspecting the damage.

I snuffled, wiped my eyes, and, turning slowly in place, tried to burn the sweep of blurry mountains into my memory.

"Dad know?"

I nodded.

"Mom?"

"Yup."

"What fun. Rex?"

"No."

"Good, I want to be there for that one. Theresa?"

"Oh, yeah." I tried to laugh. "I'll tell you about it."

And we started to walk. Just as we were about to enter the narrow, roped descent from the summit, a pretty blond girl and her boyfriend, a cute kid with big brown eyes, stepped past us. They were about Luke's age, and he turned to watch the girl after she passed. "So, all these years," he said once we were alone, "you've pretended to like her when you've actually liked him, huh?"

I didn't respond.

"That is rough, man. That is rough."

Luke whistled and moaned at the right moments in my story as we descended through spruce and into groves of maple and ash. "Tim Hawken?" he asked again when I said I had a boyfriend.

"You don't know him," I replied.

After we'd thrown our backpacks in the car, I stood on one leg with my other foot pulled up behind my back, stretching my quad. Luke stepped forward without a word, put a leg behind mine and pushed me onto the ground. He shrugged as he looked down at me and said, "I'm sorry I always make life harder than it should be. It's my job. I'm your older brother."

I scissor-kicked him so that he fell onto the gravel and into the path of an oncoming Jeep. Satisfied that his palms and knees were scraped and bleeding, I stood and waved to the glaring driver as she steered around us. *The whole summer's ahead,* I thought.

"So, you haven't told Rex yet, huh?" Luke asked when we were back on the highway. "He knows the word *gay* and all. I've heard him say it."

"Yeah, I know. I need to tell him soon. He'll hear about it from other kids if I don't."

"We should talk to him this weekend. Let's sit him down and explain it all. You can draw him diagrams, stick figures."

"This teddy bear is named Johnny," I said. "This teddy bear is named Timmy."

"See, you are in love with Tim Hawken. I knew it."

"Why do you think I have a thing for Hawken?"

"Because he's cute, dude. I'm secure enough to say that. He's a good-looking kid, and he's wicked funny and nice. Why *wouldn't* you have a crush on Hawken?"

"Okay, fine. I've always had a crush on Hawken."

Luke banged the steering wheel and laughed. "Man, I

knew it! I'm good, right? Tell me he's gay, too! I love that kid! Tell me he's gay, too!"

"No go. Very straight."

"Aw, man." Luke sank a little into his seat, shaking his head. "I thought all the nice guys were gay. That's what the girls always tell me. But girls are liars. What's your boy's name again? *Toker*?"

"Topher."

"*Topher*? What kind of name is Topher? It sounds like a carnival food. Fried topher. Sugar-dipped topher."

"Didn't you date a girl straight-up named Candy one time?"

"Candy, yeah. Not even Candace. Her parents were very nice and dumb and not much older than us."

"Topher's short for Christopher."

"Chris is short for Christopher."

"Yeah, but everyone's called Chris."

"This kid really goes out of his way to be different, huh?"

"He's very normal. You'll like him."

"Soccer player?"

"Theater."

"Ha! Normal and into theater. Right. Invite him over tonight."

"No, it'll be awkward for him. Just him and the Liddell family."

"Well, let's invite a bunch of people over. Get on your phone and start calling folks."

"What about Mom and Dad?"

"Yeah, invite them, too, I guess."

Luke called up his buddy Garret, and he beat us to our house. Garret had started working for his dad's contracting company right out of high school. His family has lived in these hills so long that there are roads named after them.

"James is gay," Luke said matter-of-factly as we shook hands by Garret's truck on the driveway. "For real. Gay. This is the Get the Parents Used to It Party. So just act normal."

"Always knew it," muttered Garret, and he yanked down the brim of his NASCAR hat so we wouldn't see him grinning at his own joke.

Derek and Hawken arrived a little while later.

"Hey, Theresa said she couldn't come," said Hawken with a shrug. "I don't know. She was super sweet all day and now suddenly she can't hang out. Weird."

I just nodded, kept my mouth shut.

Kim and Topher showed up just after I got out of the shower. I greeted them on the driveway in bare feet, and I led them around the side of the house to the porch so they were suddenly there, settled in with everyone and laughing when my parents came outside. Pleasant hellos all around, but my mother's smile was tense, and when Topher stood up to shake hands with my father, they both had the stiff seriousness of bankers. My mom asked Topher about the play. He said opening night was in a couple of weeks and rehearsals were going well, thank you. She said she was glad to hear it. Then, as Rex lobbed pinecones onto the porch, my parents went back inside.

But I could see them glancing out onto the porch from where they sat in the kitchen. They saw Derek with his arm around Hawken. They watched Garret talk to Topher about nothing at all. They saw Kim sitting on my lap, and Luke with his arm around Topher. Eventually, the conversation turned to the next day's race, the Mud 10K.

"Brutally early start," I complained. "Eight a.m. I have a rule about not running before noon."

"I have a rule about not waking up before noon," said Luke. "Have fun."

Hawken and Topher were in, though. Derek was sorry he couldn't go. He was handling his parents carefully since the fight, and they hadn't been all that sympathetic when he asked to skip church to watch Mark and me race.

"They don't want me getting into anything with Mark again," Derek explained.

There was talk of hiking up to the boulder in the meadow, but then it got late and Kim had to split, and she was Topher's ride, so everyone filed down the porch steps. Topher kissed me on the lips as he left, and then so did Hawken, and Luke sighed, "Ahh, there's still hope for you two."

CHAPTER 25

It poured that night, but it was clear again by morning. The race took place in the hills by a nearby lake. Summer camps along the shore were just stirring to life. A group of scruffy college kids with rakes trudged along the roadside, and canvas tents already clustered on the hillsides. The race registration site pointed out that most of Vermont's trails were dry enough for hiking and trail-running after Memorial Day. The Mud 10K, however, takes runners on paths that wind along high forest bogs, hence the mud in the race's name.

The starting line was in front of a long white-and-green house decorated schizophrenically with canoe paddles and snowshoes. A big map pinned to a wooden notice board showed the course following a gravel road for fifty yards, crossing a narrow little bridge, and then charging straight up a hill for half a mile. No turns. No rest. Then it veered into the woods onto a muddy roller-coaster single track, splashed for a couple of miles along high bogs, wound through thick hemlock groves, hooked up with the old gravel road again, and spat us back down the hill to the finish. Runners were invited to de-mud in the lake after the race, but not knowing that, I hadn't brought a towel.

A guy with a megaphone called: "Runners! The starting gun is in two minutes!"

"Whoa! I guess I'm not warming up." I took off my sweatshirt, and both Topher and Hawken reached for it. Hawken stepped back, hands up.

"Do you see Mark anywhere?" Topher asked me.

"Honestly, I haven't been looking for him. It's not like I'm going to speak to him or anything. I'll run, and we'll go home."

"Sounds good," said Topher. "Maybe he forgot, anyway. Maybe you can just relax and enjoy the scenery."

"Yeah. Yeah, maybe," I said, failing to keep a note of hope out of my voice.

"He's right there, you morons," said Hawken, nodding toward a field where runners were stretching and jogging in circles. Mark sat on the grass by himself, staring at the lake. He wasn't stretching or warming up, and he was so careful not to look in our direction that it was clear he had seen us, too. He wasn't smiling, but he wasn't frowning, either. It must've been painful for him to know that his former best friend, Hawken, stood so close by and didn't even want to talk to him. I thought back to what his dad had said about his mom. *He never hears back from her.* For a moment, I felt bad for the kid.

The man with a megaphone called: "Runners! Please come to the starting line! We have a few announcements, and then we'll be off!"

Pats on the back from Topher and Hawken and then I shuffled into the crowd of runners hopping in place, stretching their quads, setting their watches. The guys right around me had gray beards. I'd have to find someone else to pace me, I thought.

The course, the announcer assured us, was marked better than it had been the previous year. "Watch out for deep holes around the bogs," he warned. "Let's make this year the first without any trips to the hospital."

I looked back over my shoulder at Topher, wide-eyed. He shrugged and gave me a thumbs-up. Standing on my toes, I scanned the mass of runners and quickly located Mark, much closer to me than I'd expected, just a few yards to my left, the same distance from the starting line as I was. He saw me see him and looked away up the first long, steep hill.

Twitchy with adrenaline, I tried swinging my arms and accidentally hit the guys behind me and in front of me. Neither seemed to notice. Everyone was tense, waiting for the gun. I shook out my legs. Closed my eyes.

"Runners take your mark!"

I would lean forward at *Set.*

CRACK!

Where was the *Set?* We were already running, the crowd a weird amoeba, changing shape as it propelled itself forward, a few pieces breaking off and sliding away into the lead. The graybeards were keeping up with me, so I figured I'd pace myself with them for a while up the hill, then take off when we neared the top. The abandoned road was all ruts and rocks, and floods had exposed slabs of granite, so I had to watch the ground to keep my footing. Like goats, the graybeards climbed quickly and without losing breath. They knew the road well. I'd been trained in track to never look behind me in a race, but I glanced to my sides, and Mark wasn't there. Things were off to a good start. The hill was killing me, though. We weren't even a mile into the race, and I was already wishing we were done. I listened for the breathing of the graybeards. Winded, but still keeping pace. We'd run together long enough, I decided, and made my move, pulled ahead by a few yards and, feeling smug, imagined them cursing my youth. Then three of them, two on one side, one on the other, came even with me, and glided on past. I struggled to catch up again, but for the rest of the race I saw only their backs, far ahead. *They've been doping,* I told myself. I wrenched my guts up the final hundred yards of the hill by myself, gasping, keeping my pace by picturing Mark scrambling up the hill behind me.

At the top there was flat, open ground. Piles of rocks here, stacks of logs and tangles of brush there. Off to the right, bonfires had scorched a patch of ground encircled by stumps. The forest swallowed us up again on the other side of the clearing. A few hundred yards into the woods, a big white arrow limed on the dirt pointed us left onto a narrow trail that led through waist-high ferns, a strange fluorescent-green jungle in the dark woods. If I hadn't been keeping myself poised on the edge of unbearable pain, I would've enjoyed that stretch.

I had been wondering how I would know that we'd reached the bogs, but you couldn't miss them. First, the air turned cool and smelled like wet dog, then the ground grew spongy and a little later gave way to black soup. The runner in front of me was wearing tiny blue shorts and trying to avoid the muddiest patches by running up along the edge of puddles. I slopped straight on through them, and when I saw the trail widen for thirty yards or so, I splashed past him, leaving him to tiptoe around the messy spots. I zeroed in on the next guy in an orange shirt ahead of me. I could hear Tiny Blue Shorts right behind me, breathing angrily. He dashed straight through the black mud now, and seethed just behind me for a couple of miles, all the way around the bogs.

When the trail turned to hard dirt again, Orange Shirt picked up the pace and I cursed under my breath. I wasn't sure if I could keep up, but I knew there was a hemlock grove, then a gravel road that was all downhill to the finish line. Sure enough, soon we were running under enormous hemlocks, and the trail turned soft beneath a blanket of needles. I caught up to Orange Shirt, stayed with him as though I had him on a leash. It sounded like Tiny Blue Shorts was still right behind me. Just as we reached the middle of the clearing at the top of the hill, the runner behind me pulled even. I resisted looking over at him, but out of the corner of my eye, I could see that his shorts were neither tiny nor blue. They were long and black. I glanced up.

Mark. He looked over at me quickly, and he managed a tiny smirk. I opened up my stride and dug in as we hit the downhill. There was no way to avoid the holes and ruts in the road, except by hurdling them. We passed Orange Shirt on either side, throwing ourselves forward so carelessly that I was sure I'd lose my footing, tumble, and skid across gravel into a ditch at the side of the road. Somehow we both stayed on our feet, gasping, arms flailing, the world a banging green blur. Mark pulled ahead. A hundred yards to go. My hands began to tingle and my head swam as we sprinted out of the woods onto the paved road lined with spectators who might have been cheering, but I couldn't hear them over the blood rushing through my head and my gasping breaths. All I could see was the finish line ahead and, just beyond my reach, the bigot who had belted me in the eye. Our names were shouted excitedly from a loudspeaker full of static, Mark's name first and then mine. When I caught him, I would grab his shirt and yank him to the ground. I was tightening every muscle and drawing even—I might've been screaming, the memory of that final stretch feels like screaming—and the finish line bounced closer as Mark pulled away again. I stretched my left arm toward him and then we were done, stumbling in the grass beyond the white line flanked by men in yellow jackets, and someone I didn't know thumped my back and yelled, "Courageous finish, son! So close!"

I staggered away from the crowd on shaky legs. It couldn't have happened this way. It wasn't supposed to happen this way. I closed my eyes, gasping, hands on my head, sweating and shivering. I walked way off across a field, clung to the chain-link of a baseball backstop, and stared out toward the lake. I wanted to drown the part of me who lost.

When I finally turned around, Topher and Hawken were walking toward me. Topher carried water and orange slices.

"Well, you were supposed to beat the bad guy," Hawken shouted when they were still twenty yards away.

I shook my head in disbelief. "It turns out he's a really fast bad guy," I answered when they were closer.

"Mark puked," Hawken said. "Right in front of a bunch of little kids. Typical."

"Do you want to jump in the lake?" asked Topher, eyeing my legs.

I looked down. They were caked in black mud up to my knees. "Nope," I said. "I just want to get out of here. I'll put my jeans back on before I get in the car."

Topher and Hawken traded stories about teachers all the way home, and I sat in the passenger seat, reading the label on my Gatorade bottle.

I'd been so close.

My father decided it would be best if my mom talked to Mrs. Foster by herself, and he told Luke he'd need his help to run a few errands. By the time I came home, he had made another one of his lists that took up the entire back of an envelope. They stuck around until the Fosters arrived at our front door.

Aaron had both ears pierced. Two little silver squares. He didn't wear earrings in school. The rest of his outfit: a white polo, blue baseball cap, khaki shorts, blue shoes with white soles, no socks. Very low-key for him. He gave me a hug and shook hands with everyone else.

I recognized Jack from Rex's soccer games and school plays, a wiry little athletic kid who didn't say much. He and Rex banged out the back door ten seconds after he'd walked in the front. I'd seen his mom around at school events, too. She was tall and thin, with high cheekbones. Her eyes were pale gray, and she didn't wear much makeup. One of her wrists jangled with copper-colored bracelets, and she had a lizard tattoo above her ankle. She took my hand in both of hers when I said hi. "So good to see you, James," she said quietly, and she wasn't being fake. She must have recognized me the way I recognized Jack. "Listen, you'll have to forgive me for what I said the night you called about Aaron. I was just so upset—"

"It's okay," I interrupted. "Really. Don't worry about it. I understand." I glanced at my mom, gave her a look meant to say *I'll explain later.*

"I've felt terrible about it. Anyway, you look great."

"Well . . ." My mom laughed.

"Even with the trophy." She touched her own right eye and smiled. "Dangerous is a good look for you."

"No missing teeth, at least." I shrugged. And then, I don't know why I said it: "No brain damage."

Aaron looked away.

"So nice to meet you." My dad came to the rescue. "Luke and I will be home around four," he told my mom. "James, give us a hand carrying this stuff to the car." Next to the garage door, he'd stacked a couple of big boxes bulging with old clothes for the Salvation Army. My mom led Aaron and his mom into the kitchen.

"I screwed that up," I said as I fought a box into the back of the car.

"You didn't screw up anything. Neither of you is missing teeth, and neither of you has brain damage. Now go play with your new best friend."

He cracked himself up.

Mr. Kelly was walking his dog past the bottom of the driveway as Luke backed the car onto the street. My dad lowered his window and shouted hello, but Mr. Kelly ignored him. I wondered if he had heard about me.

★ ★ ★

I found Aaron sitting in the middle of the deck, legs out-stretched, smiling into the sun. He looked like a much happier, much more relaxed kid than the one I knew in school. Our moms sat inside at the kitchen table, sipping iced tea.

"Your house is really nice," he said when he saw me.

"Thanks. All my hard work's paid off, I guess. Hey, I've never seen you with earrings. They new?"

"I just don't wear them to school. Why attract attention, you know?"

I nodded. I wanted to say that the earrings would attract less attention than some of his other fashion choices, but I didn't. I pulled his letter from my pocket, and he clapped excitedly. "Listen," I said, handing it to him. "I owe you an explanation about all this."

"Did you really write it?" he asked, folding it up and tucking it in his pocket.

"Yeah, I did."

"And everything you said is true?" He squinted up at me in the sun.

I nodded.

"Then don't bother with any explanation. Those are the only things I care about it. You have no idea how happy this letter made me. Don't say anything that might spoil that."

Suddenly it seemed possible to forgive Theresa. We might become friends again.

I sat down next to him. "I'm glad it made you happy,

dude. You know, I read it over again, and it's not much of an apology."

"It was more of an apology than anyone else has ever offered." He picked up a pinecone and began tearing it to pieces. "And I haven't always been the friendliest."

I laughed. "If anyone's been keeping score, I think my pals and I are way ahead in the Being Jerks category."

He threw the pinecone off the deck, into the yard. "I'm sorry about that time I said you smelled like a sneaker."

"What? I don't remember you saying that."

"Oh my God, yes you do! I said it right behind you in the hallway when we were freshmen. You had to have heard me. You turned around right away. I thought you were going to hit me."

"I swear I don't remember that." I laughed.

"Anyway, you've been nicer to me than some people were. Especially during that hellish week right before I got punched. You were never one of the worst."

It was a grim pardon.

"I called you a homo once," I said after a moment. "I remember it really clearly. You took my seat on the bus during that field trip to Montpelier when we were sophomores. I think I was probably trying to impress Mark. No, I know I was trying to impress Mark."

"Honestly, I do not remember that happening."

"You don't remember someone shouting *homo* at you in public?"

"Do you know how often that kind of thing's happened to me?"

My own problems seemed to shrink next to his. "You hear a lot of that kind of stuff, huh?"

"There are plenty of days when I don't hear anything like that, but there aren't too many days when I don't feel as though . . . I don't know. It always feels like other guys want me to disappear. Every day. I can tell they just wish I didn't exist."

He pulled his cap down as if he were trying to disappear right then.

I didn't know what to say, because it was true. Some guys did wish that Aaron didn't exist. They didn't know what to do with him. *He's a boy,* they think, *but not a real boy.* And then I realized that they'd think the same thing about me now, too.

"You know," I said, "I think the thing that scared me most about admitting that I'm, you know, gay or whatever isn't so much that people would taunt me by saying 'Oh, James likes other boys,' but that they would say stuff like, 'Oh, turns out James isn't a boy after all.' You know?"

Aaron nodded and curled his legs in, sat cross-legged. "Well, they've always said that about me, so I guess I was never that worried about it. I never bought into what they meant by a real boy, anyway."

"Yeah, I guess that makes sense," I said. "But it actually makes me really angry. Like, so angry I want to punch someone."

"Don't punch anyone."

"I'm not going to hit anybody." I laughed. "I'm not looking to get into any fights. But, dude, this morning, I wanted to win that freaking race so badly." Aaron tilted his head, confused. I'd forgotten that he didn't know about it. "I ran this race against Mark. The Mud 10K."

"Excuse me?"

"You run around some bogs up in the hills. Mark and I signed up for it a while ago, back in April, before"—I waved my hand—"everything happened. Anyway, the race was this morning, and I was ahead of him right up until the end. I lost by like—" I reached out my arm and grasped at the air. "I really wanted to be able to walk past that guy and with just one look say, 'You got beat by a gay kid. We win.'"

"Ha," said Aaron, stretching his legs out in front of him again. "*We* win!"

"For real. That would've been so sweet, you know? You get that sort of chance once in a lifetime maybe, and I blew it. I totally blew it."

Aaron was grinning and shaking his head, but he held a respectful silence for a few moments while I pitied myself.

"James," he finally said with exaggerated patience, "that race was not called the Cosmic Gay Vengeance 10K. It was called the Mud 10K. You ran through a bunch of mud. Which is gross. As far as I'm concerned, no one who gets that filthy is a winner. Also, think about it: if you had beaten Mark and then even looked at him the wrong way, he would've taken a baseball bat and smashed your head like a melon. I'm sorry, but I'm glad you lost. If you had given Mark a reason to kill you, I would have been left with no boy friends. Male friends, I mean. Not boyfriend. You know what I mean." He shifted back to sitting cross-legged. "How are your parents handling everything?"

"They're coming around. I don't know what my mom expects yours to say about it all."

Aaron shrugged. "She probably just wants to hear that she didn't do anything wrong. And that even though you're gay, you're normal. She's normal. My mom's had a lot of time to process it all, and she's pretty level-headed. I'm sure she's saying the right things."

"When did you tell her?"

"I was thirteen. She wanted me to play a team sport. I would have none of it. 'I'm gay' was number four on my list of ten reasons it was a bad idea."

"You just slipped it in there, huh? Smooth."

"Right between 'I'm allergic to Gatorade' and 'The other boys smell like sneakers.'"

"You're starting fights again, dude."

"I'm joking!" He laughed. "You don't smell like a sneaker. The sweater you lent me smelled liked wood smoke and Old Spice."

"It's seen a lot of campfires. Are you sure you don't want your PEZ dispenser? I can go get it."

"No, he's yours. Keep him."

"Why the pink alligator?"

"They didn't have any white ones. Have you seen the albino alligator in San Francisco? He's on YouTube."

And that's how we spent the rest of the Fosters' visit that afternoon: watching YouTube videos. First we checked out the albino alligator, then we watched what seemed like every single other video Aaron had found over the previous two months. He had me cracking up the entire time. I was actually a little disappointed when his mom announced that it was time for them all to go home.

My mom found me washing dishes in the kitchen soon after they split. "Did you know that Aaron is a writer, too?" she asked.

"He's written some bad poetry," I said. I'd read some of his poems in *Sin Qua Non*. They're incoherent.

"He writes a lot. Like you," my mom went on. "His mom said he let her read some of it when he was in the hospital, but she couldn't get through it all. 'If only those kids understood how much he dreaded going to school every day,' she said."

My mom was getting emotional. I deliberately clanged a pot against the side of the sink to snap her back to the here and now.

"I told her how and why you got your black eye. I hope that's okay."

"I think she'd probably heard. But it's okay."

"Do I ever get to read what you're scribbling up there?"

"Maybe sometime." I dried my hands on a dish towel and stuffed it through the handle of the fridge door. The I Heart Vermont magnet that used to hold the photo of Theresa and me caught my eye. The photo was gone.

"Topher's picking me up in a few minutes."

"Are you really going out dressed like that?"

I was wearing jeans with a hole in one knee and a Henry's Towing T-shirt. "You're right. I'll put on a tie," I said over my shoulder as I left the kitchen. "Also, I might get my ears pierced."

No response from her.

As I entered my bedroom, I glanced out the window. No moose. I found my keys in my coffee can of change, slipped the pirate key off the ring, and dropped it back among the coins. And there was Aaron's snaggletoothed PEZ dispenser, half-buried. I grabbed the pink alligator by its head, pulled it from the pennies and nickels, and stuffed him in my pocket.

Topher and I drove up 91 North, way up past Bradford, our windows down, the music loud, the hills electric green, and summer vacation stretching off ahead of us.

"No! Keep heading north!" I yelled when Topher veered up the exit ramp to turn around by Wells River. "They'll never find us in Quebec! Keep going!"

We took winding back roads home, past rusting tractors and a rope-tow ski hill yellow with flowers, past a goat standing on top of a dilapidated doghouse, past a clawfoot bathtub overflowing with spring water that gushed from mossy rocks on the roadside. On a gravel straightaway, far from any barn or house, we pulled in beside a pasture. Sitting on the fence rail in the shade of a big maple, we pet a pair of brown horses that had wandered over while we kissed.

Rex was talking to himself when Luke and I arrived at the door of his room that night. We could hear *Meet the Beatles* playing, the only album he ever listens to if given the choice. For Christmas, along with the shock collar, I gave him *Let It Be* and *Abbey Road*, but he refused to move beyond 1964. His hair was even looking moppy for a while. Too bad it's blond. Luke opened Rex's door quietly, without knocking, and Rex was hunched at his desk, his back to us. Action figures battled across an open book. One soldier, wearing yellow snorkel gear and fins, dangled from a shoelace noose tied to his desk lamp, and Rex was threatening Chewbacca in a voice that sounded like a cross between a frog and a snake. We crept in behind him, holding our breaths to keep from cracking up. When Luke barked "Rex!" he screamed, spun, and chucked the Wookiee, hard, shattering a framed photograph on his dresser. It was a photograph of Rex and me from a couple of years ago, arm in arm and sweaty after a backyard soccer match.

"That's an auspicious start," muttered Luke.

Without slowing down, Rex began throwing action figures onto the floor. "I was reading! Why are you interrupting?" He was fighting back tears.

"Whoa, dude, relax!" Luke had his hands on Rex's shoulders. "No one's busting you for anything. Believe me. James is the one we're here to laugh at. Slow down."

"I was reading," Rex said again. "Look." And he pointed to two opened books, one about sharks and one about WWII fighter jets.

"You go after them both at once, huh? You're a hungry little reader!"

"Yes," he replied, standing rigidly and looking at his desk, clearly desperate for us to leave, to let him spend his evening free from humiliation and abuse. I felt bad for him. Luke and I never came looking for him. He knew something was up, and he was scared.

I dropped down onto his bed. "Hey, Rex," I began. "Relax. For real, man. I need to talk to you." I thumped the bed so he'd sit down. "And Luke's here to, uh, listen."

"To listen with you, to cry with you, to laugh when appropriate," Luke confirmed.

Rex looked up at Luke and me sadly, and then crawled onto the bed and sat cross-legged on his pillow. When he'd arranged himself comfortably and Luke had settled into the desk chair, Rex winced a little and asked, "Are you sick, James?"

I could see his eyes fill with tears, and for a moment I thought I was going to lose it.

"No, dude." I tried laughing. "I'm not sick. I'm not dying or anything. Don't worry. But I have to talk to you about some pretty complicated stuff that might take you some time to understand. Okay?"

He looked to Luke, who nodded his head, and Rex nodded back.

I stretched, cracked my knuckles, and sighed, "So, where to begin? You may have already heard about some of this, Rex. I don't know if kids at school have said anything to you about me or what."

He stared at me blankly, and then asked, "You got arrested?"

Luke cracked up.

"No." I shook my head. "I didn't get arrested. I'm not sick, and I'm not going to jail. Here's the thing. You know how I was sort of kind of but not really dating Theresa for a while?"

"She's pregnant." Rex nodded knowingly.

"Unlikely," said Luke.

"No, she's not pregnant, but that was a good guess. Anyway, the thing is that even though I was sort of going out with Theresa, I actually would rather have been going out with someone else." I paused for dramatic effect. "And the someone else is a boy."

Rex looked from me to Luke and back again, then rocked back, smiling, and said, "Aw, c'mon! You guys!"

Luke shrugged. "No, dude. He's serious."

For some reason I was worried that Luke would say it before I could, so I said quickly, "Yeah, I'm serious, Rex. I'm gay. For real. And I want you to know what that means, why it shouldn't bother you."

He just stared at us both, frozen. Not even a nod of the head.

"So," I began, glancing at Luke for reassurance, "the thing is, it's been really hard for me to admit this, not only to other people, but even to myself. It's been really hard. I've known for a long time, but I was scared to talk about it."

Rex's eyes were wide and unblinking.

"I didn't know whether Mom and Dad would kick me out of the house, whether I'd lose my friends, whether you and Luke would ever speak to me again."

"That last one's still up for debate, Champ," Luke said, grabbing and shaking Rex's knee, but failing to make him smile. "We can discuss it later, when James goes downstairs to watch figure skating."

"Anyway, I didn't know how any of this was going to go over, but some stuff happened at school that sort of forced me to come out of the closet."

"He doesn't know what that means."

"Yes, he does. You know what that means, dude? To come out of the closet?"

"To say that you're a f-f-f," and Rex stopped himself, reconsidered, and said solemnly, "To say that you like to have sex with children."

When Luke saw that Rex was actually crying, that he had his hands over his face, and that he shook away my attempt to put a hand on his shoulder, he stopped laughing.

"Rex! Dude! James does not like to have sex with children! That's not what 'come out of the closet' means, and that's not what gay means either." Turning to me, Luke whispered, "Good grief, you are making a mess of this!"

I glared at him. "Rex, would you listen to me? I don't like children! I like other guys—like, my age and older."

Luke started laughing again.

"A little older. Not old, old. But like a couple of years—I like guys the way you thought I liked girls."

Rex had taken his hands away from his face by this point, but he was still sniffling and wiping his nose with his sleeve. "You're gay, James? For real?"

We nodded at him.

He was twisting the toe of his sock. "Did you know you were gay because you kiss other boys?"

Luke bit his lower lip and hid his face behind his hand.

"Yeah, I guess," I stammered. "But I knew it even before I kissed another boy."

"And if you kiss another boy, that means you're gay?"

"Dude, has anyone explained any of this to you?" I asked, and Rex looked doubtful. "Nobody's explained any of this to you."

"First," Luke jumped in, leaning forward, "if you've kissed another boy, Rex, you're not necessarily gay. If you really, really liked it, you might be a little gay."

"I didn't really like it," Rex said.

"Then I wouldn't worry about it, man," Luke whispered, and we exchanged wide-eyed looks.

"Look, Rex. Here's what this gay thing means. One more time. I like boys, men, the way Luke here, and most other boys, like women. The way you probably will, too. Just because you kiss another boy doesn't mean you're gay."

"Probably depends on the kiss," Luke interrupted, "but the main point is that James has a boyfriend, who you already know and like—"

"Tim Hawken," Rex said.

Luke doubled over.

"No, not Tim Hawken," I groaned. "Topher. You remember Topher."

"Do Mom and Dad know?"

"Yes," my mom said, entering the room as though on a gust of wind. "Yes, we do." She was smiling but had clearly been crying silently. She wiped tears from her eyes.

"Are you kidding?" I yelled, standing up. "You were listening this entire time? We asked you to stay downstairs!"

"But then I heard the crash," she said lamely.

Luke pointed to the broken glass in the framed photo.

Part of me was angry that she had been eavesdropping, but I was sort of glad that she'd heard me talking gently to Rex for once instead of telling him to shut up.

"Well, it's good that you heard the whole thing, I guess," said Luke. "That saves young Rex here the trouble of announcing all over again that he's gay, too."

"I'm not gay!" Rex shouted, and he hit Luke with his fist as though he were swinging a hammer.

"Even if you are, dude, it doesn't matter, right?" Luke said, grabbing Rex's wrist before he could take another swing. "Even if you are, it doesn't matter. That's the whole point of this conversation. James likes other boys, and it doesn't matter."

Rex was looking at his feet.

"For real, Rex. You got it? Don't worry about what other kids say. If they call James a fag or a homo, or if they call *you* a fag or a homo, you tell them to go to hell—"

"No, you don't," said Mom.

"You tell them to go to hell, Rex, because they're being jerks. You got it?"

Rex nodded without looking up.

"Is Derek ever coming over again?"

"Yeah, of course. We're still friends."

"And Pother?"

"Yeah, Topher will come around again, Rex, but even if he's out of the picture, I'm still going to be the same way. I'm still going to be me."

"But with better hair," added Luke.

My mom clapped and sang, "I think it's time for ice cream!"

Rex sat still, as though he were afraid to go until Luke and I had declared the meeting officially adjourned.

"You guys go downstairs," I said. "Rex and I will follow you in a minute."

They left and closed the door, and I stared at the ground until I heard their feet on the stairs. Rex was still sitting stiffly on his pillow.

"Rex, I'm sorry that kids are going to make fun of you because of me, dude."

He didn't say anything.

"And I'm sorry that this is all going to be sort of confusing for you."

Still not a word, not a sound.

"I hope we're still friends." I had to admit that sounded pretty crummy, considering how often we'd fought over the past few years. But Rex put his hand on my shoulder and just kept it there without speaking.

"You okay?" he asked after a while, dropping his hand.

"Yeah, I'm okay. You?" I grabbed him around the waist and pulled him next to me, my arm around him. For a second I thought he was going to crawl into my lap.

"I thought gay guys acted like girls."

"Some of them do."

"How come you don't?"

"I don't know."

"Well then, how come you like other boys?"

"Dude, I do not know. I do not freaking know. I wish I liked girls. It'd be a hell of a lot easier."

"But you like that boy Topher?"

"Yeah, I do. He's really nice."

"You're in love with him?"

"That might be taking it a little far, but, yeah, I like him."

"Is he cute? Do you think he's cute?"

"Yeah," I said eventually. "I do think he's cute. Yeah."

"I'm allowed to tell other kids to go to hell?"

"Sure, dude. Go for it."

"Can I use the F-bomb?"

"If Mom and Dad don't hear you, you can even use the F-bomb."

Rex stood up. "Can I practice in the house?"

"No. Let's get some ice cream."

"I'll come down soon. I'm going to stay and think for a while."

Just as I was closing his door, Rex called, "James!"

I stuck my head back in.

"It's why you got punched?"

I nodded. "It's why I got punched."

He stared at me. "Someone might punch you again?"

I shrugged. "Yeah, man. Something might happen again." I shut his door with a click.

I went down by myself and joined Luke and our parents for a hushed conversation over strawberry and vanilla. The four of us never sit around eating ice cream. Luke and I had gone out earlier to buy it as a consolation for Rex.

From my seat at the kitchen table, I noticed a photo stuck on the fridge where the picture of Theresa and me had been. I got up, pretending that I wanted to put one of the cartons back in the freezer.

It was the photo Hawken took during that party at Derek's. I glanced back at my mom, but she didn't look up. She must have found the photo on my desk.

I leaned against the kitchen counter and stared at Topher and me, black-and-white against the fridge. He has his arm draped around my shoulders. I look like I don't care who's watching.

ACKNOWLEDGMENTS

To everyone who read early drafts or offered sound advice, thanks for all your patience and generosity. Special thanks to Sarah Allen-Lloyd, Christie Anderson, Eric Bennett, Louise Brooks, Cerelle Centeno, Christopher Eliot, Sean Feehan, Beth Graubert, Liz Greenberg, Sean Lally, Catriona Legrady, Paul Legrady, Franci McMahon, Kt Partridge, Langley Partridge, Andrew Saunders, Emily Silver and her Creative Writing Classes, Barb Sorenson and her Women's Lit Classes, Meghan Sterling, Evelyn Weiser, and Keith Witty.

Thank you to my outstanding agent, Rebecca Podos, and the excellent team at HarperCollins: Jon Howard, Jen

Klonsky, Elizabeth Lynch, Maya Packard, Kristen Pettit, Jenna Stempel, Lillian Sun, Kari Sutherland, and Elizabeth Ward.

Finally, thanks to my family and friends. Most of you didn't read a word of this book until its publication, but it wouldn't have come together without you.